"Flannery runs in the same ~~company~~ and his gung-ho colleagues, with lots of war games, fancy weapons, and much male bonding."

—New York *Daily News*

"Clancy and Cussler need to look over their shoulders."
—*Library Journal*

". . . A maven of mach speed mayhem, intricately moves the pieces around his global chessboard, until many bodies, plane crashes, and a running sea battle later." —*Booklist*

"Flannery's characters are believable, both good and bad guys. The plot is well designed, the dialogue crisp, and the pacing speedy." —*The Cleveland Plain Dealer*

"Sean Flannery's novel serves the oldest and most primal of literature's purposes—to divert us, to transport us, and to allow us to dream." —*The Washington Post*

"Sean Flannery is good at what he does—very good."
—*Minneapolis Star Tribune*

"Nonstop action on land, sea, and air as the CIA, FBI, KGB, and Soviet Military Intelligence pool wits and resources to apprehend a deadly sociopath."
—*Publishers Weekly* on *Counterstrike*

"*High Flight* ends the twentieth century with a bang. Russia verses Japan, with the U.S. caught in the middle. Perhaps it's time. There's a lot of techno and a lot of thrills in *High Flight*. Better strap in and hang on when you go for this ride." —Stephen Coonts on *High Flight*

THE TRINITY FACTOR

Sean Flannery

A TOM DOHERTY ASSOCIATES BOOK
NEW YORK

This is a work of fiction. All the characters and events portrayed in this book are either products of the author's imagination or are used fictitiously.

THE TRINITY FACTOR

A Forge Book
Published by Tom Doherty Associates, LLC
175 Fifth Avenue
New York, NY 10010

www.tor.com

Forge® is a registered trademark of Tom Doherty Associates, LLC.

ISBN: 0-812-53877-3

First Forge edition: August 2001

Printed in the United States of America

0 9 8 7 6 5 4 3 2 1

This book is for Dean and Colleen Moon, my biggest fans and best friends, not necessarily in that order.

Better thy heart, three person'd God; for, you
As yet but knock, breathe, shine, and seek to mend . . .

—John Donne

"Trinity," Dr. J. Robert Oppenheimer, Jr., breathed the single word. "We'll call it Trinity."

ACKNOWLEDGMENTS

As is customary in books of this nature, the author thanks the numerous persons who have helped him. First, therefore, I would like to thank my editor, Michael Seidman, for his help with the idea, the shaping of its execution, and for his encouragement.

I'd like also to thank Jim Bryant, Public Information Officer, White Sands Missile Range, N. M., for his help at the site of Trinity; George Romero, Socorro, N. M., who showed me how this could be done; Millard Hunsley, Albuquerque, N. M., who provided invaluable background material for the period 1943–45; and Verna Wood at the Albuquerque Public Library, who was infinitely patient and helpful with maps of the area for that period.

I would also like to thank the dozens of other persons around the state of New Mexico for their kind assistance during the research period.

PROLOGUE

At exactly 5:29 and 45 seconds in the misty, predawn darkness of July 16, 1945, a brilliant light flashed, and a thunder that mankind had never heard before rolled across the southern deserts of New Mexico. The Americans had tested the first atomic bomb at a site codenamed Trinity.

Its success meant the speedy surrender of Japan, something the Russians ostensibly did not want at that time. But even more than that, its success ended what may have been the biggest double cross in history.

Joseph Stalin knew about the American efforts in the race for the super weapon. His knowledge came from a nearly unimpeded spy network. He also knew that if the test was a success the war in Japan would be over before his troops could participate in an invasion of the Japanese mainland. If that had happened, Japan today would be a divided country, much like Germany.

It was imperative, therefore, that Stalin learn all he could about the bomb, and perhaps even sabotage it. This during a time of lend-lease, when the Soviet Union desperately needed the material and assistance the United States was providing.

But isn't it curious that none of the more than three hundred Soviet spies in this country during the war were captured and brought to trial until after the war? Isn't it curious that the government's case against Julius and Ethel Rosenberg had so many holes in it? And isn't it curious that the A-bomb's chief scientist, Dr. J. Robert Oppenheimer, Jr., supposedly had Communist leanings and friends?

But even stranger than all that is the fact that the Russians came up with their own atomic bomb before the British—who shared in our research.

BOOK ONE

1943

1

MOSCOW

Major Sergei Dmitrevich Runkov of the GRU—the Soviet Military Intelligence—left the communications center in the basement of the Lubyanka Prison and waddled down the corridor toward the elevator, his 160-kilogram bulk stuffed impressively into his bedraggled army uniform.

Major Runkov was in a foul mood this evening, and was sweating heavily, despite the damp chill that permeated the lower levels of the prison compound.

He was carrying a bundle of message forms in a file folder with two red stripes diagonally across its front, signifying top secret material.

At the elevator, two officers, neither of whom he knew, glanced at the file folder and then scowled at Runkov. It was a mistake on their part.

Runkov's right eyebrow arched. "You have a problem, captain?" he growled at one of the officers.

The other man, a lieutenant colonel, stepped forward. "It is you who apparently have the problem, major," he snapped. "What is your name and your unit, and what exactly are you doing carrying top secret material out of here?"

"Runkov. GRU. And what I am doing with these messages is none of your goddamned business, comrade."

The elevator had arrived, and Runkov reached out and pushed back the iron gate. The lieutenant colonel tried to stop him by placing his hand on Runkov's arm. The GRU officer spun around out of the officer's grasp, surprisingly light on his feet, and, centimeters away from the man, he said menacingly, "Do that again, comrade colonel, and you will likely lose your arm and very probably more."

The other officer paled. "See here . . ." he started to say, but his superior officer stopped him.

"Sergei Runkov?" the lieutenant colonel asked, his voice now polite.

Runkov glared at him and barely nodded his head.

"I see, major," the officer said. "Please forgive us the intrusion."

Runkov snorted, turned, reentered the elevator, and, without waiting for the two officers to join him, crashed the iron gate shut and slammed the control lever to the right. The elevator rose with a lurch as the captain, who now looked definitely ill, turned to his colonel.

"The Bear?" he asked. The colonel, who looked no better, nodded.

At sixty Runkov had well earned his nickname, the Bear, which in no way was a reference to the Soviet Union's symbol, but rather an indication of his impressive bulk, as well as his ferocity.

At the time of the Revolution, Runkov, who had come from poor peasant stock along the Volga northwest of Moscow, was a member of the Red Army, and in the fighting had proven himself over and over again. At that time his nearly two-meter frame had been packed with 125 kilograms of meat, and he could and often had crushed men to death with his arms in a bear hug. Thus his title.

After the Revolution he had transferred out of his regular army unit into the newly formed Cheka Registry Department, the forerunner of the GRU. And his reputation spread so that during the purges of the late thirties he survived without even a hint of trouble.

He had been married, but his wife had died two years ago, and his childless marriage was now nothing more than a vague, indistinct memory.

Upstairs, he charged out of the elevator and moved down the wide corridor toward his office like a battleship crashing through the sea, neither moving aside nor slowing down for any obstacle.

His chief assistant, Sergeant Vladimir Doronkin, who had been with him since shortly after the Cheka had been formed, jumped up from his desk when Runkov barged into the room. The man, normally almost as unflappable as Runkov, looked definitely shaken. "I tried to get you downstairs, but you had already left," he said breathlessly.

Runkov ignored him as he crossed the outer office and went into his own cubicle, slamming the file folder down on his desk. He slumped into his specially built chair, loosened his tie, and poured himself a stiff shot of vodka from a bottle in one of his desk drawers.

When he had thrown back the drink and taken a deep breath to calm himself, he looked up at his aide, who had followed him into his office. "What hell has broken loose now, Vladimir Nikhailovich?" he asked gently.

"Comrade Beria's office sent over a messenger for you. He is waiting downstairs."

"That fairy!" Runkov exploded, pounding his massive right fist on the desk top. "What in hell does he want?"

"No, Sergei . . . no . . . it is not him. It is Marshal Stalin himself. He wants to see you."

Runkov snapped up. "When?"

"Now," Sergeant Doronkin said. "Immediately."

Runkov smiled. "So," he said, sitting back in his chair. "The 'man made of steel' has deigned to send for me at long last."

Sergeant Doronkin, who had served his major well over the years, and who loved and respected the man, had to look nervously over his shoulder. What the major was saying was treasonous, punishable by death. But Runkov was totally unperturbed. "There is a car waiting for you downstairs," said the aide.

"Yes." Runkov was smiling. He got ponderously to his feet and began straightening his tie. "Quickly now," he said. "Get me the current files on Klaus Fuchs and on the American Manhattan District Project."

"Yes, sir," Doronkin said, pleased that his boss was not going to completely ignore the summons, as he had other summonses before. When Stalin himself called, a man either moved fast or lost his head. It was simple.

A light drizzle was falling in the warm evening as Runkov emerged from one of the side doors of the prison and climbed into a waiting car. It was an American lend-lease Chevrolet painted an olive drab. The U.S. insignia on the doors had been covered over with a red star, and red flags adorned both front fenders.

An air force colonel was waiting for him in the backseat, and as soon as Runkov closed the door, the man indicated for the driver to take off.

The car proceeded through the courtyard, past the black statue of Felix Dzerzhinsky, the founder of the State Secret Police, and then sped through the gate and headed toward the Kremlin along the deserted Yaroslavskoye Road.

"So, Sergei Dmitrevich, what do you think of our new summer offensive?" the colonel asked pleasantly.

Moscow was still under a blackout, despite the Nazi setbacks, and Runkov could barely make out the colonel's features. "If you've asked me that to be polite, colonel, don't. I do not engage in pleasantries. And if you've asked that because you desire my military assessment, also don't. My opinions go through channels."

The colonel chuckled. "The Bear," he said, half to himself. "Why is it, comrade major, that you feel you must constantly live up to your fierce reputation?"

"Stupidity," Runkov growled, looking directly at the man. "Inefficiency. Mendacity."

The colonel interrupted him. "You would do well to curb your tongue, or you may lose it along with the rest of your head."

"There would be none to shed a tear, least of all me," Runkov snapped, and both men fell silent as the car rushed through the night.

It had been two weeks now since he had sent his summary of intelligence operations in the United States directly to Marshal Stalin. For the first couple of days afterward, he had braced himself for the expected storm of protest. What was a GRU major trying to do by sending such a report directly to Stalin? Was the man mad?

But nothing had happened. Absolutely nothing. And as the days had stretched into the first week, Runkov's mood had blackened.

And, now that Stalin had finally acknowledged him, he thought bitterly, it was only to send a car and driver from the NKVD. Beria would be at the meeting, he supposed, and so would that fool Merkulov. But with Stalin he was going to have to watch his tongue.

A few minutes later they were admitted through the Kremlin gate. The driver took them slowly past the Great Palace, and then parked in front of the main administration building.

Inside the ground floor their credentials were checked, as was Runkov's bulging briefcase, before they were allowed to continue along a wide, spotlessly clean corridor to another pair of guards at the elevator.

There they were required to submit to another complete security check.

On the third floor a third check was required, and a civilian aide escorted them down another wide corridor and into a large suite of offices, where a second civilian aide took over the escort duty.

Finally they were led through a wide set of double doors into a huge room furnished with nothing more than a long conference table under an ornate chandelier. There were no paintings on the walls, no sideboards or cabinets, no chairs, only the table and thick wine-red drapes completely covering the several large windows along one wall.

Two older men in baggy, unpressed, gray suits stood around the table, and when Runkov and the air force colonel entered the room, they both looked up.

"Marshal Stalin will arrive momentarily," their aide told them, and he left, quietly closing the large doors after him.

The colonel escorted Runkov to the table, but he did not have to make any introductions. All three men knew each other. The older man to the right was Lavrenti Pavlovich Beria, who was the head of the Internal Affairs Police—the NKVD—which watched over all Soviet industry, as well as Siberia. The man to his left was Vsevolod Nikolaevich Merkulov, the chief administrator of the State Secret Service, or the NKGB.

That these three men were together in one room— the heads of the NKVD and the NKGB, as well as a high-ranking officer of the GRU—was extraordinary, and Runkov's pulse quickened. All three services maintained an intense, often bloody rivalry. It had been Stalin's contention from the very beginning that such rivalry would keep the separate security apparatuses on their toes. But it also fostered intense distrust and hatred.

The two men nodded to Runkov, who set his briefcase on the table, which was strewn with maps that obviously outlined the recent Nazi setbacks.

Beria looked at the air force colonel. "That will be all, comrade. Thank you for your kind assistance."

The colonel nodded stiffly, turned, and left the room. A moment later a rear door opened and Joseph Stalin, wearing a neatly fitting, plain military tunic and well-pressed gray trousers, entered the room and crossed quickly to stand at the head of the table, Beria to his left, Merkulov to his right, and Runkov directly across.

Stalin appeared to be in high spirits; his complexion was ruddy, his health good. His ebullience, Runkov thought, was no doubt due to the way the war had been going this past month. But the most striking figure of the supreme Soviet leader was the aura of absolute power that seemed to surround him, or rather radiate from him like heat from an open-hearth furnace.

Runkov did not let Stalin's apparently good-natured mood delude him into thinking that this was going to be easy. The dungeons here in the Kremlin itself were filled with the screams of dying men who had misjudged their leader.

"I've passed on copies of your report to Comrades Beria and Merkulov," Stalin said to Runkov without preamble. "It is their studied opinion that your contentions are nonsense."

Runkov stiffened. This was starting out badly, dangerously, but he managed a very slight smile, nevertheless. "Their reaction is understandable, comrade marshal, because they simply do not share your unique perception."

Something flashed deep inside of Stalin's eyes, but then the supreme Soviet leader threw back his head and roared with laughter. Beria looked incredulous, and Merkulov was white.

For just a moment Runkov was certain he had seriously blundered, but it was too late now to turn back.

"I did not call you together this evening for bloodshed," Stalin said when he had recovered. "Convince us, Sergei Dmitrevich, that we are wrong and you are right."

Stalin was the only man on this earth whom Runkov feared and respected. He was going to have to play this carefully—very carefully.

"If by some chance the Americans are successful in their efforts to build this new super weapon—it is being called an atomic bomb—then the war will end to our disadvantage."

"The German scientists . . ." Merkulov started to protest, but Runkov cut him off.

"No longer have the industrial resources necessary to manufacture such a weapon. They are working on it at this moment, but very soon they will be preoccupied elsewhere."

"The Germans are no threat?" Stalin asked softly. There was a dangerous edge to his voice, and Runkov could feel the sweat rolling down his sides from his armpits.

"I did not mean to imply such a thing, comrade marshal," he said. "The Germans are still a serious threat, but not in this."

"Will the Americans succeed in their efforts to construct such a weapon, or will they not?" Stalin demanded, raising his voice and thumping his right fist on the table top. Beria flinched.

"The Americans *may* be successful," Runkov answered. "And if they are, it will make our position unacceptable."

Stalin turned to Beria, his eyes flashing. "What about our efforts in this matter?"

The Internal Affairs chief seemed on the verge of fainting. "Such a weapon is impossible in the near future," he said carefully.

"What if Major Runkov is correct. . . . What then, my dear Lavrenti Pavlovich? What then?"

At first Beria said nothing, although his mouth was working, but Stalin's iron gaze remained locked into the man's eyes, and he finally had to shake his head. "I do not know," he said softly.

"What about you?" Stalin shouted, turning to Merkulov.

"The first I heard of such a weapon was through Major Runkov's reports," the NKGB chief said quickly. "My opinion is that the idea of such a device is farfetched at best. Perhaps someday, far in the future, such a weapon could be perfected. But surely not in time to make any significant difference in the war with Germany."

"But what about after the war, comrade marshal?" Runkov asked.

Stalin leaned forward, his clenched fists on the table in front of him. "What about after the war, Sergei Dmitrevich?"

"If the Americans should manage to develop this weapon, our position after the war will be unacceptable."

"They are our allies, we should demand to share in their research," Beria said.

Stalin ignored him, his attention completely on Runkov. "What is it you suggest?"

Runkov felt a little thrill of triumph, and he reached out to open his briefcase, but Stalin stopped him.

"I don't care about your maps or your timetables. I want your suggestion." Stalin straightened up. "Given a free hand, what would you do?"

This was it. "Two things, comrade marshal," Runkov said without hesitation. He had been waiting for this moment for two weeks now, ever since he had received word from Klaus Fuchs that there was a possibility that he and other British scientists might be sent to the United States to help with the American efforts to build the new weapon. "Or rather a two-pronged attack." He paused briefly.

"Continue," Stalin roared in impatience.

"The first would be to dramatically increase our U.S.

network to gain as much information as we possibly can in as short a time as possible. This information would be instantly relayed to our own scientists, which would greatly accelerate our work."

"And the second?" Stalin asked, his voice like ice.

"Stop the American efforts, or at least slow them down, which would give our scientists time to catch up or perhaps surpass their efforts. Whoever controls this weapon could control the world."

Stalin seemed to draw inward for a moment, deep within his own thoughts. "It would also guarantee that the Americans would have to continue the war with conventional weapons, ultimately weakening their position when it's over," he said absently. And then he looked up. "The spy network is understandable, but how would you slow the project?"

"There are two men deeply involved with the American efforts, which is called the Manhattan Project. The first is its chief scientist, Dr. J. Robert Oppenheimer, Jr. And the second is an army general, Leslie R. Groves. I propose that both men be assassinated as soon as possible."

"Come now, Runkov," Merkulov snapped. "Even I expected more than that from you. In your report you estimate that there may be as many as ten thousand people working on the project. What would the assassinations of two men accomplish? Very little, I'd say. Why not sabotage their production facilities?"

"The production facilities are too diverse. Dozens of American industries are working on the project, so far as we can determine. But there is a hierarchy with the project's scientists. Dr. Oppenheimer is so important that many have left their university posts just to come work with him. He is highly respected in this field."

"That from the traitor Klaus Fuchs?" Merkulov said angrily.

"Fuchs is a traitor, but he is a knowledgeable scientist. Even the British, as stupid as they are, understand that."

Merkulov glanced at Stalin, whose gaze remained locked on Runkov.

"Go on," Stalin said softly. It was impossible to read anything from the hooded expression in his eyes.

"Eliminating Oppenheimer would not stop the project. Certainly not. But it would seriously hamper the American efforts."

"And the general?"

"General Groves works for the Army Corps of Engineers. No doubt he has the ear of Roosevelt in this. He is a man who gets things done. He also is a man who has no effective second in command. Eliminate him, and the project would again be seriously affected. Eliminate both men at the same instant, and the project would perhaps never fully recover."

Again there was a long silence as Stalin seemed to ponder what Runkov had told him. It almost seemed as if he was somehow troubled. When he looked up at last, there was a grim expression on his face that made Runkov very uncomfortable.

"Spying is one matter, Sergei Dmitrevich. We are their allies and we deserve the information. But assassination is something totally different. Such an act could never be traced to us. Never. Do I make myself perfectly clear?"

"Valkyrie," Runkov said in a hushed tone.

"You would bring him back for this?"

"Yes, comrade marshal," Runkov said. "But in such a way that no one outside this room other than my assistant would know about it."

"Indeed," Stalin said.

"Then I have a free hand in this, comrade marshal?" Runkov dared to ask.

Beria and Merkulov started to protest, but Stalin ignored them. "One provision," he said ominously. The room was again absolutely silent. "Your head, Sergei Dmitrevich, should you fail, will be served up on a pike atop St. Basil's so that all may gaze upon the features of the most infamous traitor since the czars."

AUGUST–OCTOBER 1980

2

It was a stiflingly hot evening, with little or no sea breeze from St. George's Bay on the Mediterranean. Traffic was light in the city, even though the military curfew had been recently lifted, and was concentrated toward Ra's Bayrut and Hamra Street where the fashionable Anglo-Saxon residential sections were located.

In spite of the continuing strife with the Christian forces in the southern half of the country, and despite the continuing presence of Iranian troops, Beirut had reverted somewhat to its old carefree, cosmopolitan ways. The people seemed relaxed, if not completely happy.

There was one person in the city, however, who was neither happy nor relaxed. Her name was Jada Natasha Yatsyna, as of this moment, chief of station for KGB activities in Lebanon.

She stood behind her desk, a green-shaded lamp the only illumination in the small, very plain room, and idly fingered a stack of files she had just finished reading.

Beside the files on her desk was a stack of message flimsies ready to be sent in the morning by radio to Moscow. All of it had to do with recent assessments of the Lebanese political situation and its relationship with the PLO, the Iranian troops, and the southern Christians. The situation here was deteriorating, at least from the Soviet viewpoint. She'd been telling her bosses at Dzerzhinsky Square that for the last two years. But no one would believe her, and arms continued to be secretly brought into Lebanon for the day that an all-out war would occur.

Jada sighed deeply, trying to quell the uneasy feeling in her stomach. She was tired, which was evident from the lines of her face, the hollows beneath her eyes, and her sunken cheeks. At one time she had been a pretty woman—fashionably shapely and tall, with well-proportioned legs.

Lately, however, and over the past couple of years, she had lost weight slowly but steadily, so that now most of her clothes hung on her spare frame. She had taken to using a small amount of makeup every morning to hide the weariness in her face.

Jada went around her desk and at the door flipped off the light with a shaking hand. Before she went out of the room, which was located in the Referentura, the most secret section of the Soviet embassy, she checked her watch; the luminous dials clearly read 12:37 A.M. She had barely one hour to go.

She opened the door, stepped out into the brightly lit corridor, and blinked, confused for a moment, half in her office and half out into the hallway. Everything was as it should be, everything was normal. And yet for a brief instant it seemed as if her entire body had been wrenched violently from one world into another. For most of the evening she had been thinking about what she was about to do, and why she had come to this. It was nothing more than another link in a long chain of events she had initiated carefully more than a month ago. But now that it was nearly here, she was deeply frightened, and confused.

During this long night her thinking had also turned to another time. To a man she would never see again, to the loneliness she had endured, or had somehow managed to survive over the past thirty-five years. Coming out into the well-lit corridor was like coming back into the real world after an evening of fantasy, and it took her a moment to adjust.

She left the door open and stepped back into her office, where she picked up the sheaf of message forms she had nearly forgotten, then went back into the hallway, shutting and carefully locking the door behind her.

She would have to be careful, she told herself, not to do anything out of the ordinary. Not to make any obvious mistakes. They were watching her. They had always watched her. Never sure of her. Never completely trusting her.

Down the corridor, which was garishly painted a faded mustard yellow, she stopped at the communications center window and rang the buzzer. An instant later a young man slid back the tiny metal door.

"Good evening, Colonel Yatsyna," the man in a Soviet army uniform said politely.

Jada handed the message forms through the window. "I want these out in the morning transmission," she said wearily. "A double-A priority should be sufficient."

"I'm just sending out the overnights now . . . I can fit these in with the others."

"It is not necessary, Petrovich. Later this morning will be fine."

"As you wish, colonel," the young man said.

"Yes," Jada replied, "as I wish." She turned without another word and trudged down the corridor toward the stairs, which led up to the street level.

The young man leaned through the narrow window and called after her. "Have a good evening, Colonel Yatsyna." But she did not hear him as she rounded the corner, went through a heavy metal door and then up the stairs, slowly, her right hand sliding along the railing.

At the head of the stairs she showed her identification to the night duty officer as a matter of routine, signed out in the log, and was about to turn and leave when the OD suddenly jumped up from behind his small table.

"I almost forgot, Colonel Yatsyna," he said.

She looked at him. "Yes, lieutenant?" she said, her heart accelerating.

"Will you be in at the usual time in the morning?" the man asked politely. But there was something in his eyes. Something he was hiding. She was sure of it.

She took a step closer. "An unusual question, is it not, lieutenant?" she said harshly.

The man backed down slightly. "Mr. Berinski didn't want to bother you this evening, but he asked me to ask you when you left. He would like to see you in your office first thing in the morning. That is, if you are coming in."

Jada could feel the bile rising sharp from her stomach. They knew! Somehow they had found out. Despite her carefully laid plans. Despite the extreme care she and the others had taken, they knew.

She forced an unnatural calmness into her voice, and nodded. "Yes, lieutenant, you can inform Mr. Berinski that I will be in my office at eight."

"Yes, comrade," the OD said, and he sat back at his table as Jada turned, went across the main entry hall, and left the building through the thick, ornately carved wooden door.

Despite the heat of the evening, Jada shivered as she went around the side of the building to where she had parked her Ford Cortina. The cream-colored little car was a wreck, but it was a luxury here in Beirut for a Soviet officer, even one of her rank.

She unlocked the door, climbed in behind the wheel,

and started the engine, but did not immediately back out of her parking place.

She pushed her immediate fears out of her mind in an attempt to calm her nerves, which were at the raw edge. But then the other thing intruded, as it always did. She had been alone for thirty-five years. She did not have a husband. There were no children. No home or apartment in Moscow to return to. No one or nothing to care for. None of that. She shook her head slowly and closed her eyes. Hers had been an entire lifetime wasted. Gone down the drain, as the Americans would say.

And yet there had been so much hope for the future when she was a little girl growing up south of London. Before World War II, her life had been one of gentility. Good music. Good literature. Fine, cultured friends whom her parents would entertain in a gracious manner that was lost to her now.

"Christ," she said, opening her eyes. Where had it all gone? What had happened to the dreams? What had happened to the future?

She cranked her window down, flipped the headlights on, backed out of the parking space, and headed around the embassy building to the front gate, where she stopped for the security check.

A young man, his automatic rifle slung over his shoulder, came out of the guardhouse, snapped to attention, then opened the heavy iron gates.

She smiled and saluted casually, then proceeded through the gate, turning right on Rue Mar Elias. She slowly worked a zigzag path through downtown Beirut, as if she was merely out for an aimless evening drive. But as she drove she constantly checked her rearview mirror for any sign that she was being followed.

Beirut was a strange city. It was composed of an odd mixture of the old and the new, of the east and the west. She drove past modern high-rise office buildings that intermingled with the twisted streets of the bazaars, past the Byzantine Place Des Martyrs downtown, along the waterfront district, and finally picked up the Avenue Charles Helou, which led to the main seacoast highway. The Lebanon Mountains were only a few kilometers to the east, St. George's Bay to the west, and Al Buwar, thirty-five kilometers to the north.

No one was behind her. She had not been followed as far as she could tell, and as she drove she again let her mind wander. This evening, as during the past few weeks, she had permitted herself the luxury of nostalgia. Or rather, she had deluged herself with remembrances of things past. It had been an exercise in futility, she knew that. Had she verbalized her thoughts, she could have been accused of being a rambling old woman. But she also understood that what she had been doing was nothing more than a defense mechanism—defense against the loneliness of an old lady. At this point in time she definitely felt like an old woman, and yet this evening, and for the next weeks she would be needing all the strength she could muster, both mental and physical.

The decision she had made, had been making over the past couple of years, had been a difficult one. A decision that had caused her a great deal of pain and uncertainty. But the events that were coming up, that surely would be happening soon, would be even more trying to her. Perhaps too trying.

The city was behind her, finally, the highway angling north off the peninsula on which it was built, and in the distance far out at sea, she could see the lights of a low-flying airliner—either an Alia coming into Beirut, or more likely an El Al on its way to Tel Aviv.

There was no traffic in her rearview mirror, the highway dark; only the glow of the city lit the horizon behind her. And at this moment she felt more alone than she had ever felt in her life. She gripped the steering wheel more tightly and pressed down on the accelerator, the little car surging forward into the night.

* * *

It was nearly 1:30 A.M. by the time she crossed the railroad tracks about five kilometers south of the small town of Al Buwar. She flipped off her headlights and slowed down, first checking again to the rear to see if she was still alone on the highway.

Satisfied that the road was clear, she turned off the highway onto a narrow, rutted, sand road that was little more than a path down to the sea. A hundred meters off the highway she stopped, shut off the engine, and sat back in the seat, her hands still tightly gripping the steering wheel.

At this point she could still turn back, she told herself. She could start the car, back up to the highway, and return to her apartment in Beirut. In the morning she would meet with the fat pig Berinski, and listen to his usual complaints, and life would continue as it had for all these years. If they suspected her, she could somehow brazen it out.

In a couple of years it would not matter anyway. Nothing would matter. She squeezed her eyes shut, blocking off the tears that threatened to well up. Alone. So goddamned alone.

There was no one here in Beirut for her. No one back in Moscow. No one anywhere.

After a long time she opened her eyes, sighed deeply in an attempt to calm the butterflies in her stomach, then took the keys out of the ignition and got out of the small car. She opened the trunk and from the compartment beneath the mat where the spare tire and jack were kept, she took out a large flashlight and a .380 Beretta automatic wrapped in a dirty rag. Checking the weapon's clip to make sure it was loaded, she snapped the slide back, levering a round into the chamber, then turned to look back toward the highway, which was still deserted.

She closed the trunk lid and, leaving the keys dangling in the lock, turned and headed down the path to the beach, which was only a couple of hundred meters away.

The sky was clear and the night was bright, although there was no moon. The stars seemed to be splatters of white paint flung by some insane artist on the inside of a huge, inverted bowl. Beneath them was the dark sea.

She checked her watch, which showed it was nearly time, pointed the flashlight out to sea and began signaling—two longs, one short, three longs. Repeating the signal over and over again.

To the south she could make out the dim glow of Beirut jutting out on its peninsula into the Med, but elsewhere was darkness as she continued to signal.

And then there was a pinprick of light out to sea. She held her breath for a long moment, until the second signal came—two shorts, one long, three shorts, the inverse of her signal.

She flashed back her reply and strained to listen over the gentle sounds of the nearly calm sea lapping against the beach for the sounds of the rubber dinghy coming for her.

But then she heard another sound from behind her, up near the highway, and she snapped around. At first she could not identify what she was hearing, as she held her breath, straining to listen. But then it suddenly struck her that she was hearing the stamp of leather boots. Soldiers! They were coming for her!

She threw her flashlight down, ripped open her blouse, and struggled out of it as she hurried down to the water's edge. She kicked off her sandals and stepped out of her light pants.

The beach was suddenly bathed in lights, and from behind her someone shouted, "Halt!" in Russian.

Ignoring the command, she turned and fired five quick shots toward the road, threw the automatic down, and ran into the water until it was deep enough for her to swim.

The water was warm, the swells gentle, but it smelled

and tasted of oil and diesel fuel, as she swam as fast as she could possibly go in the direction of the signal light that had answered hers.

Behind her, on the beach, there was a great deal of commotion, and then spotlights were stabbing the darkness, searching the water for her.

Don't leave me, the thought screamed in her mind. Christ, don't leave me like this.

A flash of light stabbed the surface of the water a few meters ahead of her and then was gone. A moment later it was back, and it centered directly on her. She dove under the surface just as the rattle of a machine gun started up on the beach.

Something hard and hot slammed into her right leg, causing her to nearly cry out, and she swallowed some seawater.

"No," she screamed out loud as she surfaced. "Don't leave!"

The spotlight on the beach had lost her, and was shining twenty meters or so to the left, as several more machineguns on the beach opened up, spraying the water all around her.

She was weakening. She could feel what little strength she had ebbing away from her. Perhaps, she told herself, what she was attempting to do was not really necessary, after all. Perhaps it was nothing more than the insane desires of a tired old woman.

It would be easy, so easy, to quit now—to stop swimming and merely let herself sink beneath the surface. Down deeper and deeper, until she could no longer hold her breath, and then to inhale deeply of the warm salt water. Breathe deeply and peaceful oblivion would be hers at long last.

But then there were voices, somewhere ahead of her, and she looked up, trying to peer through the darkness.

"Sonofabitch," someone swore in English. In English!

"Here!" Jada cried out. "Don't leave, I'm here!" She

redoubled her efforts, and the machinegun fire from the beach also seemed to increase in intensity, once again sweeping her way.

Suddenly there were hands grabbing her arms, lifting her out of the water, dragging her nearly naked body against something hard, something metal. It was the submarine.

And then her world faded as she let herself go into a peaceful, dark void.

3

NORTHERN MINNESOTA

The sun was just coming up over the trees across the lake when Wallace Mahoney carefully closed the screen door of the cabin and stepped off the porch. He went around to the side of the small house and got his fishing poles and tackle box from where he had carefully laid them out last night after dinner.

It was well before six A.M., and Mahoney's wife Marge would be at least another hour in bed. By that time he hoped to have caught their breakfast.

He went back around the cabin and shuffled down the front lawn to the dock, where his thirteen-foot aluminum fishing boat, with its small, seven-and-a-half-horsepower outboard motor, was tied. He carefully laid the fishing gear alongside the landing net and live-box already on board, before he untied the bow, and carefully stepped in to sit on the rear bench.

At sixty-three, Mahoney was no longer as spry as he once had been, and yet ever since he had retired from the Company one year ago, he had felt good. Two years ago he had completed his last assignment as the Central Intelligence Agency's chief analyst out of the Moscow Embassy under the cover of trade mission specialist. There had been some trouble there that, when it was over, convinced him finally to bow out.

As Marge had told him when they returned to the States then, "Old man, it's time to quit so we can spend the rest of our days on that northern Minnesota lake you've talked about for thirty years."

And quit he had, after the navy doctors at Bethesda Medical Center had cured his problem with varicose veins in his legs.

That had been a year of intense pain, but now as he untied the rear line holding the small boat to the dock and started the quiet, well-muffled motor, he was glad he had gone through with it.

The surface of the lake was glass-smooth, reflecting the pine trees that in some places around the shore grew down to the water's edge. As he headed toward a small bay a half a mile away, he could see the ripples of feeding fish coming to the surface, and he sighed deeply. He was a contented man at long last, if not a happy one.

There had been the period of a year when he was recuperating from the painful operations on his legs and when he had gone through his extensive debriefing. Report after endless report detailing every aspect of his career, and every nuance of every decision he had been a part of, were requested. And he had complied. Hell, the reports had helped take his mind off his pain.

Afterward he had written another extensive round of reports—his studied assessments, actually, of the world situation as it stood at the moment.

The work had taken the better part of a year, and when he had finally finished—after the retirement papers had finally come through, and after the party in Langley (attended, it seemed, by half the Company) was over with—he and Marge had visited their son and grandchildren in Los Angeles.

On the way back from California, they had stopped in Missoula, Montana, where their second son Michael had worked for the Forest Products Laboratory. Michael had been murdered two years earlier by the Soviets. It was part of the trouble Mahoney had been involved with during his tenure at the Moscow Embassy.

Then, earlier this spring, they had come to northern Minnesota and within two weeks had found this small house on Schultz Lake, north of Duluth, and had settled in.

"For the duration, old man?" Marge his wife of forty-one years had asked.

"For the duration," Mahoney had said with a gentle smile. And so they had settled in to do exactly that.

The morning was cool, almost crisp, and after Mahoney had shut off the outboard motor and dropped anchor, he baited his two lines and cast them overboard, one on each side of the boat, before he hunched up his coat collar and sighed deeply again, something he had been doing a lot of lately.

He moved to the cushioned seat clamped to the center bench of the boat, leaned back, and closed his eyes. The smell of the pine trees and of the water brought him a small measure of peace. And there was absolutely no noise this morning—not even the wind sighing through the trees.

He had promised Marge that after lunch he would drive her down to Duluth, thirty-one miles away, to do some shopping. Perhaps they would catch a movie and have an early dinner before returning. In three days their first son, John, his wife, and the kids were coming out from California to spend a week, and before that Mahoney wanted to make sure the guest cottage, which had once been used as a boathouse, was ready for them.

But there was plenty of time for that, he thought. He had retired so that he would never have to worry or ever be in a rush again, and he was not going to get back into his old habits.

Marge's voice drifted across the lake to him, and he opened his eyes, swiveled around in his seat, and looked back toward his cabin. He could just make out Marge's figure standing on the dock, but she was not alone. From here it looked like two men were with her.

She called his name again and waved. With shaking hands he reeled in his lines, pulled up anchor, and started the outboard. His heart was hammering by the time he got the small boat turned around; he headed back toward his dock as fast as the tiny outboard would push him, his stomach tightening into a knot.

There were very few people who knew where this place was. His son. A couple of friends from Duluth. And of course the Company. But there could be others. He had spent his life as an intelligence officer, and during the course of his career he had made many enemies. There could be others now coming for him.

Keeping one hand on the throttle and his eyes on the dock, Mahoney reached down and opened his tackle box. He lifted the hinged tray up, and from under it pulled out a snub-nosed .38 revolver, which he stuffed in his jacket pocket.

As he got closer to the dock he let his hand rest lightly in his pocket, his finger on the trigger of the gun, and he throttled down.

The two men, both of them apparently in their mid-thirties, were dressed in business suits. Both of them were smiling.

"Good morning, Mr. Mahoney," one of them called out. "It's a beautiful day."

"It was," Mahoney snapped. He shut off the outboard and the small boat drifted to the dock. One of the men bent down to grab the edge of the boat, and Mahoney pulled out his gun and pointed it directly in the man's face. "I'll want to see some identification, son," he said.

The man's eyes widened. "I . . ." he started to say,

and from the corner of Mahoney's eye he saw the other man reach inside his coat.

"Your partner is a dead man unless you get your hand away from there."

The man complied, slowly spreading his arms away from his body, his hands open. The man bent over the boat was sweating.

"Move off the dock, Marge," Mahoney said, and she went back without a word. When she was on the lawn, he nodded toward the bow of the boat. "Tie it up to the dock. Very slowly, please."

The man he was pointing the gun at moved forward very carefully, grabbed the rope, and tied the boat. When he was finished Mahoney got to his feet and stepped up on the dock.

"Identification," he said.

Both men unbuttoned their coats, and from inside their breast pockets took out small leather wallets, which they flipped open. The carried Central Intelligence Agency plastic ID cards.

"Who sent you? Carlisle?" Mahoney asked. Farley Carlisle, who had been his boss in Moscow a couple of years ago, was now head of the Company's Directorate of Operations, which was nothing more than a euphemism for clandestine services.

"No, sir," one of the men said. "Mr. McBundy in Missions and Operations sent us to ask for your help."

"With what?"

Both men seemed very uncomfortable. "There is a defection in progress. At a rather high and somewhat sensitive level. Mr. McBundy thought you might be able to help with her debriefing. We have a safehouse in Greenwich, Connecticut. It wouldn't take too much of your time."

"Shit," Mahoney said half to himself. He looked up. "Why me?"

"You know their organization chart and methods of operation better than anyone."

"I'm needed as a lie detector?"

Neither man said a word.

"Will you gentlemen stay for breakfast?" Marge asked from where she was standing.

"We can't . . ." one of them started to say, but Mahoney cut him off.

"They're staying for coffee," he said. "We'll be up shortly."

"Of course," Marge said, and she turned and went back up to the cabin, her slippers flopping on the grass.

The three men watched her shuffle up the lawn and enter the house before they turned to look at each other. Mahoney was angry, and it showed in his expression. He stuffed the pistol back in his jacket pocket, and without a word turned and strode back up to the cabin, not bothering to see if the pair of them were following him. They appeared to be genuine, but he found that he didn't really give a damn.

He entered the cabin through a side door to his small study, where he slumped down behind his desk. The two men came through the door as he picked up the phone and dialed a number that he knew by heart.

It was answered on the third ring. "Six-six-four-eight," a woman said.

"Four-twenty-six," Mahoney replied, and the operator was gone. A moment later Robert McBundy answered.

"Yes."

"Bob, this is Wallace."

"Good morning, Wallace," McBundy said brightly. "How are you getting along these days as a man of leisure?"

"Is there an identity code for these two you sent me?" Mahoney asked.

"Yes," McBundy said. Mahoney looked up at the two men expectantly, and one of them managed a weak smile.

"Twixt defect," the young agent said softly.

Mahoney repeated the two words into the telephone.

"That's it," McBundy confirmed. "Are you with us?"

"I don't know yet," Mahoney said. "Let you know later." He hung up the phone, leaned back in his chair, and stared at the two men for a long moment. "All right, what have you got?" he finally asked.

"Her name is Jada Natasha Yatsyna. She's fifty-nine years old, and is the chief of station for the KGB's First Chief Directorate, Eighth Department."

"Beirut?" Mahoney asked, and both men nodded.

4

GREENWICH, CONNECTICUT

The farmhouse was located five miles north of Greenwich, off the secondary highway, several hundred yards along a well-tended gravel road. Ostensibly it belonged to a New York corporation attorney who liked his privacy, and the fifty acres of heavily wooded property were completely surrounded by a high wire fence. In the three years it had been used as a safehouse, none of the locals had ever bothered to try to get in. Most people in Greenwich enjoyed their own privacy, and respected the privacy of others.

For the first couple of weeks Jada was on the mend from the flesh wound she had received in the calf of her right leg. The wound was painful, but had caused no complications, nor had it required that she be hospitalized.

By the end of the fourth week she had gone through all the usual things with her interrogators, and had been quite cooperative, although at times it seemed at least to Mahoney that she was holding something back.

They had set up shop in what had once been the farmhouse's parlor; they had equipped it with a medium-sized conference table and several comfortable chairs, a portable blackboard, recording equipment, and, most importantly, it seemed at times, a large-capacity electric coffee pot.

Two technicians had come up from Langley, had installed antisurveillance equipment, and were always present during interrogations—one operating a scanning detector, and the other operating the recorder.

The chief Company historian, Stan Kopinski, had shown up in the third week with a station wagon filled with books for cross-references. Kopinski, who was nearly as old as Mahoney, seemed almost like a machine to them all. He never slept. During the day he sat in on the sessions with the Russian woman, and during the night he reviewed the tapes, cross-checking data.

Philip Braiteswithe, the Company's foremost expert on Soviet affairs, came up at least one day a week to review everything that had gone on, and usually managed to ask one or two pertinent questions that no one else had thought of.

Bob Greene and Leonard Sampson, who had graduated from New York University together twenty years ago, and who had since never been separated, were the chief interrogators. They were good, and even Mahoney had to admit it.

At times they would be gentle with the woman. At other times they would be harsh. But always they played off each other, one of them acting the heavy, the other Mr. Nice.

Usually when the all-day sessions came to an end, everyone was exhausted because of their intensity. But in the four weeks Jada had been here, they had wrung nearly every bit of pertinent information from her that was humanly possible.

And yet, Mahoney was left with the feeling that she was holding something back. Not necessarily holding back information that she did not ever want to tell them, but holding back because she was waiting for the right moment.

The routine was for all of them to have breakfast in the kitchen from seven until eight, after which they moved into the parlor for a session until noon when they broke for lunch. The session was picked up again at one and usually lasted until five-thirty or six. The evenings were spent in analysis of tapes, or relaxation.

It was just eight o'clock on a Saturday morning when Mahoney stopped Greene and Sampson at the door to the parlor. Jada and the others were already inside, waiting to begin.

Mahoney was tired from the seven-day-a-week routine, and he missed Marge, but he was troubled. And before he left he wanted to straighten it out. So far he had contributed very little to the woman's interrogation.

"What's on board for this morning?" he asked the two men.

Greene sighed tiredly. "Mop up a few details, I guess, and then we're going to split. Shouldn't take more than an hour or so."

"You two did a good job."

Greene shrugged. "She was easy. Cooperative. Wasn't much really, except asking the right questions at the right time."

"How about next week?"

"The FBI is coming on Tuesday, from what we were told. They'll be handling local details—Soviet agent infiltration to the States, as well as operations mostly out of Washington. When they're done they'll be handling her new identity."

"I'd like some time with her," Mahoney said.

"Be our guest," Greene said. "Anything specific in mind?"

"She's holding something back."

Greene and Sampson looked at each other. "We thought so, too. But we've got everything we need. If she's holding anything back, it must be some specific operational detail, or perhaps the name of someone she wants to protect for personal reasons. It'll come out sooner or later."

Sampson reached out for the doorknob, but Mahoney stopped him. "No one has asked her why she defected."

Again both men shrugged. "She's sick," Sampson said. "She wanted to end her days in a little more comfort than she could get at home."

"Sick?" Mahoney asked.

"We got the medical report a couple of days ago . . . just didn't think to show it to you."

"What is it?"

"Leukemia," Sampson said. "With treatment she has a couple of years at the outside."

"I see," Mahoney said, and he was beginning to understand.

They went inside, sat down, and without preamble began the morning session.

Over the four weeks he had been here, Mahoney had come to respect Jada as a woman of obvious intelligence. Once upon a time she had been a beautiful woman, and the classic lines of her face and body were still there. Mahoney had supposed she had merely aged badly, but now looking at her he could definitely see the ravages of the cancer eating at her body, and he felt sorry for her.

But beyond that he was certain now that something else was bothering her. Whatever it was probably held the key to the reason she defected.

They had gotten everything they needed from her—Greene and Sampson had been correct in that. She had provided them with everything from the KGB's organizational chart, so far as an officer of her rank could be expected to know it, to the complete structure and operational details of her own department, and the KGB's plans in the event of another war between the Arabs and Israelis. She had also promised to go over the details of KGB operations in the continental United States with the FBI, although she admitted that was an area she knew very little about.

And yet she had never made it clear why she was defecting. That bothered Mahoney, because he was sure there was a good reason. He had come to understand that the woman had never done anything in her life without good reason.

The others finished about ten o'clock, and Greene and Sampson both stood at last and stretched.

"Thank you, Colonel Yatsyna, for your cooperation," Greene said, looking down at her.

She managed a slight smile.

"Within a few weeks we'll have all of this in document form, and you'll have to review it all, and initial each page. We'll also ask you to sign a cover statement as well."

"I understand," Jada said, looking up at the two men. Her voice was soft, her English as good as anyone's in the room. She got slowly to her feet. "I would assume then that I have the weekend free until the FBI comes?"

Greene nodded toward Mahoney, who was seated at the opposite end of the table from her. The technicians were packing up their gear, and Kopinski was at the door ready to leave. He stopped and looked back.

"Mr. Mahoney has a few questions for you, I believe."

Jada turned to look at him, the gentle smile still on her lips.

One of the technicians looked up. "Would you like the equipment running, Mr. Mahoney?"

Mahoney stood up. "It's not necessary," he said to them, but he was looking directly at Jada. "Would you care to take a walk? It's a beautiful morning."

"By all means," she said. "I haven't been outside for a couple of weeks now."

"Do you want us to stick around, Wallace?" Kopinski asked, still by the door.

"I don't think it's necessary," Mahoney said. He had come around the table and taken Jada's arm, and together they went out the door, down the corridor, and out the back way.

The morning was bright, the sun warm, and the trees had already begun to turn their autumnal colors. A gentle breeze blew from the south, bringing with it the pleasant smell of the countryside, as well as the sea.

There were bridle paths throughout the fifty acres, and they headed slowly down one of them, and within a few minutes they were out of sight of the house.

"How far are we from the ocean?" she asked. They had left the house and started down the path in silence. This was the first either of them had spoken.

"Five or six miles," Mahoney said. He had stuffed his hands in his jacket pockets. "Do you mind if I smoke?"

"Not at all," she said.

He took out a large cigar, unwrapped it, wet it with his tongue, and lit it. She watched the process with a smile.

"Your wife must hate those things," she said.

Mahoney laughed. "With a passion, but she never says a thing."

"You're fortunate to have such an understanding mate."

"How about you?" Mahoney asked. "Did you leave anyone behind?"

She looked away, an expression of pain in her eyes. "There was someone once . . ." she started to say, but then she cut it off.

They were several hundred yards down the path. The birds were singing, and a couple of squirrels were playing around the bole of a tree. Mahoney stopped, reached out and gently turned Jada around so that they were facing each other.

"You came here looking for something," he said softly. "Or someone. What is it?"

Her eyes were misting over, but she said nothing.

"You must know you are dying of leukemia."

She nodded.

"For your long service to the Komitet, you would have been given at least an apartment in Moscow. Perhaps even a *dacha* in the country. But you did not want to be alone, you've told us. Surely you are more alone here than at home. So you came over because you were looking for something. What?"

She didn't answer him at first; instead she turned and watched the squirrels playing for a long while. When she finally looked back there was an expression of infinite weariness and definite sadness in her eyes.

"How long have you been married, Mr. Mahoney?" she asked softly.

The question surprised him, but he answered, "Forty-one years."

"To the same woman?"

Mahoney nodded.

"Do you have children? Grandchildren?"

The bitterness Mahoney had suppressed for the last two years rose to the surface from deep within himself. "I had two sons. One of them is married, with children. The other one . . . Michael . . . was murdered by your people two years ago."

Jada reached out and touched his arm. "I'm sorry," she said genuinely. "I'm truly sorry for you. But it must have been very difficult for your wife. It must still be difficult."

"I'm not touched by your concern, comrade," Mahoney said, accenting the title.

"I need your understanding, Mr. Mahoney."

"You've dedicated your life to an organization that killed my son," Mahoney said harshly.

Jada was shaking her head. "No," she said. "I dedicated my life to a man who was killed thirty-five years ago in Operation Potsdam."

"Then why—" Mahoney started to say, but he

stopped in mid-sentence. "Operation Potsdam?"

"It wasn't called that at the time, of course. It only had a code number. But it ended during the Potsdam Conference." There was a distant look now in her eyes. "I . . . we were here in this country from late in 1943 until mid-1945, when I returned to Moscow."

"There were many Soviet operations in this country during the war," Mahoney said. "What was yours?"

"It had to do with your development of the atomic bomb, and the ending of the war. We wanted your efforts to be unsuccessful."

Mahoney tried to recall what little he knew about the atomic bomb project. At the time he had been working in Europe as an army intelligence officer. "You worked with Klaus Fuchs and David Greenglass?"

"There were others as well. Many others. But no, we didn't actually work with them. They were merely our sources. We were not here to spy. We were here to stop the project. Or at least to significantly delay it."

"I knew nothing about it," Mahoney said.

She smiled. "Very few people know anything about it. We kept our secret well, although there was one man who nearly stopped us."

"Is that why you came over? Is that what you've been holding back?"

Again Jada nodded. "And I will tell you the entire story, and what it means, if you will do me one favor. It will be a propaganda victory for your government."

Mahoney started to protest. She, of course, had had nothing to do with the death of his son two years ago. Nevertheless, she *was* KGB. He did not deal with the enemy. And thirty-five years had gone by since the first atomic bomb had been tested. Whatever it was she had done during the war didn't really matter any longer.

"Please," Jada said. "It can do no harm. You're aware of the fact I am dying. Treat this as a request from a dying old woman."

"Goddammit," Mahoney swore, and he looked away. "What is it? What do you want?"

"I want to go to Trinity, the site of the first atomic bomb test. It's south of Albuquerque, New Mexico. I want to go there and see it with my own eyes. And then I will tell you the entire story. Will you . . . can you do that for me?"

Mahoney turned back to look at her. She was an extraordinary woman, and whatever the ultimate reason was for her defection to the United States, complying with her request could do no harm. She had cooperated with them, and back in Langley they would be terming this an intelligence coup.

"Yes," he said to her at last. "I'll take you down there."

"Thank God," she said, and it struck Mahoney odd that a Soviet intelligence officer would use such a phrase.

5

WHITE SANDS MISSILE RANGE, NEW MEXICO

Mahoney managed to make all the arrangements over the weekend, despite McBundy's protests. The FBI was going to be hopping mad that they could not begin their interrogation on Tuesday as planned, and the job of soothing ruffled feathers was going to fall on the shoulders of the Missions and Operations chief.

In the end, however, McBundy had come around. There were not many people in the Company who would refuse any reasonable request from Mahoney. He had kept a low profile over the death of his son, which at the time could have made spectacular headlines, and that kind of loyalty deserved a certain amount of latitude.

They flew to Albuquerque on Monday, where they stayed at the Holiday Inn. The next morning they rented a car and drove the seventy-five miles south along the interstate through Socorro, turning off the main highway onto a secondary road and crossing the Rio Grande at the small town of San Antonio.

The day was hot, in the mid-nineties Fahrenheit, and the rugged mountains all around them faded into vague blue masses in the hazy distance. They were at the extreme northern edge of the White Sands Missile Range, and entrance to the rugged test area was from a narrow, blacktopped road that came off the highway and led to a small station called Stallion Range Gate.

At the guardhouse, Mahoney showed his identification to an old man wearing a wide Stetson hat, cowboy boots, and a western shirt and jeans. A military .45 automatic was strapped to his hip.

"Mr. Bryant, the Public Information Officer, is expecting you, sir," the old man said. He pointed down the road. "He'll be waiting at administration—it's the low building on the right by the trees."

Mahoney nodded his thanks and drove slowly to the building. Several cars and army vehicles were parked in a small lot, and a tall, thin civilian was leaning up against a military station wagon, smoking a cigarette.

When they pulled into the parking lot, he flipped his cigarette away and came over to them.

"Mr. Mahoney?" he said.

"Yes," Mahoney said, getting out of the car. "You're Jim Bryant?"

"Yes, sir," Bryant said. "Welcome to White Sands Missile Range." He glanced through the car window at Jada, who had not moved. She was staring through the rear window at the mountains to the east. "They didn't tell me very much. What exactly is it you wanted to see?"

"The atomic bomb site," Mahoney said. "How far is it from here?"

"About twenty miles," Bryant said. "We can go in my car or yours, it doesn't matter. But we're going to have to be out of there in about three hours. They've scheduled an air-to-air strike over that area."

"That should be plenty of time," Mahoney said. He turned and looked at Jada, who had not taken her eyes from the mountains. "We'll take my car. You can ride in the backseat."

"Yes, sir," Bryant said. He went to his own car and from inside took out a walkie-talkie, then came back and climbed into the backseat. Mahoney slipped behind the wheel, pulled out of the parking lot, and headed south along the narrow blacktopped road.

Jada had turned forward in her seat and was holding her body rigid, almost as if she was bracing for a crash. For a moment Mahoney was sure she was goint to collapse, but as they drove across the desert she maintained her posture, and held her silence.

Several minutes later Bryant leaned forward. "There's a road to the left coming up. Take it," he said.

A hundred yards later they came to the road that led directly east, toward the wall of mountains.

"This is still an active testing range?" Mahoney asked, looking at Bryant in the rearview mirror. The young man looked very much like his son Michael, and it gave him an odd feeling.

"Yes, sir," Bryant said.

"Where is Mockingbird Pass?" Jada asked, her voice hoarse and cracked with much emotion.

"Ma'am?" Bryant said.

She turned to look at him. "Mockingbird Pass. Where is it?"

Bryant pointed to the southwest, and Jada followed his direction to where there was a low spot in the mountains.

"How far is that from ground zero?" she asked.

"I don't know," Bryant said, hesitating. "Twelve, maybe fifteen miles."

They came to a small concrete bunker just off the road, and a few hundred yards later the road ended at a T by a high, wire-mesh fence.

"Ground zero," Bryant said. "Take a right."

The road led around the fence to a gate, where Mahoney stopped the car. Bryant jumped out, unlocked the gate, swung it open, and then came back to the car, but he did not get in. "Through the gate about three hundred yards is ground zero. The fenced-in area roughly marks the original crater."

"Are you coming in with us?" Mahoney asked.

"No, sir," Bryant said. "One of the security people will be along shortly, and I'm going back to Stallion Gate with him. I'll return in a couple of hours."

"Fine," Mahoney said, and he proceeded through the gate along a narrow sand road, and they both saw it at the same time. Jada snapped forward in her seat with a gasp.

A tall, black stone obelisk rose from a cement pad in the middle of the fenced-in area, marking the exact spot of the test.

Mahoney stopped the ear and they both got out, slowly walked to the marker, and Jada stared at it for a long time. There was a cathedrallike silence here on the floor of the desert. And the mountains, which Bryant had told them were nearly fifteen miles away, seemed ominously large, as if they were no more than a hundred yards distant.

There were tears in Jada's eyes when she finally looked up at Mahoney, and her complexion was ashen. "He's here," she said. "I can feel it."

There was a wooden reviewing stand where tourists came once a year to visit the site, and Mahoney took Jada by the shoulders and led her over to it. They sat down on the steps.

"Do you want to tell me now?" he asked gently.

"Oh, God . . ." she said, her breath coming in ragged gasps. "Alek . . . my Alek."

After a long time she began to speak.

BOOK TWO

1943

6

LONDON

It was nearly midnight and the cold drizzle that had fallen all evening showed no signs of letting up soon. A chill wind blew up from the River Thames, bringing with it a myriad of smells and impressions—diesel fuel, rotting wood, cordage, and, over all, the effluvia of a city of 8 million inhabitants.

From somewhere distant, too, the smell of cordite wafted in on a chance breeze from this evening's Luftwaffe raid, and in the distance the sounds of sirens—ambulances and fire engines—drifted over the patter of rain in the streets.

Sergeant Michael Lovelace shifted his weight from one foot to the other where he stood just within the doorway of a pottery shop in Soho, on London's West End. He was a small, seedy-looking little man, but he had great patience. He had been watching the front entrance to a Greek restaurant across the street for more than an hour, and he was beginning to wonder if the man he had followed here had slipped out the rear door.

He reached up with both hands and pulled the collar of his dirty tan raincoat closer around his neck, and shivered. He was cold, tired, hungry, and most of all angry. Angry with himself for being the fool he was. He had no business being here this evening. No business following the man halfway across London every night for five nights now. And especially no business getting mixed up in this thing in the first place.

But Lovelace was a self-admitted snoop. And over the years his curiosity, if it could be called that, had won him both the admiration and the vexation of his superior officers.

He chuckled at himself, the sound thin and totally devoid of humor. He had been ordered out of Washington—hell, literally kicked out of Washington—six months ago for doing the same thing he was doing tonight: mixing in something that was no concern of his.

Across the street the door to the restaurant opened, spreading a shaft of dull yellow light on the wet pavement, and Lovelace stiffened as a man and woman emerged. The man quickly opened an umbrella, and, holding it over both of them, they hurried down the street. Lovelace sighed and relaxed. The man had been to short, too squat. He had been able to see that even from here.

The cobblestoned street was narrow, the three- and four-story buildings crowding in on it from both sides. From time to time he caught a glimpse of a narrow crack of light across the street in an upper-level window as someone pulled back a blackout curtain, but other than that the street was dark and totally devoid of life.

For a moment Lovelace let his mind drift to his small flat around the corner from his office at Broadway near Victoria. At this moment he should be settled back with a good book on his lap, a fire in the grate, a Scotch whiskey nearby, and a Lucky Strike. He had to smile at that. He had spent an hour here without a cigarette. It was some kind of a record.

He was reaching up to scratch his nose when the door to the restaurant opened again, and he froze as Lieutenant Stewart Young and another man stepped outside.

Young was tall and very thin, almost gangly, with a bowler hat perched ridiculously atop his narrow head. The other man was powerfully built, and wore no hat. Even from where Lovelace stood he could make out the man's thick facial features. Bulgarian, perhaps.

Young seemed nervous, highly agitated, and he glanced both ways down the street before his hand darted beneath his dark raincoat, and he withdrew a fat manila envelope.

He waited a moment until the heavyset man produced a small white envelope, and the two men exchanged them, said a few words to each other, and then started away in opposite directions.

Lovelace stuffed his right hand in his coat pocket, his fingers curling familiarly around the grip of his Smith & Wesson Police Special .38, and he stepped out of the shadows.

"Leftenant Young," he called out softly as he was halfway across the street.

Young swiveled around, nearly stumbling over his own feet. "Good lord," he said.

From out of the corner of his eye, Lovelace saw the Bulgarian sink down into a crouch. He turned as he withdrew his pistol and fired two shots at the same moment the heavyset man was raising his own gun.

Without waiting to see if he had hit the man, Lovelace snapped around in time to see Young bringing up his own pistol.

"Don't," Lovelace shouted, as he brought his gun around with both hands and pointed it directly at the lieutenant.

At that moment sirens sounded all around them, and as tires screeched on wet pavement, headlights and flashing red lights bore down on them from both directions.

"Put it down!" Lovelace shouted again, but Young was like a wild man, apparently not hearing a thing but the sirens.

He seemed to be doing a macabre little dance on the sidewalk, as he looked both ways down the street at the approaching police vehicles. Then he glanced at Lovelace. A moment later he raised the pistol to his own temple and fired.

"No," Lovelace screamed too late, and he raced forward toward the fallen man. He hadn't wanted this to happen. Not this, goddammit!

Car doors were slamming, sirens were still sounding, and he could hear several men running toward him. "Halt," someone shouted from his left.

He skidded to a stop a couple of yards from Young's body and started to slowly turn around, holding both of his hands far out to his sides.

"Don't move," someone else shouted, this time from the right, and Lovelace stood stock-still.

Strong hands snatched the pistol from him and shoved him around to face the headlights.

"Bloody hell, it's Lovelace," a familiar voice said from farther back, and a moment later he was looking into the scowling face of his direct liaison duty superior, Major Chadwick Faircloth.

"Good evening, major," Lovelace said, keeping his voice as calm as he could. He had bungled it and there was going to be hell to pay. He let his hands fall slowly to his sides.

Faircloth half turned away. "Stand down, people," he shouted. "He's one of ours." He turned back to face Lovelace. "I hate to admit."

"I think they're both dead," Lovelace said, glancing over at where Young was lying sprawled on his back. Half the side of his head was covered in blood, and a dark, glistening pool had formed beside him on the wet sidewalk.

"They bloody well are, you stupid bastard," Faircloth

said, barely able to control his anger. He shook his head. "What in hell were you doing here?" he asked, but then he held out his hand. "No, don't tell me. You can explain it all to the colonel." He stared at Lovelace for several long moments, and then finally turned away and began issuing orders for ambulances, ID teams, and someone to come and clean up the mess.

Lovelace slowly walked over to where Young's body lay, bent down over it, and pushed the man's raincoat aside. From an inner pocket he withdrew the white envelope the Bulgarian had handed over, and opened it. Inside were twenty dirty, well-worn, five-pound notes. A hundred pounds.

"He was being blackmailed and needed the money," Faircloth said from behind him.

Lovelace looked up, then put the money back in the envelope and the envelope back in the dead man's pocket, and then he stood up.

"Their setup all the way?" he asked.

Faircloth nodded, his intense anger of a few moments ago evaporated. "They thought so. The poor bastard. He was a fairy and thought we didn't know it," he said, staring down at the dead man. "But he was a hell of a good cipher man. We didn't give a damn if he was the Queen of Sheba."

"What was he selling?"

Faircloth looked up, an expression of weariness on his features. "That's just the hell of it—he wasn't selling a thing. We were using him as a plant. Coded returns, dummy troop movements, and the like, with a key. We wanted the information to get back to Berlin so we could nail down their conduit. If they had swallowed it, we would have had a field day."

"Sorry," Lovelace said, looking down again at the dead man.

"Sorry, hell," Faircloth snapped, his anger flaring again. "You had no business on this one. You're a liaison man, nothing more."

"If I had been told, none of this would have happened," Lovelace said. He could feel his own anger rising. "Christ, all Woodsworthe would have had to say last week was that it was a special operation, and that I would be told about it sooner or later. I wouldn't have gone after him."

Faircloth nodded. "If it's any consolation to you, Lovelace, none of my people spotted you."

Lovelace managed a slight smile, although he did not feel that great. "I didn't see your people, either."

Faircloth shook his head again. "You're such a damned good cop—it's too bad you can't learn to keep your nose out of other people's affairs."

"That's a contradiction in terms, major."

"I suppose," Faircloth said. He glanced down at the dead man, and then back up at Lovelace. "Let's go, then," he said, and he turned on his heel and went down the street to where his car was parked.

Lovelace followed him and climbed in the passenger side as Faircloth issued a number of other orders to his people. Then the major climbed in behind the wheel and backed the car down to the corner, where he turned around.

A moment later they were headed through Soho toward Broadway, the windshield wipers flapping back and forth in a soothing rhythm. Lovelace pulled out a Lucky, lit it, and inhaled deeply, briefly wondering if they allowed prisoners at Leavenworth as many cigarettes as he smoked each day.

Six months ago. Washington, D.C. It seemed like a million miles and as many years away.

"What in hell are we supposed to do with you, Lovelace?" his superior officer had asked rhetorically.

When he had tried to answer, the captain held up his hand. "No. Please, I don't want to know that."

They were in the Pentagon Security Office, and outside the captain's tiny cubicle, Lovelace could hear the hubbub of activity—telephones ringing, typewriters clattering, and the low murmur of a dozen voices.

He had been in similar situations in a hundred offices around the country during his seventeen years of military service; beginning as a clerk typist at the Fort Hood Military Police Depot in San Antonio and stretching from one end of the United States to the other, Lovelace had become a cop. A damned good cop, but one who never seemed able to leave well enough alone.

The first incident had been at Fort Bragg, where Lovelace happened to discover that the base commander had been pilfering supplies and selling them to downtown merchants. The commander, a lieutenant colonel, had received ten years at hard labor for his escapade, and Lovelace had been reassigned without promotion. The colonel had been Old South money.

Another incident involved the Officer's Club in New York City, which Lovelace discovered operated a highly successful bordello. When he had exposed that setup, he had caught a district command officer, Lieutenant General Hubert Briggs, literally with his trousers down. Briggs resigned his commission and retired to a small farm in Massachusetts, and Lovelace, still a corporal, was reassigned once again without promotion.

"What I do want to know," the captain asked sincerely, "is why you don't just get out of the army? Hell, the Inspector General's office doesn't even want you." There was no rancor in his voice. "But I'm sure that any police force in the country would take you."

Lovelace smiled. "There's a war going on, captain, in case you hadn't noticed," he said softly. "Besides, I need three more years for my retirement."

The captain shook his head in wonder, opened a file folder, and handed a single sheet of paper across the desk. "Your orders came over this morning." When Lovelace took the paper, the captain smiled and shook his head again. "If you fuck this one up, you'll be in big trouble." He laughed. "This time I think they've finally got you boxed in."

Lovelace looked down at his orders, and he too had to smile. The captain was probably right this time. He had been assigned as special U.S. Army G-2 liaison between General Eisenhower's staff in London and the British Secret Intelligence Service (the SIS) headquarters.

"I'm to be a paper shuffler, then," he said, looking up again.

The captain stood up, a broad smile on his face. "You got it, sarge. No more cops and robbers. But, more importantly, I've got you out of my hair." He came around his desk and pumped Lovelace's hand warmly. "I want to wish you all the luck, and I really mean that."

A paper shuffler, Lovelace thought, as he took a deep drag from his cigarette. He looked over at Major Faircloth, who was concentrating on his driving.

"Is Colonel Woodsworthe in his office at this hour?"

Faircloth glanced at him and nodded. "He was waiting to see how our operation turned out this evening."

"Great," Lovelace said dourly.

"How in bloody hell do you get into these messes?" Faircloth asked. He was totally without anger now. "I took a peek at your file when you came to us, and good lord, it's a wonder they hadn't set you before a firing squad years ago."

"It's easy," Lovelace said absently. He took out another cigarette and lit it from the stub of the first.

Six days ago, during the usual Monday morning tea-and-crumpet staff briefing, Lovelace had noticed a red-tagged file sitting on Colonel Woodsworthe's desk. There had been a glossy photo of a man paperclipped to its cover, and he had asked about it.

The colonel had pushed the file aside and shook his head. "Not for you," he said.

"Who is he?" Lovelace asked. The several other officers in the office, Faircloth included, looked with amusement at the exchange. Lovelace's reputation had preceded him.

"See here," the colonel fumed. "I told you it's none of your bloody business."

Lovelace shrugged and stubbed out the butt of his cigarette in the colonel's spotless ashtray. "Just curious, colonel. No offense meant."

Woodsworthe's eyes went incredulously from Lovelace to the ashtray and back to Lovelace. No one smoked in Woodsworthe's presence. The ashtray, purely ceremonial, had been given to him by the King, and he was angry now. Once again his goat had been gotten.

"And before you show up at another staff briefing, sergeant, do something with that uniform tunic—it's filthy!" the colonel shouted, his face turning red.

"Sure," Lovelace said absently, but he was staring at the photo and the code number on the file. He had been around SIS long enough to identify the index number. The man whose photo he was looking at was in all likelihood a Nazi agent. Probably someone within the service itself, which would explain the colonel's sensitivity about it.

When he returned to his cubbyhole of an office later that morning, he placed a call down to archives, giving them the code number he had memorized.

"Colonel Woodsworthe has that file, sir," the WAAF clerk said over the phone.

"I know that," Lovelace replied. "I just came from the man's office, but like the fool I am I forgot his duty assignment. Could you look it up for me?"

"I'm sure that the colonel would be happy . . ."

"Look," Lovelace interrupted, lowering his voice conspiratorially. "I'm in a bit of a jam with the colonel as it is. I'm on my best behavior. If I go barging back into his office now requesting information I should already have, he'll hit the ceiling."

The woman was silent for a moment, and then she laughed. "All right, luv, just a sec."

Lovelace sat back and put his feet up on the desk and smiled. A few seconds later the woman was back.

"He works in Cipher School, Communications Division."

"Bletchley Park?" Lovelace asked, dropping his feet from the desk top and sitting forward. The Park was where the British were decoding Nazi Enigma messages. It was their most sensitive project.

"Until recently," the young woman said. "He's been reassigned here in analysis. Is that all?"

"Yep," Lovelace said. "I wasn't aware that old Barnes worked out of this building."

"Barnes?" the woman said, confused.

"Yes, Joseph Barnes," Lovelace said in mock surprise. He repeated the file number. "Barnes *is* the man we're talking about?"

"I can see why Colonel Woodsworthe would be mad at you—you've apparently gone and mixed up your files. I don't know anything about this Barnes, whoever he is, but the index you're talking about belongs to Lieutenant Stewart Young."

"Thanks," Lovelace said. "You saved me from a fate worse than death. If the colonel had found out what I was up to, he'd have my head for sure."

"Anytime," the woman said. "And good luck," she added before she rang off.

Faircloth parked at the rear of the SIS building, and they entered through a back door, which the major unlocked with his own key. Down a narrow, dimly lit corridor, they came to the large entry hall at the front of the building, where they signed in with date and time. Then they took the wide marble stairs, with ornate iron railings, up to the third floor.

At the top landing they stopped, and Faircloth seemed to study Lovelace's eyes for a long moment. "I suppose that over the years a fellow like you would have built up quite a list of enemies."

Lovelace nodded, but said nothing. He had always liked Major Faircloth, who had seemed to him to be a decent sort.

"Is that why you carry a weapon?"

"It's come in handy from time to time."

Faircloth seemed to think that over for a moment, then grunted noncommittally. "When the lab boys are finished with it, I'll see it gets back to you."

"Thanks," Lovelace said, and together they walked down the wide corridor, their heels clattering loudly on the tile floor.

At the far end of the building, Faircloth knocked once at a plain wooden door, and Lovelace braced himself for the coming storm. He briefly wondered what his next assignment would be, if indeed there was to be another assignment, and then Faircloth opened the door and they entered the staff briefing room.

Colonel Woodsworthe, his thinning gray hair mussed, his military tunic open, and his tie undone, sat at one end of the long conference table, several maps and documents spread out in front of him. Next to him sat an American army lieutenant colonel, whom Lovelace vaguely recognized as someone he had seen around Ike's London headquarters.

Both men looked up and then got to their feet as Faircloth and Lovelace entered the room. They shook hands.

"Thanks for your cooperation at this time of night, colonel," the American officer said.

"My pleasure," Woodsworthe replied, and he glanced over at Lovelace. "Entirely my pleasure," There was a tight smile on his face.

"Will you need his report?"

Woodsworthe shook his head. "We've pretty well

pieced it together." Again he glanced at Lovelace. "Quite inventive, actually."

"So I'm told," the American officer said softly. He turned, took his wet raincoat from where it was draped over a chair, nodded to Woodsworthe and then Faircloth, and headed across the room for the door. "Let's go, sergeant," he snapped.

Lovelace shook hands with Faircloth and smiled. "Nice knowing you, major," he said, and he turned and followed the colonel out into the corridor. They headed at a brisk pace toward the stairs.

"What's it going to be, colonel—jail or reassignment?" Lovelace asked as they walked. At this moment he really didn't give a damn; he was merely curious.

But the colonel didn't say a thing until they had gone downstairs, signed out with the guards, and climbed into a staff car parked outside.

Before they pulled away from the curb he looked over at Lovelace. "You're one amazing sonofabitch," he said without anger.

"So I've been told," Lovelace said, and as he lit a cigarette, the colonel slammed the car in gear and they took off at breakneck speed along the nearly deserted streets.

After they had gone a couple of blocks, the colonel again glanced over at Lovelace and he shook his head. "Before I get you out to Heathrow, I've got to brief you."

"Heathrow?" Lovelace asked, stunned. He had expected some kind of retribution for his latest caper, but this was coming a little too fast.

"There's a plane waiting for you, but listen up now. I'm only going to tell you this once, and don't bother asking me any questions, because I don't have any of the answers."

"What about my things from my flat?"

"Already taken care of," the colonel said with some exasperation, and before Lovelace could interrupt again, he continued. "You have been promoted to captain, effective immediately. That's under direct verbal orders from President Roosevelt himself."

Lovelace sat back, his stomach fluttering.

"You're being assigned to the Counter Intelligence Corps, under a General Leslie R. Groves, in Washington. He's Army Corps of Engineers. Heads something called the Manhattan District Project. You're to report directly to him, and no one else, the moment your plane lands."

None of this was making any sense. The Army Corps built roads and bridges and dams. What did the CIC have to do with it? But before he could ask the dozen questions that had immediately come into his mind, the colonel was continuing.

"Your assignment is classified top secret, captain. From this point on, you will not discuss it with anyone, except for General Groves. And that includes me."

7

MOSCOW

General Ivan Yenikeev looked ashen, and when Runkov was ushered into his office the old man got slowly to his feet. There was a thin bead of perspiration on his upper lip, something Runkov had been noticing more of lately as the pressures of being chief administrator of the GRU wore thin.

Yenikeev was, after all, an administrator and nothing more. He had no stomach for the finer details of many of the military secret service's projects. Yet his very innocuousness apparently was the reason Stalin had selected him—it was expected that sooner or later Yenikeev would seriously bungle his job and that the GRU would be phased out of existence, probably to be swallowed up by Merkulov's NKGB. It was a typical game of Soviet politics.

"Good morning, comrade general," Runkov said, coming across the room to the wide desk. Although he had not gotten much sleep last night, he felt good this morning.

"What's this . . . what in hell is going on?" Yenikeev demanded, barely able to control his anger.

"Whatever are you talking about, general?" Runkov asked, looking directly into the man's eyes. He genuinely did not know what his boss was talking about. He had been summoned from his office downstairs a few minutes ago. No explanations.

"This business with Valkyrie, and networks in the United States, and . . ." The general broke off, unable to complete the sentence.

"Assassinations?" Runkov finished it for him.

"I'm ordering you to cease and desist, major. This time you have gone too far. Entirely too far. They are our allies."

How the old fool had found out about the project so quickly was a source of mystery for the moment, but Runkov was going to put an end to it quickly. He reached out and picked up the telephone from the general's desk. "May I?" he asked, and he gave the operator the extension number for his own office.

Yenikeev said nothing, and a moment later Doronkin answered.

"Vladimir, bring up the envelope lying on my desk, immediately."

"Yes, sir," the sergeant said, and Runkov hung up the phone.

"In just a moment, general, everything will become clear to you."

"I am ordering you, major, to abandon this insane project, whatever its exact nature is," the general said, straightening up.

Runkov just smiled as he looked the man straight in the eye, and the two of them stood there like that for a minute or two, until Doronkin arrived at the door with a plain white envelope.

Runkov moved to the door, took the envelope, and dismissed his aide. Coming back to the general's desk, he opened the envelope, withdrew a letter, and handed it over. "I think you should read that, comrade general."

Yenikeev took the letter, which was stamped top and bottom, *Most Secret*, and read it, his face turning white by degrees.

Maj. Dmitrevich Runkov is acting on my behalf in a most secret project of supreme importance to this government, and the war effort. He is to be given the utmost of cooperation at all times, with no questions asked. This matter shall not be documented through normal channels, nor shall it be discussed with any person at any time.

[SIGNED]

Joseph Stalin
Marshal

The general looked up at Runkov, again at the letter, and then slowly sat down. He handed the letter back and shook his head. "Monstrous," he said, half under his breath.

When he looked up again, there was fear in his eyes. "Get out," he said softly. "I don't want to see or hear of you or of this again."

"As you wish, general," Runkov said. He saluted, turned on his heel, and left the office, taking the elevator back downstairs.

He folded the fake letter he had written himself, stuffed it back in its envelope, and put it in his shirt pocket beneath his tunic.

Yenikeev, Merkulov, and Beria, three parts of a triangle, all wishing for the failure of this project, with Stalin at the wings waiting with a promotion for whoever was victorious. It was another of the games of Soviet politics that Runkov had learned well in his long career. All three of them had the power, but he had the cunning and the ruthlessness.

Back in his office Runkov summoned Doronkin inside and, while he was taking off his tunic and hanging it up, he began outlining his instructions.

"First of all, any word yet from communications about Valkyrie?"

"They've apparently lost contact with him. Temporarily, I'm told."

Runkov stopped what he was doing, and turned to look at his assistant. "What?" he said, flabbergasted.

"From what I'm told it has become normal for the man not to check in once a week. It has been three weeks now since his last transmission."

Runkov cursed himself for his own inefficiency. He should have known, but he had been too damned busy over the past months. He tried to think. It was very possible the man had been exposed, or perhaps Canaris' entire staff had fallen. They knew it was coming. Which left them only one way.

"Then we'll have to use a more direct means for summoning him," Runkov said, sitting down behind his desk. He pulled a pad of paper toward him, wrote a three-word message, tore the sheet off, and handed it to Doronkin. "See that this is coded and put on the C Channel for Berlin immediately."

Doronkin looked at the message, and his eyes widened. "But, major . . ." he started to say. Runkov cut him off.

"It is the only way. If the man refuses to answer his queries, this will bring him out of the woodwork."

"This could mean his death. The C Channel code has been broken by the Germans. They will understand that we have an agent in Berlin. They will be watching for him."

"Yes," Runkov said, with no satisfaction. "But if he cannot get himself out of this mess, then he's not the man for our project, is he?"

Doronkin shook his head in wonderment. "Anything else?"

"Yes, quite a lot, actually," Runkov said. "But get that message out first, and then come back here. We've got a lot of work to do, including finding him a wife. The Americans will expect it."

When Doronkin had left, Runkov rolled up his shirt sleeves, opened the file folder marked *Valkyrie*, and began reading.

His real name was Aleksandr Petrovich Badim, and he had been born in Moscow in 1912. His mother had died giving him birth, and his father had been killed five years later in the Revolution.

After the war, the teachers in the state-operated orphanage in which Badim had been placed came to the realization that the young man was quite extraordinary. Perhaps even a genius.

He had a facility for languages, and by the time he was ten could speak fluent German, Polish, English, and French, besides his native tongue. He also was quite good with mathematics and engineering. For a time he was the pride of the school, his teachers making it almost their hobby to discover at what level they could stump him. By the time he was fourteen he was already devouring college-level texts in three languages and he came at last to the attention of the State Security apparatus.

As early as 1931, Stalin had correctly surmised that the defeated Germany would, in the not-too-distant future, rise again as a world power. Adolf Hitler and his brownshirts were going to be a force to be reckoned with.

He had ordered his security people to begin setting up an agent network in Germany, and if at all possible to infiltrate the building Nazi party.

To this purpose Badim, among others, had been selected because of his brilliance, and because of his near-perfect German, and he was placed in a special school outside Moscow. For two years he was intensively trained there in espionage, politics, warfare, and weaponry, and proved to be a very apt pupil.

In 1934, when he was twenty-two, he was smuggled into Germany, where he was given a complete German identity—parents who had been killed in an accident, school records at the University in Gottingen, and a brief work record in Munich. Immediately he joined the Nazi party, as well as the army, and within a couple of years had gone through officers' school and had become a lieutenant in the Abwehr, the German military intelligence service.

From that day forward Badim had sent regular intelligence reports back to the Soviet Union, sometimes transmitting directly, and sometimes passing the information through intermediaries.

More than once he had almost been discovered, but each time the person or persons who were about to expose him turned up dead, or simply disappeared.

Over the past two years his reports had come less and less frequently, but the ones that did arrive were of inestimable value.

At this moment, Badim was a major in the Abwehr working directly under Admiral Canaris in Berlin.

Responsibility for Badim had fallen on Runkov's shoulders eighteen months ago, and a major portion of what the GRU knew of German military capabilities came directly from him.

Before this summer's counteroffensive, which pushed the Nazis back from Moscow, Badim had been indispensable. But now that the tide of war had definitely changed, Badim's presence in Germany was no longer one of absolute necessity. It was one of the reasons Runkov had suggested his name for this project, and he supposed the reason Stalin had agreed.

There was another reason Runkov had thought of Badim for this project, and that was old Admiral Canaris himself.

In the last few transmissions from Valkyrie that Runkov had personally studied, the GRU had been informed that Canaris was rapidly losing influence with Hitler. Badim had warned of Canaris' decline and probable fall as early as six months ago.

Runkov had ordered his agent to try with any means at his disposal to hasten such a downfall. Canaris was an outstanding intelligence service administrator, and with him gone the Abwehr would sink into inefficiency. But it was a dangerous game, because when Canaris fell, so would his top aides and officers, Badim included.

Very few photographs had ever been taken of Badim. It was a security precaution that the administrators of the espionage school Badim had attended had insisted on. Most of the photos that had been taken, including school pictures from the orphanage, had been sought out and destroyed.

One photograph had been snapped, however, by a GRU agent in Berlin. It showed a young, very intense, good-looking man in the uniform of the German army, standing behind and slightly to the right of Admiral Canaris among a line of several top-ranking German officers and their aides. To the left stood Adolf Hitler himself, and from the angle of the photograph it was clear that the officers were on a reviewing stand somewhere near the Reichschancellery.

Badim was tall, towering a good half head above Canaris, had square, erect shoulders, and carried an almost aristocratic bearing and posture.

He had been perfect all along for this assignment, but now it was time for him to return home to train for an even more important job.

Runkov closed the file folder, sat back in his chair, and sighed deeply. Badim had never married. There had been no time for it, nor would it have been a wise move. A wife, for a man like Badim, would have been dangerously excessive baggage. A weak point in his armor of self-defense. At least until now.

Doronkin came into the office and gingerly laid the slip of paper with the message to Badim on the desk almost as if it was some sort of dangerous animal.

For a moment both men just looked at each other, until finally the sergeant nodded. "I waited until it went out."

"Very good," Runkov said, sitting forward. "It will either bring him home, or render him useless as far as we are concerned." He smiled. "He'll have to get out without revealing the fact he is a Russian. Would you care to take a little wager on what happens, Vladimir?"

Doronkin shook his head. "No, sir."

"No, sir," Runkov repeated, and he swiveled his chair so that he could look out of the window and across the courtyard toward the Bolshoi Theater. The day was bright, the sky almost completely cloudless after last night's rain, and he pondered for a moment the project whose wheels he was setting in motion.

Badim had penetrated German security and had managed to escape detection for all these years. The work he had done for them had been brilliant, and now he deserved some kind of safe job in Moscow, away from the front line.

And yet from what little he knew about the man, he was certain that such a desk job would not be suitable. From the little that any of them knew of Badim, the man thrived on danger.

No, Runkov told himself, he would not allow himself any second thoughts about this project. No doubts. If the Americans were successful in their efforts to construct this new super weapon, they would become the ultimate power in the struggle for international realignment after the war.

It was, as he had told Stalin, a totally unacceptable position for the Soviet Union. But someday, he mused, there would come a head-to-head confrontation between the United States and the Soviet Union. And this project would be the front-runner. If it succeeded, the balance sheet would place them on equal footing with the Americans. If not?

He sighed and turned back to his aide.

"Is everything all right, major?" the sergeant asked, concerned. "Can I bring you something?"

Runkov smiled. Doronkin was a loyal soldier who would follow his master to the ends of the earth and beyond. Perhaps even to the top of St. Basil's, his head also on a pike.

"I'm fine, but now we begin our work in preparation for Valkyrie." He thought a moment, and then began ticking points off on his thick, powerful fingers. "First off, I want you to dig out the files on all female personnel in our GRU, as well as the NKVD and NKGB. She'll have to speak perfect English, preferably the American idiom, she'll have to be somewhere between twenty and let's say thirty, and she'll have to be absolutely loyal . . . if possible, not a native-born Russian."

"A tall order," Doronkin said.

"Indeed," Runkov replied. "After you've brought those files here I want you to get over to my apartment and bring back a few items, and then arrange for a couple of cots to be sent up here. I have a feeling we're going to be at this for a bit."

He stood up and started to straighten his tie. "I'm going over to see Beria and then Merkulov, to find out exactly what kind of agent networks they already have going in the United States, and if they are producing anything. When I get back we're going to have to put everything together. I don't want anyone getting in Valkyrie's way."

"Yes, sir," Doronkin said.

Runkov came around his desk, but before he grabbed his coat from the rack, he glanced down at the slip of paper with the message to Badim in English: VALKYRIE COME HOME. It would be enough to dislodge him. For some time the Germans had suspected there was a high-ranking spy in their midst. This message would prove it, and throw the suspicion on the Americans.

"Oh, one more thing," he said, and Doronkin looked up. "Find me a submarine. A German submarine in good working order."

Doronkin stared at him for a long moment, but then he nodded his head and went to the outer office, while Runkov pulled on his coat and buttoned it up. The sergeant was back a moment later with a plain white envelope.

"A messenger just came with this. Said it was for you, major."

Runkov took the envelope and opened it. "Did he say who this was from?"

"No, sir. He just handed it to me and told me it was for you. Personally."

Inside was a single sheet of paper, which Runkov unfolded, and for a moment his heart skipped a beat.

It was a letter, stamped top and bottom *Most Secret*, and was signed, Joseph Stalin, Marshal. The letter was the exact duplicate of the one he had typed himself last night here in the office. Stalin knew, and by this approved of Runkov's actions. The thought was at once comforting and frightening.

"One more thing, Vladimir," he said. "After this before you leave at night, I want the contents of my wastepaper basket burned."

8

It was still dark when the olive drab DC-3 bumped to a landing at Bolling Air Corps Base across the Potomac River from Washington National Airport. The pilot taxied to the southwest terminal at the opposite side of the field from the U.S. Naval Station.

Lovelace was dead tired. His eyes were on fire, his head throbbed, and his mouth felt gummy. They had stopped in Prestwick, Scotland, to refuel before making the transatlantic hop, then had stopped once more at Harmon, Newfoundland, before they continued down the east coast to Washington.

All through the night Lovelace had tried to piece together what little the lieutenant colonel had told him last night in London. But it was no use. The facts, as startling as they were, admitted no intelligent speculation.

He had been promoted to captain, on direct orders from the President himself. He had been assigned to something called the Manhattan District Project. His boss was a General Leslie Groves. And his orders were verbal and top secret. There was nothing more.

He had not been allowed to get off the plane either time it landed, but at Prestwick he had been given a thermos of coffee, and at Harmon there had been a C-ration breakfast and more coffee. Other than that he had been left alone, the only passenger on board.

The plane pulled up in front of Base Operations, the engines roared for a moment, then clanked to a stop, and a minute or two later the pilot came out of the cockpit. He, too, looked tired.

"Last stop, captain," he said, and he went to the door, undogged the latch, and swung it open as Lovelace unbuckled his seatbelt and got wearily to his feet.

The air smelled warm and moist. At least it was going to be a pleasant climatic change from the damp cold of London. Central heating and soft toilet paper, the two greatest American inventions, were waiting for him, and Lovelace was going to make full use of the latter, after which he was going to sleep for twenty-four hours.

The pilot was speaking to someone on the ground, and a moment later the boarding stairs were pushed into position and the pilot ducked back inside.

"Your things will be taken care of for you, captain," he said.

Lovelace came forward to the door, his raincoat open, and the pilot eyed his enlisted man's uniform.

"I'm traveling incognito," Lovelace said, and he brushed past the man and went down the boarding stairs.

The night was definitely warm, and to the west across the black expanse of the river he could make out several scattered lights that marked Washington. The city was still under a blackout, and the thought was chilling.

A green Dodge staff car was parked in the shadows across the apron from the airplane, and as Lovelace stepped away from the stairs someone climbed out of the driver's seat and called out, "Over here, captain."

Lovelace stopped in mid-stride and looked over to where the car was parked, but he could just barely make out the figure of a man dressed in a plain khaki uniform.

The ground crew was busy with the aircraft and across the apron in Base Ops Lovelace could see several men at work through the windows. He had the odd sensation that no one knew or really cared who he was or the fact that he was here. He had been transported to this spot, and then completely forgotten.

"Let's go," the man by the car called out again. "We have a train to catch."

Wearily Lovelace headed that way, and a couple of yards from the man he caught the gleam of something on his uniform collar. Another step closer and he could see that the man was wearing one star. He was a brigadier general.

"Jesus Christ," Lovelace said softly, and he stiffened and threw the man a salute.

"Nope," the man said, returning the salute. "General Leslie Groves." He stepped forward and shook Lovelace's hand. "Welcome to Washington."

The general was slightly taller than Lovelace, with broad shoulders and a husky frame. He wore no hat and his curly hair was trimmed well above his ears. He appeared to be in his late forties, and from the expression in his eyes and the stern set of his mouth even in a slight grin, Lovelace caught the distinct impression that this man would brook no nonsense.

"This has come as a surprise, general," Lovelace said. "Can you tell me what it's all about?"

"We can talk on the way to Baltimore. We've got a 7:20 to catch," Groves said, and he turned and climbed into the car. Lovelace got in on the passenger side, and a moment later they were headed across the airfield toward the main gate.

Neither man said anything until they had been passed off base, and were heading out Alabama Avenue past St. Elizabeth's Hospital.

"I had your things sent up to my office," Groves said as he drove. "My wife packed up a bag with a fresh uniform, some clean socks and underwear, a toothbrush, and razor. It's in the trunk. You can clean up and get some rest on the train."

"Where exactly are we heading, general?" Lovelace asked. He was dead tired and wanted to lie back this instant and sleep.

"Oak Ridge, Tennessee," Groves said. He glanced over at Lovelace. "From your record it would appear that you're one hell of a cop."

Lovelace chuckled. "I think at this moment General Eisenhower might disagree."

Groves laughed. "He and the British will calm down. FDR was impressed with your qualifications, and so am I. You're not afraid to step on toes, you never give up, and you don't make assumptions. We're going to put those talents to good use."

"Doing what, sir?"

"You're going to become a creep."

"A creep?"

Groves laughed again. "That's what they're calling the Counter Intelligence Corps boys. Colonel Lansdale's handling security for the project, but you're going to be working directly for me. I'll keep you plenty busy."

"What if I don't accept this assignment?" Lovelace asked on impulse.

"No one refuses me, captain," Groves snapped. He glanced over again. "And let's get one thing straight right now—I don't take any bullshit from anyone. That includes scientists, industrialists, and especially not prima donna cops. You were picked for this assignment the same way everyone else on the project was selected; you have a particular talent, and we need it."

For some peculiar reason Lovelace had the feeling he was going to enjoy working for Groves. "Tell me then, general, just what is this project, and where exactly do I fit in?"

"We're building an atomic bomb," Groves said, a hard edge to his voice. "And you are going to make sure that no one finds out about it, or interferes."

Lovelace pulled out a cigarette and lit it with unaccountably shaky hands as they continued through the early morning darkness past Anacostia Park and over the border into Maryland.

During his six months liaison to the British Secret Intelligence Service, he had picked up bits and pieces of information about several British and American projects, among them radar, jet aircraft, and something to do with a raid on a heavy-water plant in Norway. The last had never been fully explained to him, but the manner in which it had been treated had alerted him to the fact that it was of supreme importance. He had heard the word "atomic" once during a briefing involving the raid, but then, too, no explanations had been given.

They picked up the Baltimore Highway near Hyattsville, and when they had accelerated to the nighttime speed limit of fifty-five miles per hour, Groves reached down and picked up a bound file from the seat between them, and handed it to Lovelace.

"This is a copy of a summary report we put together for FDR and Churchill. Damn few people have seen it, and you will not discuss it at any time with anyone but me. Is that understood?"

Lovelace nodded, and Groves reached down and flipped on a light below the dash. "Read it now. This will be the only time you'll ever see it, but by the time we get down to Oak Ridge, I want you to know exactly what is going on, because I'm going to put you to work immediately."

Lovelace stubbed out his cigarette, sat back in the seat, and idly thumbed through the thick file for a few moments. The pages were filled mostly with charts, graphs, and other scientific diagrams, along with maps and a few sketches and photos of what appeared to be huge industrial plants under construction.

"Why me?" he asked softly.

Groves looked his way. "What?"

"I said, why me, general?"

"I've already explained that . . ." Groves began, but Lovelace interrupted him.

"If I am to be privy to the information contained in this report, if I'm to be working directly for you, and if, as you say, you're not going to put up with any bullshit, you're going to have to be straight with me, general. I can't and won't work in the dark. I'll have to know everything. And that includes why I was selected for this job. The real reason."

For a long time Groves held his silence as they sped through the night toward Baltimore. There was very little traffic on the highway, and the dash light cast a reflection of the general's face on the inside of the windshield. Lovelace stared at it.

"Because you're a screw-up cop," Groves said at last. "Or at least that's your reputation, but I saw something different in the record. You've been transferred from every duty station you've ever been assigned to because of your habit of poking your nose where it doesn't belong. There are quite a number of people still serving prison terms who disregarded your abilities."

"How did my name come up in the first place?"

Groves smiled. "General Briggs and I are old friends. He still calls you that 'sonofabitch,' but he said you were the best damned cop he ever had the misfortune of running into." Groves looked over at Lovelace. "He was involved with the New York City Officers' Club a few years back."

"I remember," Lovelace said, and he, too, had to smile.

"I'm giving you a free hand in this, Lovelace. I want you to poke your nose into anything that interests you. There'll be no person or no place where you won't belong or can't investigate. Everything is open."

"Including you?" Lovelace asked, again on impulse.

Groves laughed out loud. "Including me," he replied, and without another word Lovelace opened the report to the first page and began reading.

America's entry into the race for the "nuclear secret," as it was called, had its feeble beginning in the spring of 1939 when the Navy Department awarded a fifteen-hundred-dollar research grant to study the feasibility of using a rare isotope of uranium to power submarines. Then it was in October of that year when a Hungarian scientist, Leo Szilard, afraid of what Adolf Hitler might do if the Nazis unleashed the nuclear secret, convinced Albert Einstein to write a letter to President Roosevelt outlining the danger.

It was this letter, which suggested the possibility of an atomic weapon of unbelievable power, that convinced the President to at least investigate.

To this end a secret advisory committee on uranium was formed, and by February of 1940, the committee had appropriated six thousand dollars for the purchase of graphite and uranium ore for research.

By July of that year, a new group, this one called the National Defense Research Committee, was formed to further investigate the feasibility of coming up with enough fissionable material to make a bomb possible in time to affect the outcome of the war. It was about this time that the Americans began to become seriously worried about research efforts into the same possibilities.

But it wasn't until the second half of 1941, when the high-powered Office of Scientific Research and Development was formed, that the work began in earnest.

That year three hundred thousand dollars was spent on research grants to sixteen separate universities; all publication of papers involving any aspect of nuclear research was voluntarily halted; and on December sixth, one day before Pearl Harbor was attacked, the committee of scientists investigating the bomb possibility was given six months to come up with a go, no-go recommendation.

The S-1 group reported back to Roosevelt on June seventeenth of 1942, with the recommendation that if an all-out effort to build the bomb began immediately with a budget of at least a hundred million dollars, such a weapon might be constructed as early as June of 1944.

FDR gave his go-ahead the same day, and on the eighteenth the Army Corps of Engineers was selected for the job, and the Manhattan District was created. In September, General Groves was assigned to head the project.

The concept of an atomic bomb was actually quite simple, and was based on a theoretical conclusion that if enough fissionable materials were to be suddenly assembled in one lump, an explosion millions of times more powerful than TNT would occur.

There were two difficulties with the execution of the theory, however: The first was refining enough of the pure fissionable material, and the second was somehow assembling it instantaneously into what the scientists were calling a critical mass.

The latter problem was being studied at a laboratory outside of Santa Fe, New Mexico, at a place called Los Alamos. The lab was code-named Site Y. Heading this project was a University of California scientist, Dr. J. Robert Oppenheimer, Jr.

The first problem, however, was the one creating the most difficulties.

Two kinds of materials could be used for an atomic bomb. The first was a rare isotope of uranium, for which a huge industrial complex was being built at Oak Ridge, Tennessee. The second was plutonium, for which another huge plant was being constructed in a remote section of Washington State near the town of Hanford.

The combined work force of these two plants numbered in the tens of thousands of men and women, and involved dozens of companies around the country.

And yet, Lovelace was shocked to read, no one, including the scientists, was certain that any of this would ever work. It was a huge gamble.

They were just entering Baltimore when Lovelace finished reading the report, and he closed the cover and looked up at Groves, who had a slight smile on his lips.

"Amazing, isn't it?" Groves asked.

"Insane." He laid the report back on the seat between them, his mind racing. If such a weapon could actually be built, it would be monstrous. And yet, weren't tanks and flame throwers and ordinary bombs monstrous as well? The only difference here was the scale of destruction.

But that wasn't his problem. His concern was security. And how in hell could a project involving tens of thousands of people be made secure? It was impossible. It was a situation in which a security officer had to fail.

"It's either us or the Nazis," Groves said.

Lovelace looked at him. "Is that all, general?" he asked softly. "I mean, is that the only reason we're building this thing?"

They came around a corner, a block from the train depot. "I'm a military officer, Lovelace. I was given a job to do, and I'm going to do it to the best of my abilities. It's not my place to ponder the philosophical or moral aspects of this thing." He glanced over. "I called you in as an extra security measure, not to act as a conscience for the project."

Lovelace managed a tight little smile, and he shook his head. "Colonel Lansdale seems to be handling security as well as can be expected. Anything I might do would only amount to a drop in the bucket as far as that's concerned."

"Look," Groves said, raising his voice, "we've gone over that already. I want you in on this."

"You've got me, general. Only if I'm to be given a free hand, I'm going to do this my way."

"Which means?"

"Which means simply that there is nothing I can do that would effectively increase your security. What I am going to do, however, is cover your rear door. You've gone and left it open."

A startled expression crossed Groves' face, but he said nothing until they had pulled up in the train station's parking lot, where he shut off the headlights and the engine. "What do you mean?" he asked.

Lovelace tapped the cover of the report lying on the seat between them with a tobacco-stained index finger. "Just how important to this project is Dr. Oppenheimer?"

Groves' eyebrows rose. "Very."

"And Dr. Fermi?"

"Almost as important."

"And yourself?"

"What are you getting at?" Groves snapped impatiently. He looked at his watch. "We've got only a few minutes before our train leaves. Out with it, man."

Lovelace leaned forward. "Colonel Lansdale will watch out for infiltrators. I'm going to work on the theory that someone would like to see this project stopped."

"Sabotage?" Groves said incredulously. "Impossible. The processes are spread out too far. Nothing anyone could do would seriously hurt us."

Lovelace shook his head, then formed a pistol with his right hand, his finger pointing directly at Groves' head. "What if, general, you were to be assassinated? And what if Dr. Oppenheimer and perhaps Dr. Fermi and a few others were to be taken off the project? Permanently. What then?"

Groves had turned white, and for a long moment he said nothing. Finally he gathered up the report on the seat and opened his car door, but before he got out he looked back, a pinched smile on his lips. "I'm glad you decided to join us, Lovelace," he said. "But I promise you one thing."

"What's that, general?"

"If I'm assassinated, you're fired."

9

It was shortly before eight on a chilly, rain-swept morning when Abwehr Major Alek Badim emerged from his staff car, crossed the sidewalk, and mounted the steps to the large stone building at 74-76 Tirpiz-Ufer, Nazi Intelligence Services Headquarters.

He was a tall man, aristocratically handsome, with dark hair and eyes, and an apparently natural, easygoing smile. But this morning he was in a sour mood. What he was doing, what he had been doing over the past months, went against his grain. Canaris was a good man, who along with his chief assistant, Colonel Hans Oster, had been opposed to Hitler from the beginning.

There had been rumors of plots against the Fuehrer's life almost monthly, it seemed, from as early as September of 1939, when Poland was attacked.

And that constant threat was the wedge that Badim had used to begin the long process of prying someone so high in rank away from the strings and levers of power. Canaris and Oster would fall, and with them presumably the entire Abwehr within a matter of months, certainly in less than a year's time.

But that accomplishment, which was partly of Badim's doing, and partly of Canaris' doing himself—the admiral seemed incapable of keeping quiet about his views—gave Badim little or no satisfaction. Over the past two years of his assignment to Canaris' staff, he had come to admire the man because of his obvious intelligence tempered by a good and gracious manner.

He nodded absently to the sentries at the front doors, and took the stairs up to his office on the second floor. As he emerged from the stairwell he saw Colonel Oster hurrying down the corridor, out of breath and red-faced.

"Alek, thank goodness you're here," the husky, white-haired man puffed.

Badim stood with his hand on the doorknob the top button of his tunic undone, and waited until the colonel reached him.

"Have you heard?"

"Have I heard what, colonel? I've only just now arrived," Badim said. His voice was sonorous, well-modulated, obviously cultured.

The colonel seemed to regain some of his composure, and he took a deep breath, letting it out slowly. "All hell has broken loose," he said. "You'd better come along—the old man is in a fit. I've never seen him like this."

"What's happened?" Badim asked, forcing himself to remain calm. Inside he could feel his gut tightening.

"He spent most of the night with Hitler and Keitel in a railroad car in the station, and now Himmler is screaming for blood. Something about an intercepted message on the C Channel. Someone has bungled this thing pretty badly."

"You're not making any sense. What message? Who has bungled what?"

The colonel looked at him for a long moment. "Come on, he's waiting for you. I'll let him explain it. But

Himmler has asked for you personally." He turned and hurried down the corridor, Badim falling in behind, taking off his leather gloves, hat, and greatcoat as he walked.

That the Reichsfuehrer wanted to see him was not in itself unusual. But how Canaris would view the summons was another matter.

Lately Oster had seemed to be in a constant state of lather, and it was obvious to Badim that something had been hatching for some time now. But Canaris rarely lost his temper, although his sharp tongue was often used to make disparaging remarks about anything that was bothering him at the moment . . . including the Fuehrer himself. It was these casual remarks that Badim had made use of in his careful campaign to unseat the admiral.

But this morning, if Oster's agitation was to be taken at face value, something big was happening. And against the strong possibility that his cover might be involved, Badim began to review his plans for escape. Through his long years in Germany he always had such plans in the back of his mind, no matter where he found himself.

Canaris' secretary, a young Abwehr lieutenant, was sitting morosely behind his desk in the outer office when Oster and Badim came in. He looked, then jumped up stiffly at attention.

Oster paid no attention to him; instead he crossed the room, knocked once on Canaris' door, and went in. Badim laid his things over a chair and followed Oster inside, softly closing the door behind him.

Canaris stood behind his desk, his back to the door, staring out the window at the overcast, rainy morning. For several long moments it didn't seem as if he was aware that anyone had come in. Then Oster cleared his throat, and he turned around.

He looked bad. His hair was disheveled, his eyes red-rimmed, and there was an unhealthy gray pallor to his skin. When he motioned for them to sit down his hand shook.

"Did Hans fill you in?" he asked as they took their seats across the wide desk from him. He remained standing for the moment.

"No, sir," Badim said, looking up at him. "Just that there seems to be some kind of trouble, and the Reichs-fuehrer wants to see me, but not why."

"I was rather hoping you could tell me that," Canaris said. His voice was ragged, and soft, as if he had a cold.

As Deputy Chief of Foreign Intelligence Activities, Badim had often hand-carried Abwehr reports to Himmler's office. Canaris knew that. But what the admiral did not know—or at least Badim hoped he didn't know—was that Badim had often handed Himmler other reports that never showed up on any Abwehr staff budgets. Reports on Canaris' and Oster's activities. It was these reports that Himmler had been using to sidestep the Abwehr in his drive toward deposing the admiral and taking over the service himself.

"No, sir, I cannot," he said. "The weekly summary of foreign intelligence activities isn't due until Friday."

Canaris glanced at Oster, and some message seemed to pass between them, then he sighed, took a slip of paper from a file folder lying on his desk, and handed it across to Badim. "This supposedly came over the Soviet C Channel, and was routinely decoded and sent to all departments, including Himmler's snoops." He sat down.

Badim took the slip of paper on which was stamped the routine decoding and routing initials, with the label, "C Channel . . . U.S.S.R.," but his eyes were riveted on the three-word message in English: VALKYRIE COME HOME.

In English! What the hell were they trying to do? He knew they were trying to contact him, wanting a report. He had received a postcard in his mailbox from his supposed aunt in Garmisch-Partenkirchen. But this was insane.

Canaris was talking, and Badim had to force himself to calm down and listen. His life could very well depend upon it.

"Himmler is undoubtedly going to ask you about this—he hasn't the courage to confront me directly. So before you go over there I'm going to have to fill you in."

"Fill me in?" Badim asked. A small but powerful fishing boat was at his disposal on the Baltic at Stettin Bay, near the Polish border above Szczecin. If he could get to it undetected, he would have a good chance of getting past the Nazi gun-boats that patrolled the sea.

"On Project Valkyrie."

For a moment Canaris' words did not sink in, but then Badim's mind cleared and an icy calmness descended over him, as it always did in times of extreme danger. They wanted him home so desperately they had been willing to use the C Channel, which they knew the Germans had broken months ago. But they had sent the message in English, apparently in an attempt to convince the Germans that the Americans or British had an agent here.

"Who is this Valkyrie? Any ideas?" he asked, but Canaris shook his head.

"Not who, Alek, what."

"We are aware of your true feelings about the Fuehrer and how the war is going," Oster broke in. "But we hesitated to bring you in on this because we wanted to keep the Abwehr's actual involvement to an absolute minimum. You can understand the risks involved for everyone concerned."

"But now someone has bungled it," Canaris snapped. "It may be too late for all of us, unless you can convince Himmler that the message actually is what it appears to be: The call for an American or British agent to get out."

"Can you do it?" Oster asked.

Badim handed the message back to Canaris. For just a moment he wondered if they knew, and this was just some kind of a loyalty test, but then he dismissed the notion. Evidently Canaris and Oster were involved in some project with the code name Valkyrie. It was just pure blind luck. "Yes," he said, nodding. "I'll do what I can."

"Good," Oster said, breathing an obvious sigh of relief.

"But what exactly is this Project Valkyrie?" Badim asked. It seemed strange to be speaking his own code name out loud.

"I can't tell you that, Alek," Canaris said, obviously sincere. He got to his feet. "Hans and I are not directly involved in it, but unless you are successful with Himmler, all hell will break loose, and a lot of good men will be lost."

Badim got to his feet and smiled. "I'll do my best, Herr Admiral."

"Thank you," Canaris said, and Badim saluted, turned on his heel, and left the office, retrieving his things from the chair.

Badim was a pragmatist. He had known all along that when the end came for Germany it would probably be impossible for him to get out. When the end came the Americans, the British, and the Free French would be attacking from the west, and his own countrymen from the east. And except for a handful of men in Moscow, no one in the world knew Badim as anything other than an Abwehr major. A Nazi. The enemy. His contacts here in Germany knew him only as a German who was doing work for the Communists for money.

Despite that sure knowledge, however, for as long as he had worked in Germany Badim had gone through the motions of always keeping an escape route open for himself. Often his plans for escape would change, as did his circumstances. But always in the back of his mind were his orders that if and when escape became necessary, it would have to be done in such a way that no one suspected he was a Russian. It would endanger all of his contacts still in Germany, and could even lead to the complete exposure of the entire Soviet network here.

He stopped at his office only long enough to tell his aide that he would be at Prinz Albrechtstrasse with Reichsfuehrer Himmler himself for the remainder of the day, and then went outside, where he dismissed his driver and took the car, a black, four-door Mercedes with official OKW plates.

The situation now seemed almost tailor-made for his escape, if he could get out of Berlin and make the two hundred kilometers to Stettin Bay before the alarms sounded.

As far as Canaris and Oster were concerned, he was with Himmler. But when he didn't show up at Prinz Albrechtstrasse, Himmler's office would call Canaris.

For a while the accusations would fly. Canaris would believe that Himmler had thrown Badim in the Gestapo dungeon for questioning. Such things happened all the time. Himmler, on the other hand, already suspicious of Canaris, would be certain that the admiral had either hidden Badim away somewhere, or had arranged his death.

In any event, Badim would cease to exist as an Abwehr major within a few hours if all went well, or cease to exist totally if something went wrong.

It was an incredibly long and dangerous twelve hundred kilometers up the Baltic and then into the Gulf of Finland to Leningrad, traveling only at night, but it was the only way, and Badim was prepared and willing to try it.

He did have one regret, however, in leaving Germany. And that was another plan that had been at the back of his mind for some time now.

When the end finally came, he had promised himself, he would personally kill Himmler. Now he would miss that opportunity.

10

LOS ALAMOS, NEW MEXICO

State Road 4 wound its way up into the pine-studded mountains north of Santa Fe, and the morning was crisp, almost cold, filling the battered, olive-drab Chevrolet with its chill as Lovelace rolled his window open.

For nine days now he had followed General Groves around from one end of the country to the other without, it seemed, more than an hour or two of sleep in each twenty-four.

But none of it seemed to have any effect on the general, who was driving this morning. A car had been waiting for them at Dorothy McKibben's, who ran the project's clearinghouse in Santa Fe, when they had gotten off the overnight train from Chicago, and Groves had insisted they get up to the laboratory immediately without stopping for breakfast.

First it had been Oak Ridge, Tennessee, where a vast plant was under construction for the separation of the fissionable isotope of uranium; then Hanford, Washington, where another huge plant was under construction for the manufacture of plutonium, which also could be used to build a bomb; then Milwaukee, where rare pumps were being designed and manufactured; and Decatur, Illinois, where something called barriers were being invented; and on to Detroit, where Chrysler was building diffusers; and Allis Chalmers, General Electric, Westinghouse, Kellex, Union Carbide . . .

The names and places Lovelace had seen over the past week and a half read like a litany of American manufacturing and scientific genius.

But, he thought wryly, security for any of the operations was impossible. Last night on the train from Chicago he had again brought up his doubts about keeping the project a secret.

"No other way to build the bomb that we know of," Groves had said offhandedly. He was writing a report and he hadn't bothered to look up. "We'll just have to live with it. Do the best we can."

Do the best we can: The words ran through Lovelace's mind. But what good would "the best" do? The entire project leaked like a sieve. There was no way possible to keep even a semblance of security in something that involved more than twenty thousand people from all walks of life and several dozen foreign countries.

Most disturbing of all to Lovelace was that many of the scientists, including Dr. Oppenheimer, were believed to either be Communists or have Communist leanings.

They crossed a railroad trestle, which spanned the Rio Grande, here only a narrow, silty stream, and as the dirt road strewn with boulders and potholes wound its way even higher into the mountains, Groves concentrated entirely on his driving.

A new road was planned for later in the year, but for now the dirt path was the most direct access to the laboratory, which until recently had been nothing more than a boys' school.

At least here, Lovelace thought, security would be reasonably tight, if for no other reason than the remoteness of the site.

"How many people are up here now?" he shouted over the laboring car engine.

Groves didn't take his eyes off the road. "Around two thousand, including my own people," he said. "But that number is growing daily. By the end of the year there should be three times that many."

Lovelace again fell silent. Everything in the project was big, and was being done in a hurry. Factories had been constructed before processes were invented. Manufacturing firms were given government contracts before they even knew what was expected of them. Scientists were recruited even before there was a place for them to work.

He shook his head. It was insane. But he understood the urgency of the work. The Germans, it was believed, were working on their own atomic bomb. If they came up with the weapon first, the war would be lost.

They came around the last curve and the road flattened out, revealing a ramshackle collection of hastily constructed wooden buildings and Quonset huts. New buildings were being erected, bulldozers were cutting new roads, and mounds of supplies seemed to be stacked everywhere.

Much of the makeshift town was enclosed behind a tall, barbed-wire fence, and they were stopped at a guardhouse manned by four enlisted men carrying weapons.

Groves rolled down his window as two of the guards approached the car. They came to attention and saluted.

"Have you got Captain Lovelace's security pass ready?" Groves snapped, returning the salute.

"Yes, sir," one of the men said. He handed Groves two of the ID cards, each with a large alligator clip attached, saluted again, and waved them through the gate.

A quarter of a mile down the main road, Groves pulled up and parked in front of a large stone-and-log building. Before they got out of the car, he handed Lovelace the ID tag.

"This gives you access to every building on the post. But if you start poking around the scientists they'll howl like stuck pigs, so you'd better have a good reason for everything you do."

"Is Dr. Oppenheimer here?" Lovelace asked, clipping the pass to his tunic lapel.

"Yes, and you'll meet him: You'll also get to meet Colonel Lansdale. He arrived here yesterday to inspect security arrangements."

They got out of the car and went up to the building, which was on a slight rise above the street. Before they went inside Lovelace turned and looked over the camp. Utility poles and electric lines were strung everywhere, and there seemed to be a great deal of activity going on throughout the post at a breakneck speed.

"What do people in Santa Fe think about all this?" Lovelace asked.

Groves, his hand on the latch, turned back and chuckled. "About the same as the people in Tennessee and Washington State think about those operations. They know something is going on, but not what. The latest rumor from town is that we're experimenting with a captured German submarine up here."

Lovelace looked at him in open amazement. "A submarine? In the mountains?"

"It's much better than some of the other stories that have circulated. We've been accused of doing everything up here from manufacturing Roosevelt campaign buttons to running a nudist camp or a home for pregnant WACs."

"Any of them ever come up for a peek?"

"We get an occasional visitor," Groves said. "But we just inform them politely that this is a government installation with access forbidden and they go away.

We've had no serious trouble yet, if that's what you mean. But I'll let Colonel Lansdale fill you in on our security arrangements."

Groves led him through the building to a large room filled with a couple dozen folding chairs all facing a portable blackboard. Inside were two men: Dr. J. Robert Oppenheimer, Jr., and Colonel John Lansdale. Oppenheimer was a thin man with short-cropped, wiry hair, large ears, ascetic face, and manner. Lansdale, on the other hand, looked like nothing more than what he was: a harried army colonel with too much on his mind and too many responsibilities.

Groves quickly made the introductions and then excused himself. "I'm going to snoop around for a while this morning," he said to the others, then turned to Lovelace. "When you're finished here, take the car back to town and turn it in at Dorothy's. Take the first train back to Washington. My secretary will be expecting you, and will give you all the help you'll need setting up."

"You're not coming back with me?" Lovelace asked.

Groves shook his head. "Nope, too much to do here, and then I've got to get up to New York—Kellex is screaming bloody murder about something."

"Will you have time for me this afternoon?" Oppenheimer asked. His voice was soft, almost effeminate.

"I'm taking the overnight up to Chicago. You can ride along with me and take the morning train back."

"All right . . ." Oppenheimer started to say, but Lovelace interrupted him. He could not believe what he was hearing.

"Wait a minute," he said. The others looked at him, and he turned to the scientist. "Dr. Oppenheimer, do I understand that you leave this camp on a regular basis?"

"I'm not a prisoner here," Oppenheimer said.

"I understand," Lovelace replied. "And I'm sorry if I implied anything of that nature." He turned back to the general. "Can I be open here?"

"Shoot," Groves snapped impatiently.

"How often do you and Dr. Oppenheimer leave this camp together?"

Groves shrugged. "Once a month, perhaps. Saves time all the way around if I can get Oppie's briefing on the train ride up to Chicago."

"And it gets mc out of here," Oppenheimer said. "Why?"

"If I were an assassin, the train would be an ideal place to take out my two primary targets. You and Dr. Oppenheimer."

"See here—" Oppenheimer started to protest, but this time Groves cut him off.

"Can't be helped, Lovelace. You'll have to work around it. I hired you as an independent creep, which does not mean I'll allow you to rearrange schedules or movements."

"I see," Lovelace said. And he did see. His job, which until now had been impossible, had just become tougher.

11

MOSCOW

It was early evening and the night was pitch black under
a heavily overcast sky as Alek Badim, driving a canvas-
topped lend-lease jeep, turned into the gate at Lubyanka
Prison off Yaroslavskoye Road. He was dressed in civilian clothes.

Two soldiers, both armed with rifles, came out of the
guardhouse and as Badim pulled out his identification
papers one of them held back, his weapon at the ready.

"Dawbrih y Vyechehr," the nearest guard said, taking
Badim's papers.

"Good evening," Badim snapped harshly. "I am here
to see GRU Major Runkov."

The guard studied the papers, which Badim had doc-
tored himself from documents he had stolen from his
own section in the Abwehr, and which identified him
as an interdepartmental investigating officer from the
NKGB, then looked up. "Are you expected, sir?"

"Absolutely not," Badim roared, snatching the papers
away from the young man. "And straighten up in the
presence of a superior officer."

The soldier stiffened to attention, as did the other young man nearer the guardhouse.

"I'm here on an inspection tour, so I would strongly suggest you stay away from your field telephone for the next five minutes. Do I make myself clear?"

"Perfectly, comrade colonel," the soldier said weakly.

Badim made a show of angrily slamming the jeep into gear and continued into the courtyard.

One side of the huge complex was used as a prison, while the other side, which at one time had housed the All-Russian Insurance Company, was now used as headquarters for the various branches of the secret service. He parked the jeep outside one of the entrances to the newer section, which was under construction, but before he climbed out he sighed tiredly. He was tired, and wanted nothing more than to sleep for a week or so. But there was no place in Russia, except here with Runkov, that he could feel totally safe.

During his long trip up the Baltic to Leningrad, he had had plenty of time to think about Runkov's extraordinary message to him on the C Channel. At first he had been angry with what he considered an incredibly stupid blunder. But later, as he gave it more thought, he came to realize that Runkov must have had very compelling reasons to summon him in such a fashion. And whatever those reasons were, they had driven Badim to come here immediately and confront the man.

He closed his eyes and his hands gripped the steering wheel so tightly his knuckles turned white.

She was a fishing boat that had been outfitted with a powerful Mercedes Marine diesel several years before the war had begun. The boat had been kept in fine repair by its previous owner up in Wolgast, and three months ago Badim had initiated the paperwork necessary to impound the boat in the name of the Reichsnavy. The illegible signatures on the paperwork could never be traced back to him or even to the Abwehr itself. And as far as the previous owner was concerned, the boat was lost to him for the duration of the war.

He had ordered the naval office in Rostock to send two men down to move the boat from Wolgast to Anklam on the Peene River, and from there six weeks later, Badim had himself moved the boat one evening into Stettin Bay, running it up the river into the swamplands below Ueckermünde.

Finally he had entered the necessary documentation into the Reichsnaval system to show that the boat—which had been called the *Hildegard II* but had been redesignated the PB 757—had been destroyed by fire.

As far as the Reichsnavy was concerned, then, the boat no longer existed.

He had gone back up to Ueckermünde twice to check on the boat, which was still marked with its naval insignia, but if anyone had discovered it hidden in the swamps, no one had disturbed it.

By 10:00 A.M. of the morning he had left Berlin in response to the C Channel message, Badim had driven north to Prenzlau, where he had purchased a half liter of dark red waterproof paint, a five-centimeter lettering brush, and a sanding block. From there he had continued north, taking a back road into Ueckermünde itself, then doubling back toward the tiny village of Eggesin.

Halfway between the two towns, however, he had driven his staff car off the lonely road, managing to get it far enough into the tall grasses and low brush so that it was invisible to passersby. From there he had taken his purchases and slogged on foot across the swamp upriver to where he had hidden the boat.

The day was cold and the rain had not let up, so that by the time he had reached the boat he was soaked to the skin and thoroughly chilled. Because of his preoccupation with his discomfort, he did not notice that the cabin hatch was slightly ajar, the lock jimmied, until he had jumped from the river bank onto the deck.

Suddenly he saw it, and he dropped his things as the

hatch came all the way open and a large man stepped up on deck, a determined expression on his face and a pistol in his hand.

Without hesitation Badim kicked out, the toe of his boot catching the man on the wrist, causing him to drop the gun. In the next instant Badim was on him, chopping once with the side of his hand at a spot between the man's eyes, then slamming his palm into the end of the man's now broken nose, driving the nasal cartilage and shattered bones into his brain.

The man convulsed once, then fell back down the ladder into the cabin with a loud crash.

Badim remained where he was for several long moments, listening for sounds of anyone else aboard, but everything was deathly still, except for the light patter of the rain. Finally he let himself relax.

He went down into the tiny cabin, stepping over the man's body, and looked around. The food and clothing Badim had stored aboard weeks ago had been pulled from the cabinets and piled in the middle of one of the bunks, the blankets loosely tied around the treasure.

The brass barometer had been pulled from the bulkhead and the shortwave radio had been taken off its brackets and laid on the table.

Badim turned back to the man's body and quickly searched it, coming up with a couple of Reichsmarks and a few pfennigs, plus papers identifying him as Conrad Hertl, from Greifswald, which was seventy or eighty kilometers to the northwest. His labor card showed that he was a fisherman, but what he had been doing here was a mystery, unless he had been working out of Ueckermünde and somehow happened on the boat.

Badim spent the afternoon straightening up the cabin, and then listening to the naval shore patrol frequency on the shortwave.

He changed clothes with the dead man, putting his own watch and identity disc on the body, which he placed in one of the bunks, and then he laid down in the other bunk, where he instantly fell asleep.

When he woke it was nearly ten o'clock, and within an hour he had eaten, untied the boat, started it, turned it around, and headed downriver toward the bay, the powerful diesel engine barely rumbling as he idled it.

Just before he reached the bay, he pulled on a naval pea coat and hat, then ran up the Reichsnavy ensign.

Within minutes he had cleared the town's harbor facilities and was out in the short chop of the bay, the night pitch black under the heavily overcast sky, heading across to the channel that led out into the open Baltic Sea.

In times past the channel had been on the Polish side of the border, but now it was guarded by German soldiers, who he expected would give him no trouble this evening. Naval patrol boats used the channel on a constant basis. His only trouble, if any came, would be from other naval units.

A strong spotlight shone on him as he closed on the channel marker lights, and he stepped out of the wheelhouse and waved. No one challenged him as he passed the gun emplacements, and within an hour he had passed Odra Port and was in the Pomeranian Bay . . . on his way home.

Later that evening he had wrapped Hertl's body in a large piece of canvas, which he had soaked with diesel fuel to hold down the eventual smell, and had stuffed the body in the bilge beneath the cabin sole.

He opened his eyes and looked up at the secret service building. Six days it had taken him to make it up the Baltic and into the Gulf of Finland to a section of deserted shoreline fifty kilometers south of Leningrad.

At first he had run with his navigational lights on, flying the German ensign. But later, as he got farther north, he had run only at night, lights out, the ensign overboard, laying to, hidden along the shoreline during the day. It was during these hours that he had siphoned fuel from the barrels lashed on deck into the main tanks, and then gotten a few hours of sleep.

On the third day he had used the sanding block to remove the German navy insignia from the hull just below the gunwales, and the red paint to reletter the boat the *Hildegard II*.

The leftover paint, brush, and sanding block had gone overboard.

Several times he had had to drastically alter his course to avoid German patrol boats, and twice he had had to run for shore, hiding in back bays. But on the evening of the sixth day, he had put ashore south of Leningrad in a small dinghy.

Before he abandoned ship, he had soaked the cabin and deck with diesel fuel and kerosene from the lamps, making sure the body was well soaked, turned on the engine, tied the wheel so that the boat was running out to sea, and then he had set fire to it.

When they found the boat, if they found her before she burned to the waterline and sank, on board would be the body of Abwehr Major Alek Badim . . . possibly a deserter, possibly murdered on Admiral Canaris' orders, or perhaps even done in by Himmler's Gestapo.

Now he got out of the jeep and tiredly went into the building, where he showed his NKGB identification to the clerk and signed in.

"Major Runkov is on the fourth floor, comrade colonel," the clerk, an older man with one arm missing, said pleasantly. "Just a moment and I'll call his aide to come fetch you."

"No," Badim said softly. "It is not necessary. I am here on an inspection." He felt sorry for the man.

The clerk smiled. His face was white and covered with a thin sheen of perspiration. He looked sick. "If you don't mind my saying so, colonel, you're taking on quite a task by inspecting Major Runkov."

Badim returned the smile, and nodded toward the

man's empty sleeve. "When were you wounded?"

"Two months ago, Leningrad."

"You should not be on duty this soon," Badim said with compassion.

"If I weren't here an able-bodied man better suited for the front would have to do this. We all must do what we can."

Badim reached out and patted the man's hand. "Don't call up. I'd like my visit to be a surprise."

The clerk smiled again. "As you wish, colonel, but I'd like to be a little bird in the window to see the major's reaction."

Badim turned, went down the narrow corridor, and took the stairs up to the fourth floor. Three days ago he had stepped ashore onto Soviet soil for the first time in years, and it seemed strange. In Germany, despite the Nazi setbacks, there was a great deal of gaiety and brightness—plenty of food, glittering parties, and a general sense that somehow the Fuehrer would pull them out of their troubles.

But here at home everything seemed to be dark and brooding; the towns, the countryside, and the people all seemed to be existing under a dark shadow. Even his own language seemed heavy and depressing to him after the German he had spoken and thought in for the past nine years.

He paused at the stairwell door to the fourth floor corridor, the impression that he was a stranger in his own home coming strongly over him. But then he sighed again, pushed open the door, and stepped into the hallway.

There was a lot of activity here, people coming and going, but no one paid him the slightest attention as he strode purposefully down the corridor to Runkov's office and opened the door without knocking.

Sergeant Doronkin was standing at a large table piled with maps, books, and a great number of file folders, his back to the door when Badim came in. He turned around.

"Can I help you, comrade . . ." he started to say, but then his complexion went pale. "Sonofabitch," he swore softly.

Badim closed the door behind him. "Is that any way to greet an officer, sergeant?" he asked.

"No . . . I mean, I'm sorry, comrade," Doronkin said, flustered. "We haven't heard a thing for the past ten days. We didn't know what to expect."

"Tell me, sergeant," Badim said, nonchalantly placing his right hand in his coat pocket so that his fingers touched the German officer's issue Luger there. "Is your major a sane man?"

Doronkin's gaze went from Badim's hand back to his eyes. "It is not as you think, comrade," he said. "There is an assignment for you. A very important assignment, and we had to get you out of Germany."

"There was no other way?"

"You did not answer your queries."

"So you forced me out, making sure I'd have to return home or be killed."

Runkov's door opened, and he was standing there. "Exactly, Aleksandr Petrovich," he said. "And now if you are going to shoot us, get it over with or else come into my office. We have much to do."

Badim had never met Runkov, of course. He had never met any of his control officers. They had only been encoded names on the orders he had received from time to time. But now, seeing the man who had controlled him for the past eighteen months, the man who had authorized the carefully maneuvered fall of Canaris and Oster, and who had sent the incredible message on the C Channel, the anger went out of him.

Runkov was no fool, it was obvious to Badim. Ruthless, certainly. But definitely not a fool.

He withdrew his hand from his coat pocket, and a look of relief passed over the sergeant's features.

"Send for the girl," Runkov said, and, motioning for Badim to follow him, turned and went back into his office.

Badim took off his coat, but before he went into Runkov's office, he turned to the sergeant. "The gate sentries and the one-armed clerk downstairs believe I am an NKGB colonel here on a snap inspection. And there is a jeep in the parking lot that I stole outside the train depot."

Doronkin smiled and nodded. "I understand, sir. It will be taken care of. And welcome home."

"Thanks," Badim said, and he went into Runkov's office, where the large man was already seated behind his heavily laden desk, pouring two glasses of vodka.

The office was a mess. A cot was set up in one corner, but it was piled with papers and files and several maps of the United States marked with blue and red grease pencil. Other maps and charts were pinned to the walls, and the room smelled of stale smoke, liquor, and an unwashed body.

Badim folded his coat and carefully laid it atop the papers on the cot, and before he sat down across from Runkov he took out a German cigarette and lit it, inhaling deeply.

"Vodka?" Runkov asked, holding the glass out, but Badim waved it aside.

"I've developed a taste for cognac over the last nine years."

Runkov smiled, pouring Badim's vodka into his own glass. "I suppose you've developed a great many German likes and dislikes."

"Purely out of necessity. Self-preservation," Badim flared, but instantly held himself in check. He was tired, and he could feel his weariness eating at his self-control.

Runkov took a deep drink of the liquor. "How is your English? American idiom?"

The question surprised Badim, but he answered it honestly. "Rusty."

"With training, say for a couple of months, could you pass as an American?"

Badim thought about it a moment, but then nodded slowly. "Of indeterminate heritage, perhaps, but yes."

"How's your health?"

"Excellent."

"Your nerves?"

Badim laughed, the sound devoid of humor. "As well as can be expected."

Runkov did not smile. "Stand up, take off your shirt, and turn around," he ordered.

Badim wanted to crawl off to bed somewhere, but he complied, and as he turned around slowly he could feel Runkov's eyes on him, measuring, searching. But for what?

"You'd be a salesman of some kind, I suppose. You'd have to have a limp, otherwise you'd be in the service."

Badim sat down again. "The Americans are our allies."

"So were the Nazis at one time," Runkov said absently, toying with the glass of vodka in his massive paws. He was silent for a long moment, as if he was deep in thought, and when he finally looked up there was a grim expression in his eyes. "I'm sending you to the United States on a *Mokrie Dela*."

"Assassination?" Badim's distaste was obvious.

Runkov nodded, and suddenly it all fell into place for Badim. The extraordinary message forcing him out of Germany, the question about his German likes and dislikes, and his American idiomatic English. He was going to be sent to the United States to assassinate someone, but with a fail-safe. If he was caught he would be identified as an Abwehr major. A Nazi. Not a Russian. It was ingenious.

But he had nothing against the Americans and he said as much to Runkov.

"Neither do I. They're an inventive, straightforward people."

"Then why am I being sent to assassinate someone?"

"Two people, actually," Runkov said. "And the reason is quite simple. The Americans are *too* inventive. Left alone they will almost certainly develop a new super weapon that would make things quite impossible for us after the war."

"The atomic bomb," Badim said, half to himself. So it was true.

A startled expression had crossed Runkov's features. "Where did you hear that?" he asked sharply, and Badim looked up.

"I knew the Germans were working on such a weapon without much success, and it was believed the Americans and British were doing research on it as well, but with even less success."

"The Americans will succeed," Runkov said. "Left to their own devices."

"Then why don't we just steal the secret?"

"We will, but even with that it would take our scientists a long time to catch up. Perhaps too long a time."

"I'm being sent over to slow the project down. Kill two key men."

Runkov nodded. "Will you accept the assignment?"

Would he accept the assignment? What an odd question. Badim turned it over in his mind in an attempt to make some sense of it. He had never been asked such a thing in all his life.

From the time he had been an orphan under the care of the State, his life had been very carefully controlled. He had rebelled, certainly, but within a very narrow path, never really straying far from his superiors' wishes.

He understood intellectually that other people made choices . . . major decisions about their own lives. But such things had always been a wonderment to him. Duty and honor. He was a product of the State. He did what he was asked to do.

And now, for the first time in a long while, Badim

had to wonder if there wasn't something missing inside of him. Some function of human behavior that he had not been born with, or had never learned.

He understood perfectly well what Runkov was saying to him. After the war, when Germany was being divided up, and when world power was being parceled out, there would have to be a strong place for the Soviet Union. Delaying the American efforts toward building the super weapon was a necessity. He could see that clearly.

But was there another understanding of what Runkov was saying to him that he should be aware of? A feeling suddenly grew strong in him that he was a stranger not only to his own land and people and language, but to himself as well.

He looked up out of his thoughts finally, and nodded, the action almost in self-defense. "Of course," he said softly.

"Very good," Runkov replied, and there was a knock at the door. "Come," he snapped, looking up.

The door opened and Sergeant Doronkin stuck his head in. "The girl is here."

Runkov got to his feet. "Fine, send her in." He turned to Badim. "Part of your cover in the United States will be a wife. The girl is here now. Her English is perfect."

Badim got up and turned as a young woman came through the door, and his mouth fell open.

"Aleksandr Petrovich, I'd like you to meet Jada Natasha Yatsyna," Runkov said, but Badim barely heard him as he continued to stare at the girl. She was the most extraordinarily pretty woman he had ever seen.

BOOK THREE

SUMMER 1944

12

CAPE COD

Alek Badim paused at the metal-runged ladder that led
up from the Control Room into the conning tower and
turned toward the captain who had taken them this far.
In the dim red battle lights the man's face was barely
visible.

It had been a strained voyage around North Cape
from near Murmansk, then across the North Atlantic,
rendezvousing with their supply ship for fuel north of
the Faerøe Islands. By day they ran deep and silent to
escape detection from Allied patrols, as well as other
German U-boats. Only by night did they risk coming to
the surface to recharge their batteries.

The man and his tiny crew had done a brilliant job
bringing them across, and for just a moment Badim was
undecided about following all of Runkov's orders . . .
especially those determining the fate of these fine men.

On the one hand he could see the sense of what Runkov had planned. He understood perfectly well that if
the operation fell apart for some reason, the blame

would have to be placed on the Germans, and no one else. That was paramount above all else. He had a job to do. A very important job that had the wholehearted support and approval of Marshal Stalin himself.

Yet on the other hand it came down to a question of being a Russian with loyalty to the State, or being totally useless.

All through the winter he had trained with the girl outside Moscow, learning American history and customs, learning engineering and physics in the field of nuclear power, and learning everything there was to know about Groves and Oppenheimer so that he and Jada knew them as well as any mother would know her sons.

Runkov had told him what would have to be done once they reached the eastern coast of the United States, but the knowledge was kept from the girl. She was too soft, too emotional to understand the necessity.

But, he wondered at this moment, as he had all through his training, was he strong enough to accomplish it?

They had come aboard the captured German submarine at Gremikha thirteen days ago, and had sailed within the hour. For the most part, during the crossing, Badim had kept to himself, sharing a bunk in the officers' quarters with the young first mate. During the man's off-watch hours, Badim had stayed in the officers' mess reading from the boat's supply of German literature, trying to clear his mind for the coming assignment.

Then, earlier this evening, with the tension aboard running higher than it had before, the first mate had come to his cubicle, knocked once on the bulkhead, and shoved back the curtain.

Badim had been lying on his back, fully dressed in his dark trousers, dark turtleneck sweater, and soft-soled shoes, his right arm flung over his eyes. He had taken his arm away and looked up.

"Is it time?" he had asked softly.

The young first mate had nodded, his face garish in the dim red battle lights. "Yes, sir. The captain requests your presence in the Conn. We'll be taking you off within the hour."

"Has the woman been informed?"

"Yes, sir," the mate had said. "She is getting ready."

Badim had gotten out of his bunk, and had followed the young man forward to the control room, where the captain had nodded up toward the conning tower.

"We're at periscope depth. Go on up and take a look, see what you think," the man had said.

Badim sighed deeply and without a word climbed up into the cramped cubicle and raised the periscope, flipping the handles out.

He leaned forward to the eyepieces, and the distant shore leaped out at him in the darkness, ruggedly, the waves breaking on a rocky shoreline. They were about a thousand meters offshore, and to the north at least two or three kilometers, he could just make out the lights of what appeared to be a small village. It would be North Truro, which was directly on Highway 6, a road running the entire length of Cape Cod and all the way back up to Boston.

He studied the patterns of the waves against the rocks, imagining himself and the woman in the rubber dinghy. It would be difficult getting ashore, but not impossible. They would get wet, but that could not be helped.

Leaning his weight against the periscope, his arms draped over the handles, he closed his eyes.

Groves and Oppenheimer. He understood full well now why they had to be assassinated. But the other thing. Was it necessary?

"Absolutely," he could hear Runkov's bellow echoing in his ears. "Make no mistake about it, Aleksandr Petrovich, every stage of this project has been carefully worked out. Each must be accomplished to insure success."

The girl was wide-eyed and innocent. This was a sacred mission to her, the most distasteful aspect of which was Badim himself, whom she could not stand.

"You are crude, cruel, and thoughtless, comrade," she had told him one month ago when he had shown no remorse over the fact that they were being sent to the United States to kill two men and possibly more.

All through their early training she had been of the belief that Badim also found their assignment distasteful. A necessity of war, with the approval of the government, but a crime, nevertheless.

When he had not agreed with her, when she had finally understood that he was doing nothing more than following orders, apparently with no emotion, she had asked Runkov to take her off the assignment.

The major had refused, of course, and Jada could do nothing else but comply. But she did not have to like it or Badim, and she had told him as much on more than one occasion.

And now he wondered, looking up and then stepping back so that he could lower the periscope, what would she think if she knew the entire story? Would the fact that he felt terrible about what he was going to have to do tonight make any difference to her?

Badim climbed back down to the control room where the captain, first mate, and navigational officer were waiting for him.

"Is it to your liking, comrade?" the captain asked.

"It will do," Badim replied.

"Then get the woman and stand by at the forward hatch. I'm going to surface only long enough for you to get off with the rubber raft, and then we're getting out of here."

Badim stared at the man for a long time. He was forty-five, born in Vladivostok, and had distinguished himself on the Halifax-to-Murmansk lend-lease convoys as one of the few Russian naval officers in the almost exclusively British, American, and Dutch fleet.

The others in the crew were mostly faces without personality. But young. So young. Most of them were in their late teens or early twenties.

Runkov had cautioned him not to think about the crew, but the captain was an able, courageous man, and Badim admired him.

"Good luck," the man said, and he turned away.

Badim nodded at the first mate and navigational officer, then turned and went aft where Jada was just coming out of her cubicle. She looked sickly in the dim red light, her eyes wide, her wonderfully expressive mouth half parted.

"Are we there?" she asked softly in English.

"Yes," Badim said. "Get your things and get up to the forward hatch. I'll be along in a moment." He started to brush past her in the cramped companionway, but she put out a hand to stop him.

"Whatever differences we've had . . . whatever I've said . . ." she started, but then stopped.

Badim managed a tight smile. "We have a job to do," he said. "When we are finished with it, we can settle our differences, if there are any."

"I just wanted to say that I won't give you any trouble. I'll do whatever you tell me to do."

He stared into her eyes for several long moments. She was beautiful, and she had more depth than any other woman he had ever met. But that would have to wait.

"Get your things. I'll be right with you," he said, and he went past her and ducked into his own cubicle, where he shoved the heavy curtain across the opening.

For a moment he stood there listening to the sounds of the boat. The drive motors were in neutral, but the generators supplying their electricity hummed, and the air coming through the ventilators made a gentle hushing sound.

It was no good thinking about the crew. There was a good chance they could not make it back home anyway. And even if they could, there was the chance they would be killed in action somewhere. The war was far from over, and many good men would die before it was.

He bent down, reached under his bunk, and fished out the small, American-made, canvas sack he had brought aboard with him, and took it over to the tiny fold-down table under the ship's intercom.

He pulled out of the sack a screwdriver, a pair of wire strippers, and a small tubular device that looked like a tiny telescope with a single wire sticking out from each end. This he laid gently on the tabletop.

He held his breath for a moment to make sure no one was coming, and then quickly removed the four screws holding the intercom to the wall. The plate came loose and he eased the entire unit out of its slot in the bulkhead, and laid it gently on the desk top without disconnecting any of the wires.

Near the back of the narrow recess in the wall he could see the two plain yellow wires Runkov had told him would be there. Working quickly now, the sweat beginning to form on his forehead, he stripped the insulation off the ends of both wires, then gently picked up the tube and connected it to the circuit.

For a long, sick moment, he thought about what he was about to do. Then he reached out with both hands and sharply telescoped the tube together. There was a soft crunch of broken glass, and inside the device the released acid began eating at a thin plate separating the two wires.

It was a simple acid fuse. In four hours it would connect the explosives that had been packed against the submarine's fuel tanks and around the torpedo rooms with a series of dry cells.

The explosions would be terrible, Badim thought, as he shoved the tube with its obscene wires farther back into the recess and then screwed the intercom unit back in place.

For days, bits and pieces of the wreckage would wash ashore. Letters with German postmarks, tins of German food, bits and pieces of Reichsnavy uniforms and equipment. There would be no doubt in anyone's mind that a German submarine had exploded, for some unexplained reason, off the coast of Massachusetts.

The rubber dinghy would be found as well, telling the authorities that one or more German agents had come ashore before the U-boat had exploded. A manhunt would begin. For Germans, not Russians, and certainly not a man with a limp whose wife was young and lovely.

Badim stuffed his tools back in his sack, grabbed his summer-weight navy blue jacket from its hook, and went out into the companionway. He hurried forward into the torpedo room, where Jada was waiting with two crewmen.

"Ready to go, sir?" one of them asked.

Badim nodded, and the young man reached overhead and hit the intercom button. "Ready up here, captain," he said.

Immediately there was the sound of rushing water being pumped out of the ballast tanks, and the deck tilted slightly back.

Outside he could imagine the bulk of the conning tower rising out of the sea. Would anyone be out there watching this way? Would they know what they were seeing?

One of the crewmen scrambled up the ladder and spun the hatch lock wheel. A moment later some water sloshed down the tunnel, followed by a blast of fresh, cold air.

"Are you ready?" Badim asked Jada, looking at her. She seemed nervous, almost on the verge of collapse, but she nodded.

The other crewman had scrambled up the ladder, and Badim motioned for Jada to go up. A moment later he followed her up the ladder and scrambled onto the deck, which was so low in the water it was nearly awash.

The crewmen had taken a small rubber raft from a waterproof locker and pulled the cords on the CO_2 cartridges, which inflated the tiny boat in less than ten seconds, and then shoved it overboard.

They helped Jada aboard the pitching boat, and then Badim.

"Good luck," one of them said softly, and Badim waved, then unfolded the oars, slipped them in their locks, and started away from the submarine toward the dark shore.

13

Michael Lovelace sat at his desk in his cramped office on the fifth floor of the War Department Building on Virginia Avenue. His coat was draped untidily over the back of his chair and his tie was loose. There were files strewn about the office, and the walls were filled with photographs and charts.

It was shortly after four in the morning and this section of the building was deserted. Groves had left for home around midnight, leaving Lovelace behind to review the latest files Hoover had sent over.

His mouth tasted foul and he had a splitting headache, but beyond that there was a vague uneasiness in his gut. It was the same feeling that he had had on numerous other occasions when the apparent facts of whatever investigation he was on didn't add up.

On the one hand, Colonel Lansdale was doing as fine a job as possible keeping the lid on the mammoth project. Even the FBI and the people here in the War Department knew only that Groves and the people who worked for him were involved in some sort of secret war project. Nothing else.

But on the other hand, he thought, there were too many apparently insignificant little details that did not add up.

He categorized his thoughts tonight for the tenth time as he reached for a cigarette and lit it. Item. Oppenheimer had been a Communist, and had admitted to General Groves that he had been approached by an old university friend for information about the bomb. Yet Groves had denied his own CIC chief's recommendation that Oppenheimer be pulled from the project. And Groves had the backing of Roosevelt himself.

Item. On the surface Hoover had been and continued to be highly cooperative with Lovelace's requests to see any and all files on known or suspected German agents operating in this country. Yet the FBI director refused to allow Lovelace to sit in on interrogation sessions.

Item. Secretary of War Stimson and everyone else in the department refused to discuss any aspect of the project with Lovelace, always referring him back to Groves, who had become too busy to discuss anything with him.

"You've got a job to do," the general snapped. "Do it, and make sure I have a weekly report on my desk."

Item. President Roosevelt was scheduled to meet with Churchill in Quebec later this summer to discuss a scientific exchange program. If the President agreed, it would mean British scientists would be added to the project. Stalin had not been invited to participate in the conference, and that meant potential trouble from the Russians.

Lovelace shook his head, looked at his cigarette, and stubbed it out in an overflowing ashtray on his littered desk, then got to his feet, stretching tiredly.

Over the years he had built up a network of friends in the various police forces around the country, including the FBI. They were detectives or operations men with whom he had worked from time to time, and with whom he had built a rapport. It was a network of mutual respect that knew no chains of command.

Item. The most disturbing item of all. The operational reports his friend Marvin Willis, an agent with the FBI, was sending him were somewhat different—usually more complete—than the ones that came over routinely from Hoover himself. Why? And what else was Hoover holding back?

He reached for his coat and went around his desk to the door as he pulled it on. Before he went out he stopped to look at the photos pinned up on the walls. All of them were known or suspected German agents operating in this country whose movements were being monitored by the FBI or some other governmental security agency. But none of them had so far approached Oak Ridge or Hanford or Los Alamos, nor had any of them made any attempt to make contact with General Groves.

Not even his old-boy network in and around Washington had given him any indication that Groves was in danger from these people. Which meant one of two things. Either Groves was being set up for an assassination by someone no one knew about, which was an admittedly valid possibility, or such an attempt was not being planned, in which case Lovelace was wasting his time.

He opened the door and stepped out into the darkened corridor just as his telephone rang, the strident noise jerking him out of his contemplations.

He reached it on the second ring. "Yes," he said.

"Do you know who this is?" a voice Lovelace instantly recognized as Willis asked.

"Yes, I do. What have you got?"

"Maybe nothing, but listen up . . . I've only got a moment. A German submarine exploded a couple of hours ago sixty-five miles off the northern end of Cape Cod."

"Any survivors?"

"No," Willis said softly. "But this is an odd one,

which is why I called you. A Mrs. Margaret Owens, she's a great-aunt of one of our staffers, called earlier this evening with a wild story about a Nazi invasion. She lives in North Truro, which is a little town a few miles south of Provincetown on the Cape. We relayed the information to the Coast Guard, and they were the ones who intercepted the sub. Only before they could drop charges on the boat, she ran, and a few minutes later exploded."

Lovelace tried to think. "Anything else?"

"Plenty," Willis said. "Mrs. Owens also told us that a landing party had come ashore, and just a few minutes ago the old man himself called and told us to keep this one under wraps. Said he didn't want to start a panic. A couple of our people from the Boston office are going out to see the woman later this morning."

"They haven't left yet?"

"No," Willis said softly. "But even if you disconnect most of her story as hysteria, there *was* a submarine, and there *may* have been a landing party. Maybe the person you're looking for."

"Thanks," Lovelace said, a part of his brain already trying to figure out how he could get up there before the FBI arrived. "It's probably a long shot, but I'll check it out."

"Good hunting," Willis said, and the line went dead.

He hung up the phone, then unlocked the bottom drawer of his desk and took out a thin booklet marked *AAA Priority Materiel/Services*, and opened it to the section on transportation, not really knowing why he was doing it. At the beginning of this assignment Groves had handed him the list with the admonishment that it should only be used in a genuine emergency, when all other methods failed. This situation hardly could be classified an emergency, but he was glad for the chance to be doing something . . . anything.

He dialed a number halfway down the list, and after five rings a sleepy, gruff voice answered.

"What is it?"

"Colonel Pearson, this is Captain Michael Lovelace, Counter Intelligence Corps."

"You work for Groves, don't you?" the man said, his voice suddenly awake.

"Yes, sir. I need some quick transportation this morning up to Provincetown on Cape Cod."

"Hold on a moment, captain," Pearson said.

While he was waiting Lovelace removed a cigar box from the open desk drawer, and from inside it selected a thin leather wallet from among several and stuffed it in his pocket. When he had replaced the cigar box in the drawer, Colonel Pearson was on the line again.

"A P-47 will be waiting for you at Bolling, Base Ops. Will you be needing return transportation?"

"Yes, sir, probably," Lovelace said, and as he talked he took his .38 Police Special with its sawn-off barrel out of the drawer and stuffed it in his pocket with the ID wallet.

"The aircraft and pilot will have to be back here by noon. I'm assuming you are declaring this an emergency."

"Yes, sir, I am," Lovelace said.

"Then I'll expect a written report when you get back. Countersigned by General Groves, of course."

"Of course, sir, and thanks," Lovelace said, and he hung up the phone. He closed and relocked his desk drawer, shut off the office lights, and hurried down the corridor to the stairs, which would take him to his car in the basement.

It was a long shot as far as he was concerned—he had been honest with Willis. But he had built innumerable cases on even thinner leads before, and he had a gut feeling about this one.

It was nearly 5 A.M. by the time Lovelace had made it across town, over the Anacostia River Bridge, down to Bolling Air Corps Base, and had signed in at Base Ops.

A Republic P-47 Thunderbolt with British Air Force markings was parked on the ramp, its engine turning over slowly. One of the ground crew helped him climb up on the wing and struggle into the cockpit next to the pilot, a freckle-faced young man who looked to be no more than fifteen or sixteen.

As soon as Lovelace was strapped in, the pilot gave the ground crew the thumbs-up sign, the chocks were removed from the wheels, and they were moving down the north-south runway. Any talk was impossible over the powerful engine sound.

Lovelace sat back, his head against the seat rest, and closed his eyes, glad for the chance of an hour's rest before he had to get to work.

What would he find, if anything? The woman's story about invasion forces had to be discounted, of course, although her call had resulted in the interception of the submarine. He was probably on a wild goose chase. But maybe, just maybe there was something to this, after all. Chasing after this story was better than what he had been doing these past months, in any case.

It was shortly after 6 A.M., and the sun was coming up brilliantly over the ocean by the time they touched down at the small airfield outside Provincetown. And it was nearly 7:30 A.M. by the time he had talked the local Coast Guard station commander into the loan of a gray staff car for the morning.

The day was warm and pleasant, and as Lovelace drove he forgot for a time the doubts that had been gnawing at him lately about his value to the project. Once again he had become nothing more than a glorified paper shuffler. He was sure that even General Groves was having second thoughts about him.

So far the only thing he had accomplished was to convince Groves to hire an effective second in command, and to carry a pistol wherever he went. Beyond that the general refused to go, spurning Lovelace's repeated suggestion that he be accompanied by body-guards.

It took less than fifteen minutes to drive the short distance down from Provincetown to North Truro, which was a tiny village just off Highway 6, where he received directions from a service station attendant on how to get to Mrs. Owens' home on the beach.

Her house, a large, ramshackle, clapboard Colonial, complete with banging shutters and an iron-railed Widows' Walk on the roof, was situated in a stand of scrub pines on a slight rise overlooking Cape Cod Bay. When he parked the car out front, an elderly lady in a dirty white housecoat, floppy slippers, and wool stockings rolled down around her ankles came out onto the large front porch.

"You from the Coast Guard or the Bureau?" she shouted as he got out of the car and came up to the porch.

"The FBI, Washington," Lovelace said, showing her his ID.

"About time you showed up, young man," she said, glancing at the identification. She pointed south toward an area where the sand beach gave way to a stretch of rocky shoreline. "They came in down there about ten-thirty or so."

Lovelace looked that way as the woman came down off the porch. She pointed up to a second-story window.

"I watched the whole thing from up there," she said. "When I saw what was happening I hurried downstairs, called my nephew, and then went into the fruit cellar with my shotgun."

It was a wild goose chase, after all, and Lovelace was disappointed. He turned to the woman and smiled pleasantly. "Were there many ships?" he asked, just to be polite.

The woman looked at him, an incredulous expression on her face. "Hell, no!" she roared. "Just the one submarine, and a single landing party. Leastways, that's all I stuck around to see."

Lovelace's stomach fluttered. "You reported that?"

"Damn right," the woman said lustily. "There were just two of them in a little rubber raft. A man and a woman. I lost them when they came around the point, but they must have come ashore less than a mile from here."

Careful to keep his voice neutral, although his heart was pounding, Lovelace asked, "How do you know it was a man and a woman?"

"I saw them through my binoculars."

"Can you give me a description?"

The woman frowned and shook her head. "The light was bad and they were too far away. The man was large and the woman was small. . . . I could tell it was a woman because of her long hair."

"But you couldn't see their faces?"

"I already told you . . ."

Lovelace interrupted her. "What else did you see? Clothing? Equipment? Weapons?"

"They were both wearing some kind of dark outfits, but I didn't see if they were carrying anything."

"Thank you, Mrs. Owens," Lovelace said, his heart hammering even harder. "Thank you very much." He turned and hurried back to the car.

"Say hello to my nephew," the woman called after him, and he waved as he took off back toward the highway, his tires spinning on the loose sand.

Just because a German submarine dropped off a man and a woman here didn't mean they were agents come to interfere with the bomb project. That was stretching things too far, even for Lovelace. But it also did not mean they *weren't* here for just that purpose.

Hell, he told himself, pounding one hand on the steering wheel, all he was doing was making a plausible assumption. What if these people had indeed come to assassinate Groves? What if?

He could hear the general now. "I didn't hire you to play cops and robbers, Lovelace. Unless we get a positive indication from the Bureau that these supposed agents are here to interfere with the project, you will stay out of the investigation. Do I make myself clear?"

"Perfectly, general," Lovelace said to himself. But first he would have to be in the general's presence to hear those orders.

He stopped at the same service station where he had received directions to the woman's house, and asked the attendant, an old man, if North Truro had a police force. The man seemed indignant at such a question, and assured Lovelace that the town had a very able police force in the person of Constable Wally Smith. His office was in the town hall on the square.

There were two possibilities. The man and the woman would have made it up to the highway around eleven o'clock or so, and were either met by someone, or flagged down a passing motorist. In any event, by now they could very well be in Washington, if that was their destination.

With luck, Lovelace told himself, he might be able to find that out from Wally Smith. There could not be much traffic on that highway that time of night. And what little traffic there was, the local cop should know about.

He parked in front of the courthouse on the square, raced up the walk, and hurried inside. A woman was sitting at a switchboard behind a counter doing her knitting. When Lovelace barged in, she looked up in surprise.

"Can I help you?"

"Wally Smith, is he around this morning?"

The woman's eyes strayed toward the corridor. "Yes, sir, but he's with someone now."

Without waiting to hear any more, Lovelace walked down the hall, and at a frosted glass door with the legend, *N. Truro Police Department*, he knocked once and went inside.

A fat man with thinning white hair was seated behind a broad desk, and was facing a youngish woman in tears.

"Here . . . what's this . . ." the man sputtered, getting to his feet.

"Constable Smith?" Lovelace demanded. He reached in his pocket and brought out the FBI identification and held it out for the cop, who swallowed hard once and nodded.

The woman had seen the ID as well, and she jumped up, grabbing Lovelace by the arm. "You're here about my husband?" she wailed.

"I'm sorry, no, ma'am . . ." Lovelace started to say as he tried to disengage his arm from her grasp.

"The Germans from the submarine got him," she screamed. "I know that's what happened. I know it!"

"Now . . . now, Liz, you know that just isn't so," Constable Smith said, starting around the desk to her, but Lovelace was staring at the woman.

"What about the people from the submarine?" he asked, and the woman looked up at him in tears. Her eyes were puffy and red-rimmed. She obviously had been crying for several hours.

"Maggie called and told me about it. I got worried so I called Harvey's hotel in Boston to have him phone me as soon as he got in this morning. But he didn't call. He should have been there by three at the latest. But he didn't call, and the hotel this morning said he never showed up. They've got him. I know it!"

"Your husband was on the highway around eleven o'clock last night?"

"Midnight," the constable said. "And it's true, he hasn't shown up at his hotel."

"What kind of a car does he drive?" Lovelace asked.

"A Chevy," the woman said.

"A '38 Chevy, dark green . . . I've got the license,"

the constable said helpfully. He seemed to be enjoying this.

Lovelace tried to think it out. It was possible, just possible, that the woman was right. The man and woman from the raft could have flagged her husband down and ridden with him up to Boston. From there they could have taken a bus or train to Washington. But they would not have harmed the man unless something had gone wrong. They would not have wanted to call attention to themselves that way.

He looked at the constable. And then he decided— he was going to follow through with this, goddammit. Groves would scream and howl, and so would Colonel Pearson when he didn't show up with the plane. But he could not let it go. He felt close. So damned close.

"I need your help this morning, Smith," he said, and the constable licked his lips.

"Anything for the Bureau," he said with relish.

"First, what's her husband's name?"

"Harvey Dansig," Smith replied.

"Okay," said Lovelace. Grabbing a pad of paper and pencil from the desk, he wrote down a name, and then handed it to the man. "I want you to call this person immediately. He's a friend of mine on the Boston Police Force. Tell him Lovelace needs a favor."

"Yes, sir," the constable said eagerly.

"Give him the description of the car, including its license number, and tell them to put out an APB on it. Right away, this morning."

"Boston is a big city . . ." the constable started to say, but Lovelace cut him off.

"Tell him to check at the bus depot, train station, and airport. Tell him to instruct his people not to touch a thing, and that I'm on my way up. Can you do all that?"

"Yes, sir," the constable said. "Right away."

"Good," Lovelace said briskly, and he turned to leave, but the distraught woman grabbed his arm again.

"They've killed my husband," she cried.

Smith came around the desk and led the woman back to her chair. "I'll take care of everything," he said, looking up.

"Thanks," Lovelace replied, and he went out the door, down the corridor, past the woman with the knitting, and out to his car. The gut feeling that he was on to something was very strong.

14

It was already dark when Badim woke up. For just an instant he had no recollection of where he was, but then he opened his eyes, and through the window he could see an amber light flashing on and off, slowly, in an soothing rhythm. And from across the room he could hear Jada crying softly, the sobs low and muffled.

He reached out and turned on the light next to the bed and looked across the room to where she was seated in a large, overstuffed chair, her face buried in her arms.

"That won't do any good," he said softly, after a while.

She jerked up at the sound of his voice. Her long, light brown hair was disheveled, and her eyes were full. She had been crying for some time. "Why?" she asked, her voice hoarse.

Why, he asked himself, repeating the question in his mind as he continued to stare at her. He had tried to talk Runkov out of using her for this assignment. His argument had been that she was too young, too green to understand what they would have to do. Too naïve.

And now that they were here, they could not afford to falter. They would have to move very fast, strike very hard, and then get out.

Runkov had turned him down. Had turned them both down. She was perfect. Sweet. Innocent. The very qualities that Badim found so dangerous in her, Runkov felt would automatically swing attention away from him.

"It will be like a magician's act with cards," Runkov had explained. "His one hand is kept busy distracting his audience's attention, leaving his other hand the freedom to do its magic."

He lay back on the bed and closed his eyes, not answering her question. Instead, his mind drifted to the details of their assignment. A general and a scientist. The actual killings would be relatively simple. The timing would be difficult. Both men had to be eliminated simultaneously, or so very nearly at the same time that the security services would not have the chance to react, throwing a protective barrier around the second target.

Groves lived and worked here in Washington. Oppenheimer had disappeared months ago from his Berkeley, California, university post to somewhere in the southwest. A secret laboratory, no doubt, at which a large number of scientists were doing their work on the bomb.

The key, Runkov had explained, would be Groves. Sooner or later the general would have to meet with Oppenheimer. In all likelihood they met on a regular basis. "Follow Groves, and when he and Oppenheimer are together, take them out."

Their photographs came into his mind's eye, sharp and very clear, as did Runkov's final admonishment: "The NKVD is running the intelligence gathering network with something over three hundred agents. Some of them are good, but most of them are amateurs and will eventually be found out."

They were at the airport outside Moscow. Doronkin

was waiting in the staff car, and Jada had already boarded the huge TB-7 that would take them up to Murmansk, when Runkov had taken Badim aside.

"Two things of prime consideration, Aleksandr Petrovich," he had said softly. "The first assignment takes priority for the moment. And secondly, you must not be identified as Russian. No matter what happens, no matter what you feel you *must* do to meet those priorities, you will be protected here at home."

"The girl won't understand," Badim had said.

Runkov had waved it off. "It is of no consequence. She will keep her head, you will see to it."

There was a pressure on the bed, and Badim sensed Jada's presence. She smelled faintly of soap. She had evidently bathed while he slept. He opened his eyes and looked up at her. She was kneeling next to him, her hands on her knees.

"I asked you a question, Aleksandr," she said softly.

"In public we're Peter and Lara Bradley," he said.

Jada brushed a loose strand of hair away from her eyes. "I asked you why. Why did you have to kill that man?" Her voice had lost its British accent during her training, and now was slightly nasal. He could not decide if he liked the change.

"He could have identified us," Badim said.

"As hitchhikers, nothing more. He was willing to take us to Boston. That's all we wanted."

He reached out to touch her, but she shrank back. "You know you are quite pretty," he said.

She shook her head in anger. "We are here to assassinate a general and a scientist. I can understand why we must do such a thing, God help me, I can understand it. But that poor man. Why him?"

Badim looked into her eyes. They were quite lovely. How could he tell her about the submarine exploding? The Coastal Patrol finding the wreckage. Identifying it as German. Then making the connection that a German agent or agents came ashore and killed the man?

German agents. Throw the suspicion on the Nazis. Make it abundantly clear that this is a German operation. How?

"Are you going to murder the hotel clerk downstairs because he can recognize us? Or how about the ticket clerk in Boston? Or the bus driver who brought us here? Or the cab driver? Are you going to murder them as well?"

Jada's voice was becoming loud and strident, and Badim sat up and took her forcibly by the shoulders, his face only a few inches from hers.

"Listen to me very carefully, little girl, because I will not repeat myself," he said sternly.

She hiccoughed, but said nothing, her eyes wide, her lips half parted.

"We have a job to do here, one of supreme importance to our government. We were selected for the task because Marshal Stalin himself thought we could do it. And we will. But nothing, absolutely nothing will get in the way. No matter what we have to do to accomplish this, we will do it. Even if it means forfeiting our own lives. Do you understand that?"

She nodded, her eyes even wider.

"Then understand this as well, my little Natasha. I abhor violence."

A look of surprise crossed her features, and Badim nodded.

"Yes, I abhor violence. I have nightmares about the lives I have ended, and about the lives I will end. But make no mistake, I will do what I must. And so will you."

He wondered why he had told her that. It was true . . . there were nights when he would awaken in a cold sweat. And most of the time he felt that he was holding himself in some kind of a straitjacket. It was almost a mental restraint he had to live with. Behind the controls there was . . . what? Even now he shrank away from delving too far into his own psyche.

"I'm sorry . . ." Jada said, but her voice was toneless, and after a long moment she shrugged out of his grasp and got off the bed. She went across the room to the window and looked down at the evening traffic in and around Dunbarton College, which was across the street from their hotel.

She wore a light-colored robe, with no slippers on her feet, and as Badim stared at her tiny back he felt an almost overwhelming urge to go to her, to hold her, to comfort her, to make love to her.

How long had it been since he had a woman? Six months? Nine months? A year? It had been in Berlin. Just a whore whose name he had not bothered to learn.

But with those disturbing thoughts came others. Guilt feelings for the man on the highway he had killed.

"Harvey Dansig's the name," the man had said, looking over his shoulder at Badim in the backseat. "You say your car broke down?"

"Yes," Badim said. He was wet and cold, and he was shivering. "Something happened to the steering. We ran off the road just up here a couple of miles. Thought we could walk back up to Provincetown if no one came along."

"It's a good thing I did come along, then," Dansig said. "Won't be any other traffic along here till morning, I suspect." He looked at Jada sitting next to him in the front seat and smiled. "Where you folks heading this time of night?"

"Boston," Badim said. "We were up at Provincetown on our honeymoon. I've got to be back by morning."

"Well, if we can't get your car fixed, you folks sure are welcome to ride along with me. I'm going all the way up to Boston myself. Be glad for the company."

Badim tried to tear his mind away from remembering what had happened after that, but he could not. It was as if he was being forced into watching a horror movie he had seen before.

They stopped at the side of the road and the man got out of the car, Badim directly behind him. Jada, not knowing what was going to happen, got out as well, and said something to the man, distracting him.

In that instant Badim jammed his right knee in the man's back, and with both hands over Dansig's face jerked backward as hard as he could, snapping the man's spine.

Jada screamed and Dansig collapsed without a sound, his legs jerking spasmodically. Within a minute and a half Badim had stuffed the body into the trunk, had helped the stunned Jada back into the passenger seat, and had gotten behind the wheel, the bile rising up sharply in his throat, his stomach churning.

They had driven the rest of the way to Boston in silence. Badim had parked the car around the corner from the Greyhound Bus Depot, and they had taken the first bus to Washington.

All through that morning she had not said a word to him, and even avoided looking at him, until now. And her reaction was understandable. He could not blame her.

He shook his head slowly, swung his legs over the edge of the bed, and got up. She turned around to him, the flashing amber light from the hotel bar downstairs throwing her face into harsh shadows.

"I told you on the submarine I would help you," she said in a soft voice. "And I will. I'm sorry for my outburst."

"Jada," he said, taking a step toward her. He wanted to explain something to her that even he didn't understand, but she shrank back against the curtains.

"Don't come near me," she said coldly. "I'll help you, but don't come near me."

Badim stopped in the middle of the room, staring at her. She was lovely, but frail. He wanted to comfort her. Or was it he who needed comforting?

"What do you want of me now?" she asked.

Badim continued staring at her. Runkov was wrong. She had no business being here with him. The events of the next few days would most certainly not be to her liking. And another thought briefly intruded as he watched the expression in her eyes. Another terrible thought occurred to him. If she got in the way . . . if the assignment hinged on her . . . what then?

He turned away, not able to face her. "I'm going out. Stay here," he said.

"How long will you be?"

"An hour. No more. And while I'm gone I want you to cut your hair and do something with it."

"Yes," she said softly.

Badim reached the telephone booth two blocks from the hotel ten minutes later, exactly on schedule. He dropped a nickel in the slot and dialed a number Runkov had given him for their contact.

After two rings, the phone was answered. "Good evening," a woman said in an almost singsong voice. "War Department night operator, may I help you?"

15

BOSTON

"Definitely seawater," the stoop-shouldered little police scientist said, straightening up from his microscope. He fumbled for his thick glasses lying on the cluttered lab table, and when he had them on he focused on Lovelace.

"Are you sure?"

The scientist shrugged. "I was sure six hours ago when you brought me the material from the seats. It was still wet. I tasted it. Seawater."

"The man sat in the backseat then," Lovelace asked. He was tired, and his eyes were burning.

Again the scientist shrugged. "You told me there could have been a man and a woman in addition to the driver. We know the woman sat in the front seat. Long, light brown hair. She's probably in her late teens or early twenties from the condition of the half-dozen strands we found on the seat back. And the second passenger sat in the rear seat directly behind the driver. They both were wearing wet clothes."

"Anything else?"

"They came up from the beach, that's obvious. You could see that yourself from the sand on the floor mats."

"Fingerprints?"

The scientist chuckled. "Twenty-seven different lifts, of which only six are even remotely usable. Considering the man and his wife, perhaps children, mechanics, friends, you name it, you might be several years tracking them all down."

The laboratory door banged open and Lovelace's friend, Detective Stewart Gillingham, strode across the room to them, a worried expression on his face.

"You finished here?" he said to Lovelace, ignoring the scientist. He was a large, thin man, with short-cropped hair. His suit was rumpled as if he had slept in it.

Lovelace nodded. "Let me guess . . . Captain Kennedy is on the rampage."

"Bingo," Gillingham said grimly. "He's across the street in the morgue. They're finishing the autopsy now and he wants to see you."

Eight years ago Gillingham had been a junior-grade detective on the Boston Police Force, with a series of unsolved rape-murders on his hands. Lovelace had come down from Samson Army-Air Corps Base in New York on the trail of an AWOL soldier whose psychological profile indicated he could be a sexual deviate. Together they had solved the crimes, and Gillingham had been promoted as a result. Over the ensuing years he and Lovelace had kept in loose contact, each man respecting the other's abilities.

Calvin Kennedy, on the other hand, was more of a politician than a good cop, and eight years ago Lovelace had told him so. That statement had not exactly endeared the police chief to him.

He thanked the scientist, and went with Gillingham out of the lab, up the stairs to the first floor, and then outside. Before they crossed the mall to the morgue, Lovelace stopped his friend.

"Anything from the bus depot?"

Gillingham shook his head. "There were seven buses for D.C. today, the first of them leaving at 6 A.M. We've managed to track down six of the drivers, but with so little to go on, we didn't come up with much. Every one of the buses had at least one couple matching your loose description. A man and a long-haired woman."

"How about the first bus? That would have been the one they took."

"We talked to that driver, but he couldn't remember anyone unusual. Can't you tell me what you're working on?"

"No," Lovelace said. "Ticket clerks, baggage handlers?"

"The same. Nothing conclusive. If we could come up with a more concrete description . . ."

"Yeah," Lovelace said, half to himself, and they headed across the mall.

It was late, well after eight o'clock, and he was dead tired. It had been a long night and an even longer day. He had sent the P-47 back to Bolling as soon as the pilot had dropped him off here in Boston. Before he had left the airfield, however, he had called Colonel Pearson and explained the unscheduled stop, apologizing for it, and promising that a full written report would be forthcoming.

He had not called his office, and he was sure that General Groves would be hopping mad by now. But that could not be helped. The general had given him a carte blanche when this assignment had begun, and until now he had not used it.

Sooner or later, however, he would have to confront the general. Only before that happened, he wanted something more to go on than he had now.

Captain Kennedy, a bull of a man with a beet red complexion and thick white hair, was waiting in the corridor outside the autopsy laboratory with a man in a long white coat. When he spotted Lovelace and Gillingham coming from the elevators, he broke away and came to meet them. He looked furious.

"I want to know what the hell is going on, and who the hell you think you are, Lovelace, goddammit!" the man bellowed. He looked as if he was on the verge of a stroke.

Lovelace gazed up at him, and smiled. "Good evening, Captain Kennedy, what brings you downtown so late?"

It seemed as if the man's eyes were going to pop out of his head, and his mouth worked but no sounds came out.

"Have they finished with the autopsy?" Lovelace continued. "I'd like to see the results, and talk with the pathologist."

"You'll see nothing," Kennedy roared. "I spoke with your commanding general five minutes ago, and he told me that you were to be placed on the first available transportation up to Washington, even if I had to arrest you to do it."

Kennedy had made trouble during the murder investigation eight years ago. It had been something about the pride of the force. He hadn't wanted any army enlisted man coming in and telling his people how to do their jobs.

Lovelace smiled again. "Evidently General Groves hasn't been informed. Perhaps we should call him."

A hint of doubt crossed the bullish captain's features. "Informed about what?"

Lovelace turned to Gillingham. "Could you excuse us just for a moment, Stewart? I'd like to talk to Captain Kennedy alone."

"Sure," Gillingham said, and he walked down the corridor to where the man in the white coat stood waiting.

When he was out of earshot, Lovelace took Kennedy

by the arm and pulled him aside. "You're aware that I work for the Army Counter Intelligence Corps."

Kennedy nodded, but there was mistrust obvious in his eyes. "General Groves told me that. But he was mad. Said he wanted you back in Washington."

Lovelace made a show of checking to make certain that Gillingham and the pathologist were far enough away, and then he pulled Kennedy a little closer to the wall. "What I'm about to tell you is classified information. Top secret."

Kennedy suddenly looked very uncomfortable, and he tried to back away. "I don't want any part of anything like that. . . ."

Lovelace interrupted him. "You're already a part of it, captain, and so is your entire police force, by virtue of the fact a man was killed here in your city . . . or at least his body was found here stuffed in the trunk of a car."

"No . . ." Kennedy sputtered, but Lovelace continued.

"There is a plot in progress at this very moment to assassinate Roosevelt."

The captain paled.

"That's right," Lovelace said. "His assassins are probably in Washington at this very moment. I think they are the ones who killed the poor man you found by the bus depot. And I need your help to find them. . . . President Roosevelt needs your help."

"But General Groves said . . ." Kennedy started, but again Lovelace cut him off.

"General Groves does not know you like I do. He told me to use my own discretion in telling you any of this. You can understand the panic that would occur if such a thing got out." Again Lovelace looked toward Gillingham and the other man. "We've got to work fast on this, captain. I'm depending on you not only to help us, but to keep this a secret. As far as anyone is concerned, we're looking for the murderer of a man. Nothing more."

Kennedy wet his lips, his eyes wide.

"President Roosevelt's life could very well depend upon you, captain," Lovelace said seriously. He was getting a perverse pleasure from this. "And I'm sure that when he is informed of your cooperation, he will be grateful. Very grateful."

Lovelace could see the wheels spinning in Kennedy's head. Weighing the alternatives. If Lovelace was telling him a lie, it wouldn't really matter. He would be covered because the man was a CIC agent. There were no denying that. And if by some circumstance Lovelace was telling the truth, it would be a feather in his cap. Not many police captains had the gratitude of a President.

"How can I help?" Kennedy finally said, and inwardly Lovelace sighed with relief. As much as he despised the man, he needed him and his police force, as well as the cooperation of the Washington police, which Kennedy could assure.

"In a number of ways," Lovelace said. "First of all, we must keep this absolutely secret. We're looking for a murderer, nothing more."

Kennedy nodded.

"Second, I need the results of the autopsy. Third, I want every man you can spare down at the bus depot to find someone who remembers the man and the woman. Gillingham can help with that. Fourth, I'll want to contact the D.C. police chief and inform him that you believe the murderer or murderers are in Washington. Give him whatever you've got from this end, and ask for his department's help. And finally, I'll need some transportation back down to Washington tonight."

"Can do," Kennedy said briskly and without hesitation.

"But mum's the word," Lovelace said, theatrically placing his forefinger over his lips.

"I understand," Kennedy said.

Lovelace smiled and nodded. For better or for worse,

Kennedy was on his side now, or would be for a short while.

They went down the hall to Gillingham and the white-coated man. Kennedy made the introductions.

"Captain Michael Lovelace, Army Counter Intelligence Corps . . . Dr. Hubert Miller, Middlesex County assistant coroner."

"Pleased to meet you," Lovelace said, shaking the man's hand. He was young, probably in his early or mid-thirties, and he looked almost as tired as Lovelace felt.

"Give Captain Lovelace your fullest cooperation," Kennedy said, and then he turned to Gillingham, who was staring at Lovelace in open amazement. "Come with me. We've a lot of work to do tonight."

"Yes, sir," Gillingham said crisply, nodding to Lovelace.

Kennedy turned again. "When you're finished here, captain, come across to my office. *I'll* have your transportation arranged."

"Thanks," Lovelace said, and Kennedy and Gillingham strode down the corridor.

When they were gone, Dr. Miller led Lovelace into the autopsy room, where a body covered by a white sheet was lying on a stainless steel table.

"I wish I had been a little bird on your shoulder when you talked with Kennedy. Ten minutes ago he was cursing you up one side and down the other. And suddenly after a couple of minutes of discussion, he's a pussycat."

Lovelace laughed. "We're old friends, actually."

The doctor looked sharply at him, but said nothing. At the table he flipped back the sheet to reveal the nude body of a man, with several bruises on his face, and a large triangular patch cut out of his torso, the flap of skin loosely sewn over the opening like a gruesome trapdoor.

"Harvey Dansig," the doctor said. "Age thirty-seven."

He looked at Lovelace. "What do you want to know?"

Lovelace stared down at the body for a long moment, wondering how Harvey Dansig, age thirty-seven, had spent his last day on earth, and what had moved him to pick up a pair of hitchhikers on a lonely road in the middle of the night. "Time of death?" he asked finally.

"Sometime between midnight and two—can't get it any closer than that."

"Cause of death?"

"The instantaneous fracture of the third lumbar and second cervical vertebra, which severed the corresponding lumbar, thoracic and cervical nerves."

"In plain English," Lovelace asked, staring at the man. He wanted a cigarette.

"The man's back and neck were broken at the same time, severing his spinal cord in three places."

Lovelace looked up. "Was he hit by a car?"

"Nope," the doctor said, "but he might as well have been." He sighed tiredly. "Do you want the long or the short version?"

"The short version," Lovelace said, "but don't leave anything out."

The doctor smiled. "Your killer came up behind Dansig, grabbed his head in both hands—you can see the bruises on his face—shoved his right knee into Dansig's back, and yanked hard. Death was instantaneous and totally unexpected."

"What can you tell me about the murderer?"

"He's tall, probably six-one or six-three. He's long-legged . . . his hands are large, but his fingers are narrow. He's very powerful, and he's right-handed."

"He needed the height and the long legs to get his knee up into Dansig's back, and the size of the hands and fingers could be determined by the bruises, but right-handed?"

"The bruises on that side of Dansig's face are deeper, combined with the fact that the fractures are spiral right to left, indicate a man whose right hand and arm are stronger than his left."

"Anything else?"

The doctor shook his head. "Not unless you want the long version, but you've got the high points."

"A man of ordinary strength couldn't have done that?"

"Your killer isn't a superman, if that's what you mean. But he is strong, and he knows how to kill a man silently."

"Thanks," Lovelace said absently, and he started to turn away, but something the doctor had said earlier bothered him, and he turned back. "You said death was totally unexpected?"

"That's right," the doctor said. "There were no indications that his muscles had contracted. He was totally relaxed. He was even smiling."

"As if he was being distracted . . . pleasantly?"

The doctor shrugged. "I don't know. But he definitely was not expecting to be killed."

"Thanks," Lovelace said again, and he left the autopsy lab, went down the corridor, and took the elevator up to the street level, very puzzled.

Why was Harvey Dansig killed? There was no reason for his death. No *apparent* reason, that was.

16

Jada watched the hands of the cheap alarm clock they had purchased two days ago creep toward a quarter to ten. She lay on the bed in their hotel room, dressed in a print blouse and a plain dark skirt. A Glenn Miller tune was playing on the radio, but she was only half listening to it as she tried without much success to clear her mind of the disturbing thoughts she had been having over the past three days. She kept coming back to the look on Harvey Dansig's face when he died.

He had been smiling at her. Christ, earlier in the front seat he had even winked at her, and then Alek had killed him in cold blood.

But even more disturbing than that to her were her thoughts about Alek. For some insane reason he reminded her of the image she had had as a young girl of what her perfect man would be. Tall, strong silent, but with a deep, solid intelligence.

She had been very naïve in those days, a trait she had inherited from her father, who had been a professor of history at Oxford, but who had retired early to write a series of books on the Great Russian Revolution of 1917. That naïveté was the man's one major flaw, and he had passed it on in spades to his only child.

Like many academicians, the real day-to-day world outside of dusty historical tomes was out of his reach. And for his daughter, the world was nothing more than a wondrous fairy tale.

Those were the halcyon years . . . the late twenties and early thirties . . . for her. People were basically honest, and the ones who weren't always came to justice. Women were kind yet strong . . . keepers of the home fires. While men possessed a different kind of strength tempered by gentleness—knights in shining armor and all that.

She remembered their house in Brighton, south of London, on the Channel. To her it was always a warm, sunny summer's day. There were picnics on the beach. There were the constant houseguests—writers and artists and actors who would spend the night with her father and mother arguing politics and philosophy. There were train rides up to London to see the symphonies, and the plays and the ballet. And best of all there was her father, who had raised her with love, devotion, a certain idealism, and a feel for history and languages.

By the summer of 1926 when she was just five years old, her French was as good as her English. By the time she was eight she had nearly mastered Italian and Spanish. And by the time she was ten her father had started her on the long, rugged path of Russian, which he called the "bastard language of a lovely, stoic people."

Then when she was thirteen her wonderful little world crumbled around her. It began in December of 1933 with her mother's death of an undetected brain tumor, and by the next summer her father had sold their house and they had moved to Helsinki, Finland, where he took a post at the university.

That lasted only until the fall of that year, when they

took the train the nine hundred kilometers to Moscow from where her father was accepted at a Moscow State University post.

They were given a fine apartment overlooking the Moscow River and within sight of the Alexander Gardens, and it was here at the age of fourteen that Jada made a number of important discoveries about her father and about the world in general.

Her father was an important man to the Soviets. Not so much because his field was important, but because his was a big name in academic circles. His immigration to the Soviet Union had been a propaganda coup.

Jada, whose name in England had been Marion Elizabeth Stanhope, had never questioned her father's decision to immigrate or the extraordinary change of name, or even the courses in political theory she was required to take six days a week. Her father was happy, and that was all that mattered.

Too, she found the Russian people to be warm and friendly, whereas many of their British neighbors back home had been stuffy and pretentious. And although she found the language difficult at first, she was heartened by the depth of the poetry in a land she came to learn considered that art form a national institution.

When she was eighteen she was accepted to Moscow State University on the strength of her father's position. But a year later he died.

For the first few dazed months after his funeral Jada had expected that her position at the university would be canceled, but she was allowed to remain enrolled.

The Germans had invaded Poland, the Russians had marched into Finland, and yet everyone at school expected war with Germany at any time.

Language clerks were desperately needed, and Jada, because of her perfect English, was recruited. She went to work in a drab office building near the Kremlin, where nearly a year passed before she realized that her employers were the NKVD. But by then her transition from being British to being Russian was complete . . . at least in her own mind.

Her father had loved the Soviet Union, had loved the Russian people, and had loved the idealism of communal government and ownership, and that was good enough for her.

No matter that she was constantly watched, no matter that she was constantly questioned, that her work was constantly checked. Those were necessary precautions. It was war.

Only now that they were in America, she found it hard to reconcile her fond memories of Brighton with the drab existence she had led in Moscow. Here in Washington, away from both worlds, she had a chance to compare them, and neither was satisfying in retrospect.

Alek, from what she had been told of him by Major Runkov, had led a tragic childhood. He, too, was a loner. And at this moment she desperately wanted him to be her knight in shining armor, yet she kept coming back to the look on Harvey Dansig's face when Alek had killed him.

It was a quarter to ten finally, and she got up from the bed, smoothed her skirt, put on a clean blouse, and slung her purse over her shoulder, then left the room.

Alek had been out all day, returning earlier this evening to have dinner with her at a small restaurant around the corner, and then he had left again, telling her he was going to watch General Groves' house on Thirty-sixth Street in the nearby Cleveland Park.

Last night after the ten o'clock call to their contact in the War Department, Alek had been excited. The man had told him that Groves was probably getting ready to leave for a week or more. The general had been staying late at his office, and bringing home two briefcases for the past few days. That pattern of behavior always preceded a long trip.

This morning Alek had gone out and purchased a

four-year-old Ford coupe in good condition, and had seen to its registration and gas coupons.

If Groves was getting set to meet Oppenheimer somewhere, they would have to be mobile, ready at a moment's notice to move fast.

Their room was on the third floor, and she took the stairs down and went out the back way. The evening was hot and muggy, but she was glad to be outside and finally doing something.

Alek had told her she would have to make the ten o'clock call to their contact, who was a night man in the War Department's parking garage, because he didn't want to risk losing Groves should the general decide to come home early and leave on his trip the same evening.

Now that there was a possibility that they soon would be doing what they had been sent here for, Jada was frightened. All along, in the back of her mind, she had harbored a secret hope that somehow their orders would be changed, or that it would become impossible to get to Oppenheimer, in which case they would have to return home.

Even now she hoped that the contact would tell her it was a false alarm. That Groves would be staying in Washington after all.

She reached the phone booth two blocks from the hotel with barely a minute to spare. There was no traffic on the road at that moment, and no other pedestrians, and for just a minute an overwhelming sense of loneliness, a longing for her safe, secure childhood, washed over her. But she shrugged it off, went into the phone booth, and dug a nickel from her purse.

The telephone rang as she was about to reach for it, and her hand stopped in mid-air, her heart seeming nearly to leap out of her chest.

It rang again, the noise like an explosion in the confines of the booth. It was ten o'clock. Who would be calling a phone booth? Had Alek given their contact the number?

She looked back up the street toward the hotel as a car turned the corner a block away, its red taillights receding in the distance.

The telephone rang again, and she picked it up. "Yes?" she said softly.

There was a silence on the line for a long time, and she was about to speak again, when a low, guttural man's voice answered. "Who is this?"

Jada was confused and frightened. She wanted to hang up but something made her stay on the line. But what to say? "I think maybe I must have the wrong number." She spoke the code words in desperation.

There was another long silence until the man replied, "If it's extension seven-two-one you want, you have the right number."

It was the proper response. "Then you must be the man I want to speak with about my car," she said automatically. Her heart was pounding. Something was wrong.

"Where is Peter?" the man snapped.

"Working," Jada said, not able to think of anything else. "How did you get this number?"

"Peter gave it to me," the man snapped. "But listen, there is trouble. I must seen him tonight."

"Impossible," Jada said, trying to make her brain work. What kind of trouble? What was happening?

"I must. There is danger. I'm not calling from work. I must see Peter!"

"I don't know when he'll be back," Jada said. It would be too risky to try to find him near Groves' house. But what else could she do? Her knees were weak, and she wanted to hang up the phone and run.

"Then I'll come to where you're staying and wait for him."

"No . . ." Jada said, but the man shouted her down.

"We're all in great danger. I have to see him." There was an edge of panic in the man's voice.

Oh god, Jada thought. Alek. "The Dunbarton Oaks Hotel. Room 328," she blurted in desperation.

"I'll be there in fifteen minutes," the man said, and he hung up.

Badim had parked his car around the corner on Thirty-fifth Street, and he had been standing in the shadows of a line of bushes across the street from the yellow brick house since nine o'clock. Groves had come home shortly before ten, parking his green Dodge in the driveway. A few minutes later he had come out of the house with a single suitcase, which he had placed in the backseat of the car, and then he had gone back inside.

That had been nearly fifteen minutes ago, and since then the house across the street had been quiet. Lights shone from the living room window and from an upstairs window, probably a bedroom. From time to time he could see someone moving around inside, but then the porch light went out, and the downstairs lights were extinguished.

Badim was keyed up, his mind hyperactive since his contact last night. Groves was getting set to make a move. Which could mean nothing more than a conference somewhere, probably New York or Chicago. Or it could mean he was going to meet Oppenheimer.

But he was also keyed up because of a brief article he had read two days ago in the *Washington Post*. Harvey Dansig's body had been discovered in the trunk of his car near the Greyhound Bus Depot in Boston. The police there were looking for a tall, husky man and a young woman with long, light brown hair.

The District of Columbia police had been alerted because it was believed that the killers may have come to Washington.

But it was not the facts in the article that had disturbed Badim; rather, it was what the article had not reported that had him worried.

No mention had been made of the German submarine. In fact, nowhere in the Washington, Boston, or New York newspapers was there mention of a submarine exploding off the coast of Cape Cod.

Had the fuse worked? Had the submarine exploded? Had its wreckage been discovered? And had a connection been made between the sub and Dansig's murder? Or had none of that happened?

Badim had an odd, gut feeling about this. The Americans were not stupid. And if they had made the connection, why hadn't the newspapers gotten hold of it? GERMAN SPIES SOUGHT IN WASHINGTON AREA. Those should have been the headlines.

The porch light came on again, and he stiffened. The front door opened and Groves came down the walk to his car. But he was dressed in a robe and slippers.

For a long moment the general stood by his car, looking up the street, his right hand in his pocket, but then he locked his car doors and trudged back up to the house. A moment later he went in and closed the door, and the porch light went out.

Groves was not leaving tonight. Probably first thing in the morning, Badim thought. But he would wait just a little longer to make absolutely sure.

Ten minutes later, the upstairs light went out, and a few minutes after that the lights in another house down the street went out, and the neighborhood settled down for the night.

Badim sighed deeply, then turned and slipped through the shadows to the corner, where he got in his car, started it, and headed back to the hotel.

If there was no new information from their contact, he and Jada would come back here at about four in the morning and wait for the general to leave.

*   *   *

The hotel room was dark. Jada sat in a straight-backed chair in the corner facing the door. In her lap was a German pistol with a bulbous silencer screwed on its barrel.

She had been sitting like that ever since she had hurried back from the phone booth, alternately cursing her stupidity and wishing for Alek to return.

She had been flustered on the telephone, and she had blurted out their location. It was incredibly stupid. The man had said there was trouble, and she had led him here, when she should have been leading him in the opposite direction. They had covered situations like this in their training. Set up a dummy location, from which your contact can be directed to a series of fail-safes. Now she remembered it all. But she had forgotten it on the telephone.

There was a knock at the door, and her heart seemed to stop beating for an instant. She snatched the gun from her lap, and fumbled with the safety catch. "It's open," she said softly.

The knock came again, more insistently.

"It's open," she said louder. "Come in."

The door swung slowly inward, and a short man with gray hair and a huge, red nose stood framed in the doorway by the light from the corridor. He took a step inside and then stopped, obviously unable to see Jada.

"All the way in, and close the door," Jada said, pointing the gun at him with shaking hands.

The man jerked at the sound of her voice, but he complied, softly closing the door behind him.

"Is Peter back yet?" the man asked. It was the same guttural voice from the phone.

"I'm pointing a gun at you. I want you to go to the bed and sit down."

"Where is Peter?" the man asked, raising his voice.

This is going all wrong. Alek, Jada screamed silently. She could not shoot this man. She could not!

Her finger tightened on the trigger. "Sit down on the

bed or I will kill you," she said, almost choking on the words.

The man walked carefully across the room and sat down on the edge of the bed. "I was fired from my job," he said into the darkness. "I think they suspect me."

Christ, Jada thought. "Suspect you of what?"

"Of working for you and Peter."

And she had led him here. Dear god, what had she done? "How do you know that?" She would have to keep her head.

"I don't know . . . for sure," the man said, shaking his head. He ran the fingers of his right hand through his hair, then sat forward on the bed, obviously still not able to see Jada very well in the dark corner. "They caught me up in Groves' office. Asked me what I was doing there. I told them I wanted to talk to the general about his car. But they kicked me out, and a couple of hours later my super came down and said I was through. Told me to get out."

Jada tried to make her brain work, tried to think of what she had learned from her training. "Were you followed here?"

The man reacted almost as if he had been slapped. "Followed?" he squeaked.

"Yes, were you followed? Did you take precautions?"

"I don't know," the man said, his voice on the verge of cracking. And Jada suddenly could smell liquor. The man had been drinking.

What to do? They'd have to get out of here. Now! If only Alek would return.

"But I found out something," the man was saying, his voice almost pleading. "General Groves has tickets for the ten o'clock Limited out of New York. For to-morrow morning. He's going to Chicago."

"How do you know that?"

"I saw the tickets on his secretary's desk. He's leaving in the morning. Peter has to be . . ."

Badim burst into the room, and he instantly took in the situation, his gun appearing suddenly in his right hand as he gently kicked the door shut behind him with his heel. The color drained from the man's face.

"Who is this man?" Badim snapped.

Jada had jumped up from her chair, her stomach fluttering again, but relief washing over her. "Our contact."

"There are a pair of military policemen downstairs looking for him. Gasoline black market. How did he get here?"

"I gave him our address. He was fired tonight," Jada said.

The man had recovered from his momentary shock, and he jumped up from the bed. "I got the information for you, Peter," he blurted. "General Groves is leaving on the ten o'clock Limited from New York."

"We've got to leave, now," Badim said to Jada.

"What about me?" the man squeaked, and Badim shot him in the chest. The silenced gun made only a dull plopping sound, but the man was violently slammed backward, spread-eagled on the bed.

"Alek!" Jada cried, taking a step forward. The smell of gunpowder was strong in the small room.

"Get our things together and go to the car. It's parked around back. Two minutes!" Badim snapped, and he turned and went out of the room as the bile rose up in Jada's throat, and she vomited on the floor.

When Runkov had told them there were fools within the NKVD's agent network here, he had not been exaggerating. But Jada's performance tonight had been totally inexcusable, and it made him sick to think about it.

He hurried down the corridor, his mind working at top speed. The only person who had really gotten a good look at them in this hotel was the night clerk on duty, at this moment talking with the military police.

Both he and Jada had managed to avoid close contact

with any of the other hotel personnel, checking in the first day after 6 P.M.

He took the stairs down to the first floor, two at a time, stuffing the gun in his jacket pocket. His hand curled over the grip, his finger on the trigger, the safety off.

When he had come in he had seen the MPs talking with the clerk in the otherwise deserted lobby, and he only hoped now for just a little bit of luck. Once they got out of here he was going to make sure the rest of the assignment was carried out with less sloppiness. Far less.

He pushed through the door and took the short corridor to the lobby, where the two cops were still behind the counter with the clerk, looking through the registration book. No one else was around, and they all looked up as Badim rushed to the counter.

"Mr. Bradley . . ." the clerk started to say, but the words died on his lips, as he saw the expression of deep fright on Badim's face.

"My god, it's terrible," Badim babbled. "I saw him with a dead man. He was dragging him down into the basement."

"What?" one of the cops demanded.

"A little man with white hair. He killed the other man! Just now!"

The cops and the clerk came around the counter and headed in a dead run toward the stairwell door, Badim right behind them.

Still no one had come into the lobby, and as he reached the door he withdrew his pistol.

The three men were halfway down the stairs when Badim closed the door behind him and leaned over the stairwell railing. "Hey," he shouted.

The three of them looked up as Badim fired four shots, the first hitting the clerk in the head, the second hitting one of the cops in the throat, blowing away most of his Adam's apple, and the third and fourth shots hitting the other cop, who was starting to pull out his gun, in the chest and cheek.

Calmly. Badim pocketed his gun and went back to the still deserted lobby. Behind the counter he found the page in the registration book with his and Jada's names, tore it out and stuffed it in his pocket, then hurried out of the hotel's back door.

17

PORTSMOUTH, NEW HAMPSHIRE

Lovelace drove as fast as Detective Gillingham's car could possibly go. The road wound its way through the lovely rolling hills of northeastern Massachusetts, past picturesque dairy farms and through storybook towns. From time to time he caught glimpses of the Atlantic Ocean out his right window, the afternoon sun sparkling on the water, and he wondered about the Allied soldiers pounding their way through the French countryside toward Paris. But he also wondered about the Germans being pushed back to their homeland.

Were they even now stepping up their research on the atomic bomb? A team of intelligence agents was at this very moment scouring the Italian and French countrysides for nuclear installations. Project ALSOS, it was called, but so far nothing significant had been found.

North of Newburyport, he was forced to slow down by a tractor-driven farm wagon filled with manure, but shortly before the New Hampshire border the farmer pulled off onto a side road, waving as Lovelace roared past him.

At any other time he would have enjoyed this drive through the rustic countryside, but this afternoon he was tired . . . mentally worn-out. He thought about General Groves, who was so certain that this was nothing but a wild goose chase. And about Colonel Lansdale, the head of CIC, who had agreed, privately advising Lovelace to drop it.

He also wondered what he would do if and when Groves ordered him point-blank to drop this investigation. So far that had not happened, although when he had returned from Boston after commandeering the P-47, and after upsetting the entire Boston police force, he had come perilously close to being fired.

But his argument to the general then, and now, had been the same.

"What if this man and woman are here to interfere with the project?"

"A very remote possibility, Lovelace—even you have to admit it," the general had snapped. "But assuming you're right for just a moment, why did they kill that fellow from North Truro and leave his body in his car by the bus depot in Boston? It was damned near a full-page newspaper ad telling us they had come to Washington."

"I can't answer that, general," Lovelace had admitted. "Yet. But it bothers me, too. It doesn't make sense."

"Yes, it does," Groves said. "If they are spies, they're amateurs. I think we can handle it."

"Are you pulling me off this?" Lovelace had asked.

The general stared at him for a long moment, then smiled, wanly. "If I do you'll continue anyway, won't you?"

Lovelace nodded.

The general thought a moment. "One week, captain. Seven days. If nothing turns up by then, you'll drop it."

"I'll need your backing."

"You've got it," Groves said. "Now get out of here. I have a lot of work to do."

It was shortly past two o'clock when Lovelace drove into Fort Constitution, which was the access point for the Portsmouth harbor facilities. Yesterday afternoon he had learned that a relatively intact section of the German submarine that had exploded off Cape Cod had been recovered and was being towed to the Portsmouth Navy Yard. Groves had telephoned the commander here and requested his cooperation. As a result Lovelace's reception was very crisp.

From the main gate he was immediately escorted across the Piscataqua River to the naval yard itself, which occupied two islands in the harbor. From there he was ushered into the administration building, and to the office of Lieutenant Commander Roland Gannt, Chief, Facility Security, a man in his late thirties with a broad smile. There was a chief petty officer there as well, but Lovelace never caught his name.

"Did you drive up from Boston?" Gannt asked. He indicated a chair for Lovelace.

"Yes, I did," Lovelace said. He remained standing. "Has the submarine arrived?"

"Actually, it came in last night. The weather was good and the tugs made better time than we had first hoped for," Gannt said. "It's a lovely drive up the coast road, isn't it?"

"Have you determined what caused the submarine to explode yet?"

Gannt smiled. "We've got a yard crew on it now, but I haven't seen a report so far. Would you like to go down and have a look-see?"

"If it's not too much trouble."

"Heavens, no trouble at all," Gannt said, and he came around his desk. "Be back in two shakes," he said to the chief petty officer, and he escorted Lovelace out of the building to a gray jeep with navy markings parked at the rear.

The Portsmouth Navy Yard, which had been established in 1800, now specialized in the construction, maintenance, and repair of submarines. Everywhere on both islands there was the din and apparent confusion of any shipyard. In many of the slips, two and even three vessels lay tied up, ready for departure, and in several dry docks, boats in various stages of construction or retrofitting were being worked on. "Around the clock, seven days a week," Gannt told Lovelace proudly.

He drove them across the yard to a huge, dark-gray metal building, at least as large as an aircraft hangar, from which a wide set of railroad tracks led down into the water. The building, and what appeared to be a scrap pile of twisted metal, was separated from the rest of the base by a tall, wire-mesh fence. Two armed guards were on duty at the gate, and they came over to the jeep when Gannt pulled up.

"Good afternoon, commander," one of them said, saluting.

Gannt returned the salute. "This is Captain Lovelace, Army CIC. He's come down from Washington to take a look at our latest find."

"Yes, sir," the guard said. He saluted again, and the other man swung the gate open, allowing Gannt to proceed.

"Any captured enemy submarine or piece thereof ends up here sooner or later for study," Gannt said, and he drove through the gate and parked at a side entrance to the huge building.

"Do you get much business?" Lovelace asked.

Gannt shrugged. "We had most of the pieces of a Jap submarine here a couple of weeks ago. Had to ship it to us by rail all the way from California, then put it on barges across the bay. Quite a project, actually."

They got out of the jeep, but before they went inside, Lovelace pointed to the scrap pile at the south end of the building. "What's all that?"

Gannt looked that way. "That's what's left after demanufacturing." He turned back and smiled. "We don't put them back together, you know."

Lovelace was about to ask what he meant by "demanufacturing," but Gannt evidently read the puzzled expression on his face.

"I'll explain everything inside," he said, and he came around the jeep and opened the door that was posted with an UNAUTHORIZED ENTRANCE PROHIBITED sign.

Pneumatic chisels, electric drills and hammers reverberated in the cavernous interior of the building. Set up on huge skids and surrounded by scaffolding was a barely recognizable section of submarine, most of its outer hull peeled away, and much of its inner hull gone as well, exposing a maze of piping and wiring.

Gannt had to shout close to Lovelace's ear to be heard. "This is a piece of the boat, from the bow planes aft to the vicinity of the forward batteries, including a section of the officers' quarters. In here we reverse the process of construction by pulling out every bolt, rivet, plate, and tube. When we're done we know what makes the boat run. The leftovers get tossed on our scrap pile."

At least a dozen men in greasy coveralls had swarmed in and around the section of the sub that was illuminated by strong spotlights. One of them broke away from a group of three who were removing something from the area of the torpedo room, and came across to where Lovelace and Gannt were standing by the door.

He was a large man, with a stub of a dead cigar clenched firmly in his teeth. He was wiping his hands off on a greasy rag.

"This your boy from Washington?" he bellowed.

He was probably Irish, Lovelace thought. His freckled complexion was red, and the short-cropped hair visible beneath his cap was carrot-colored.

Gannt nodded effusively. "Captain Michael Lovelace, Army CIC."

"Lieutenant Kowalski," the large man said, sticking out his greasy hand.

Lovelace shook it without hesitation, then nodded toward the door. "Can we go outside and talk?" he shouted.

Kowalski nodded, and the three of them went outside, the relative quiet a blessing.

"Did you say Kowalski?" Lovelace asked.

Kowalski laughed. "My old man was a Polack, my mother a Colleen, and I'm a Heinz 57," he bellowed. "But you didn't come up here from Washington to discuss my heritage."

Lovelace liked the man. "What have you found so far?"

"Plenty," Kowalski said, and he turned to Gannt. "Is this guy cleared for the top?"

"Yes, he is," Gannt said, his eyes narrowing. "Anything unusual?"

"Plenty," Kowalski said, eying Lovelace. "The sub was sabotaged."

Something clutched at Lovelace's gut. "Are you sure?" he said evenly.

"Damn right," Kowalski said. "We pulled a couple of hundred pounds of TNT from behind the inner hull in the vicinity of the forward torpedo room. Noticed several of the inner plates cut out and then rewelded. Wires led back to some kind of a low-battery buss bar. From the looks of it I'd say the entire sub had been loaded with explosives."

"Why didn't the TNT you found explode?"

"Faulty connection just forward of the main buss."

"Detonator?"

Again Kowalski glanced at Gannt, who nodded for him to continue, only now the man didn't seem so certain, and he lowered his voice.

"I don't know what you're working on, captain, and I guess I don't much care. But whatever your interest is in this submarine, I think you may have hit the jackpot." He withdrew a narrow tubular device with wires sticking out both ends from his coverall pocket, and handed it to Lovelace.

It was light, not more than a couple of ounces, and it had a curious odor, almost like vinegar.

"What is it?" Lovelace asked.

"An acid fuse. It was wired into the battery buss bar. We traced the wires back to the officers' quarters, where we found it installed behind the ship's intercom."

"Someone sabotaged the boat, and this was the fuse," Lovelace said absently. He was thinking about Harvey Dansig and why he had been murdered.

"There's something else," Kowalski said, lowering his voice even more. He seemed troubled.

"Yes?" Lovelace said, handing back the fuse.

Kowalski took it. "Unless I'm completely wet— which has happened before—I'd say this fuse was Russian-made."

Gannt went pale, and Lovelace suddenly felt light-headed, almost as if his mind was detached from his body.

"How sure are . . ." he started to ask, but Gannt cut him off.

"Hold it," he snapped. "This is going no further until I get some authorization."

Kowalski waved him off. "I'm only sure of death and taxes, captain, but I'd stake my reputation that this fuse is Russian-made."

"That's enough," Gannt roared. "And that is an order, lieutenant."

Kowalski looked at him and smiled tiredly. "Whatever you say, commander. How about my people?"

"Restricted to base until further notice," Gannt snapped, and he turned to Lovelace. "And you are getting out of here, captain. But I'm warning you that what you've heard here this afternoon will be classified top secret, probably 'eyes-only' to the President. As of this moment it is a navy matter."

"Sure," Lovelace said, his brain spinning to a dozen different possibilities. He looked up. "Before I go I'd like to use the telephone in your office."

18

The clacking wheels and rhythmic swaying of the moving train should have put Jada instantly to sleep. But she was wide awake. She lay on the top bunk of their compartment, aware of her heart beating against her ribs, and of her chest muscles expanding and contracting as she breathed.

It was at least three in the morning, which meant they would be in Santa Fe within four hours. It also meant that within twenty-four hours they could be finished with their assignment. If all went well.

In Chicago they had gotten close enough to General Groves in the depot to overhear him order two sets of round-trip tickets. One set from Chicago to Santa Fe and back, and the other originating in Santa Fe, on the overnight.

Alek had been convinced that the bomb laboratory where Oppenheimer worked was somewhere near Santa Fe. Groves was going down there to look things over, and was taking someone back with him on the overnight. Probably Oppenheimer, for a conference on the train.

"What if it's not Oppenheimer?" she had asked him.

Alek had shrugged. "Then we'll have to continue following Groves. Sooner or later he and Oppenheimer will be together."

As she lay on the bunk she thought about their assignment. In some respects she hoped Groves was not picking up Oppenheimer, and therefore they would not have to kill just yet.

But another part of her mind held a strong desire for it to be ended. She wanted to return home. She was tired of the constant fear, constant worry of detection. And despite the fact she was living with Badim as his wife . . . almost as his wife . . . she was lonely.

Alek, she said his name softly to herself. Aleksandr. She liked that better. It was softer. Fit the tongue better.

He had said nothing to her about her terrible mistake, giving their contact their hotel and room number. And she had said nothing to him about killing the man.

It could not be helped. The man was a danger to the entire operation. He had to be eliminated. Yet every time she thought about it, she recoiled, seeing the almost totally blank expression on Alek's face when he had killed.

Those thoughts also brought up the recurring picture of Harvey Dansig, which threatened to force her mind down into a deep, dark whirlpool.

She rolled over on her side so that she was facing the tiny bathroom door, and she held her breath, listening for sounds from the bunk below. She could faintly hear his breathing, and after awhile, he moved, then it was silent again.

"Aleksandr," she said softly under her breath. There were several men in the NKVD section where she worked who were interested in her. One of them was a full colonel. But he was an old man who constantly smelled of vodka and cigarettes. His teeth were yellow, and he never seemed to be quite clean-shaven.

Her nightgown had hiked up to her hips, and she placed her right hand beneath her thighs, and clamped her legs tightly together, the warm feeling spreading from that place.

She had never known a man. No one had ever touched her there, not even a doctor. No one, that is, except for herself.

She thought about Aleksandr lying on the bunk beneath her, and wondered what he looked like with his clothes off. He was tall. He was handsome. And he was strong.

But she also wondered about the women he had known. Had he made love to German women? He must have. He had spent nine years in Germany, and she was certain he had not lived like a monk.

If everything worked out here in Santa Fe, they would be on their way back home this time tomorrow morning. When they got back to Moscow he would undoubtedly be given a new assignment, and she would return to the language section, and the colonel who wanted her.

She shifted her legs and an almost electric thrill coursed through her body. She was wet and she could feel a flush creeping up her neck into her cheeks.

"Aleksandr," she said softly.

She wanted a husband. Children. A home in the country, possibly by the sea. But that image was mixed up in her mind with Brighton and the beach. She was a little girl, and her father was there to protect her.

But those things were irrevocably lost to her, and so would Aleksandr be lost to her once this assignment was completed.

Something woke Badim, and he opened his eyes. The train was still moving through the night, and in the dim light filtering through the window he could make out the edge of the overhead bunk, and across the tiny compartment the bathroom door, which was ajar. A thin silver of light shone under the passageway door, but nothing was wrong. Everything was as it should be.

Jada shifted in the bunk overhead, and he thought he heard a muffled sob. He was about to call her name, but then she was quiet, and he said nothing.

The luminous dials on his wrist read three-thirty, leaving them three and a half hours of sleep before they arrived in Santa Fe. The overnight back to Chicago probably left at seven or eight in the evening, which gave them a full twelve hours or more in town.

He had thought about following Groves from the train depot and somehow trailing him to the laboratory, but had dismissed it as an unnecessary risk.

If Oppenheimer did not come back to the depot with Groves there would be another time to make plans for finding and approaching the installation, which was probably not too far from Santa Fe itself.

For now, however, he would content himself with taking the overnight back to Chicago. If Oppenheimer was with Groves, he would be able to take them both out and get away.

The first step would be getting to New York City, where he had a telephone number for transportation. From there it would be across the Canadian border to Halifax, Nova Scotia, then on the Russian convoy to Murmansk.

Those thoughts brought a kaleidoscope of others—about his childhood, about the orphanage, and about his nine years in Germany.

Besides his training in Moscow before he became Valkyrie, there had been little else for him other than the State. He had been a friendless child who had only the vaguest memories of his father, a stern, authoritarian figure, and none whatsoever of his mother.

In fact, he mused now, he had never even seen a photograph of his mother. Although there were times when he found himself thinking about her, wondering what she was like, he had never developed even a fantasy picture of her in his mind. And that very fact itself was sometimes a cause for disturbance in him.

Jada shifted again in her bunk, and he called softly to her. "Are you awake?"

There was a silence above for a long moment, but then she answered timidly. "Yes, I am. Did I wake you?"

"No," he lied. "But try to go to sleep. We'll be in Santa Fe in a few hours."

She was silent for a long time, and Badim thought about her. Over the months of their training outside Moscow, the thirteen days in the submarine, and now the week they had spent in this country, he had had a chance to closely observe her. She was a lovely young woman; her naïveté was her only real fault.

On several occasions he had seen her clothed in nothing more than a bra and panties, and her image swam into his mind's eye now, but he shut off his erotic imaginings even before they began. They were here to do a job; there would be time later for the other thing.

"I'm sorry," she said softly.

"I told you that you didn't wake me, Jada. Now go back to sleep."

"No, I mean about leading our contact back to our hotel."

It had been inexcusable. And he found himself thinking that if she had been anyone else, he would have killed her then and there. It had been a mistake that could have cost them their lives.

Why hadn't he killed her?

She shifted on the bunk again, and he looked up as her bare legs came over the edge. Her feet were small and her ankles were narrow. He almost reached up and touched her.

"Go back to bed," he snapped. "We'll need our rest."

"Aleksandr . . . I . . ."

"Go back to bed," he said harshly.

"Listen to me," she pleaded. "I think . . . I think I want you to make love to me."

Badim groaned inwardly, but before he could say anything she had jumped down from her bunk, her nightgown sliding up, giving him a momentary glimpse of the backs of her legs, and her buttocks. And then she was standing there in front of him, her eyes wide.

He pushed himself up on one elbow. "When we're finished with this assignment, and back home, there will be time."

She shook her head, then gathered the hem of her nightgown in both hands and pulled it over her head, tossing it aside.

Her legs were straight and perfectly formed, the hair on her pubis was only a tuft of light brown, her belly flat, almost boyish, and her breast were small but well-rounded, the nipples erect.

He looked at her in the dim light for a long time, feeling his heart accelerate, and his breath quicken.

"You have a lovely body, Jada," he said finally, and he flipped back the covers and moved over, giving her room to lie beside him.

She came to him, and they were in each other's arms. He kissed her lips, and then her chin and tiny neck, and she responded by arching her back, pressing her breasts against his chest, a soft moan escaping from her lips.

"Aleksandr," she said heavily. "Oh, god . . . Alek . . ."

He stroked her breasts with his fingertips, then bent down and kissed her nipples.

Again she moaned. "Alek . . . make love to me . . . please . . . now." She rolled over on her back, her eyes closed, her lips half parted. "Please, Alek," she said. "Please."

He was wearing only pajama bottoms, and he took them off. Then he was on top of her, entering her, and she was incredibly tight. She cried out sharply once, but then her hips were gyrating wildly, and he was pounding inside of her, deep inside, and his memories and thoughts about everything, including their assignment, were gone, replaced by the moment.

She came almost at once, her entire body convulsing, and a moment later he released, the pleasure going on and on, and she held on to him tightly with her arms and legs, as if she never wanted to let him go, as if she wanted him inside of her even deeper.

For a long time afterward he lay on top of her, his heart slowing down, his ragged breathing quietening.

Aside from the fact that she was young and very tight, she had been a virgin, and it had not been very good. In technique, the whores he had known in Berlin had been much better. But this wasn't the same. Despite the lack of technique, which could be learned, this had been better in a different way.

He tried to withdraw, but she wouldn't let him.

"No," she said, opening her eyes and looking up at him. "Don't leave just yet. I like you . . . in me." She giggled.

"We need our sleep," he said softly.

"We have three hours or more before we get to Santa Fe," she said. "I'd like to do it again. Slower this time."

Badim had to laugh despite himself. "You're going to have to give me a little time to recuperate."

A sudden look of alarm crossed her features. "Are you hurt?"

He laughed out loud, and shook his head, then bent down and kissed her nose. "No," he said. "With men it's a little different than with women. It takes us a little longer to get ready for a second time."

"It takes you a while to get another hard-on?"

He wondered how he could have thought about killing her. "In polite society it's called an erection, if it's mentioned at all."

She sighed deeply. "I want to mention it, and I don't want to be polite. Not now."

19

WASHINGTON, D.C.

Lovelace had a splitting headache, his mouth was foul from too many cigarettes, and his eyes burned in their sockets.

Blearily he looked at his watch again; it read 11:50 A.M. Ten minutes before noon Washington time, which meant it was close to ten in Santa Fe. Groves should have been at Los Alamos by now. He should have gotten Lovelace's frantic message. And yet he had not called.

"Sonofabitch."

He sat at his desk in his office, where he had been sitting since eight this morning waiting for the general's call.

He had tried everything, but Colonel Pearson refused to cooperate, Colonel Lansdale was somewhere en route to Berkeley, California, Secretary of War Stimson was not in, and President Roosevelt was on his way up to Quebec, Canada, for a meeting with Churchill.

Two police artist sketches were laid out on the desk

in front of him, and he looked down at them again. One was of a handsome man—narrow nose, square chin, and aristocratic eyes. The other was of a woman—much younger, tiny nose, high cheekbones, and lovely, full lips.

The police chief in Santa Fe had thought he was crazy when Lovelace called this morning, but had agreed to keep his people on the lookout for a man and a woman matching the descriptions he had relayed.

"Can't guarantee much, though, captain," the police chief had said with a thick Texas drawl. "We've been gettin' a whole shitload of people coming through here as of late, if you get my meaning."

"Anything you can do will help," Lovelace had said patiently.

"Can you tell me what you want them for? I mean, are they deserters or something?"

"Murderers," Lovelace said.

"Hotdamn," the chief said with obvious relish. "I'll sure do what I can for you. Have a good day now, hear?"

The phone rang, jangling Lovelace out of his thoughts. With a shaking hand he picked it up. "Lovelace."

"This is Groves. What the hell is going on up there, Lovelace?"

A flood of relief washed over him. "Where are you at this moment, general?"

"Site Y, and I want to know what's going on up there with you. I've just been on the phone with Hoover. . . . He wants you thrown in jail!"

"General, listen to me carefully," Lovelace snapped, putting as much force into his voice as he could. "I want you to stay where you are. Don't move until I get there."

"You're not going anywhere!" Groves roared. "You're staying right in Washington. You're going to see no one, talk to no one, or do a thing. And that's an order!"

"Goddammit, Groves, listen to me! Your life is in danger. There's a very good possibility you will be assassinated if you leave Y!"

There was a dead silence on the line for a long time, and Lovelace ran the fingers of his right hand through his hair.

When the general came back on the line, his voice was deadly calm. "As soon as I finish talking with you, Lovelace, I'm going to telephone my secretary and tell her to start proceedings against you. As of this moment you are fired. You may consider yourself under house arrest. If you run, we'll find you."

Lovelace closed his eyes and sighed deeply. "General Groves, why won't you let me help you?" he asked tiredly. "I'm doing nothing more than the job you hired me for."

"You've gone too far this time," Groves snapped.

"There are compelling reasons for me to suspect that a man and a woman are here to assassinate you."

"I was informed about the submarine, and about the fuse. Good lord, even the navy is on my back about you."

"Then why won't you listen . . ."

Groves cut him off. "I don't know what you're trying to do up there, captain, but already you've brought too much attention to the project. It ends right now."

"All right," Lovelace said. "All right, but can you tell me one thing?"

"Lovelace . . ." the general warned.

"When are you coming back?"

Groves hung up.

"General?" Lovelace shouted, but there was no answer, and he hung up his phone.

His mind was spinning in a dozen different directions; it was so damned difficult to think straight. For the moment Groves was safe, and would be until he left Los Alamos. Whenever that was.

Suddenly he jumped up from behind his desk, rushed

out of his office, down the corridor, and burst into Groves' office. The phone was just ringing and Groves' secretary was reaching for it.

"When is General Groves scheduled to return?" he shouted.

The woman looked startled. "He's leaving tonight."

The phone rang again.

"On the overnight to Chicago?"

"Yes," the woman said, picking up the phone and covering the receiver with her hand. "He and Dr. Oppenheimer are having one of their overnight conferences." She turned to the phone. "Army Corps of Engineers, Manhattan District."

Lovelace stood in the doorway, staring at her open-mouthed. Groves and Oppenheimer would be together. On the train. It was a perfect setup. Perfect!

The secretary was looking at him. "Yes, general, he's right here," she was saying.

He didn't wait to hear any more. He turned and ran back to his office, where he grabbed his pistol from the desk drawer, scooped up the police artist sketches, and hurried down the corridor to the stairwell. Groves was probably ordering his physical arrest at this very moment. But they'd have to catch up with him first, and he still had one long shot remaining for getting out of town and down to Santa Fe.

The stairwell was deserted, and he took the stairs down two at a time, stuffing the pistol in his jacket pocket and the sketches in his breast pocket.

On the ground floor he raced, out of breath, across the wide lobby, at least a dozen persons gaping at him, out the front door and down the access street in front of the War Department building to Virginia Avenue one block away.

Traffic was heavy at this time of day, but he spotted an empty cab coming in the opposite direction across the avenue, and he ran out into the street to flag it down.

Horns were blaring and tires were screeching as he

made it across, but the cabby stopped for him, and he yanked open the back door and leaped in.

"National Airport, and hurry!" he shouted, and he fell back in the seat, as the cab pulled away.

"A guy could get killed that way," the cabby was saying. He was studying Lovelace's reflection in the rearview mirror.

Lovelace laid his head back on the seat and closed his eyes as he tried to catch his breath. His heart was hammering painfully in his chest and his legs were shaking with fatigue.

Until yesterday morning he had had nothing but conjecture and a few circumstantial facts to go on. But now, goddammit, everything was fitting together into a terrible pattern.

First there had been the submarine landing a man and a woman on the beach at Cape Cod. And then there had been the murder of Harvey Dansig. A murder that had been obviously done by a professional—a man trained and highly skilled in the art of killing silently.

Dansig's death had seemed so senseless at first. It was understandable that a couple of German agents had come ashore, but why would they attract attention to themselves so blatantly by killing Dansig?

But then there was the Russian-made fuse, and suddenly it was as if a veil had been lifted from his eyes, letting Lovelace see at least one portion of the puzzle with startling clarity.

A *Russian* fuse in a German submarine. The Russians—not the Germans—had set two agents ashore, but in such a fashion that it would be believed they were Nazis. It was the reason the sub had been set to blow. If it had happened according to their plan, the flotsam washed ashore would have identified the sub as German, while still giving their agents a couple of days headstart.

But sabotaging the sub told Lovelace something else as well: the man and woman were ruthless, professional, and highly dangerous. They had not stopped at killing an entire crew of their own countrymen, or even a hapless salesman who had happened to pick them up. They would certainly not stop at killing anyone who got in their way.

The next piece in the puzzle had come in Boston. Captain Kennedy had been true to his word, and had allowed Gillingham to run down the leads at the Greyhound Bus Depot. And by the time Lovelace had returned from Portsmouth with his old friend's car, Gillingham had the sketches.

"Just came up with something for you this afternoon," he said.

It was early evening, and they had met at a bar two blocks from the police department. Lovelace's train back to Washington was due to leave in two hours.

Gillingham withdrew a small manila envelope from his coat pocket and handed it across to Lovelace, who opened it and took out two pencil sketches.

"Took the coroner's description back to the depot, and came up with a ticket clerk and the bus driver for the early Washington bus, who remembered them," Gillingham said.

Lovelace studied the drawings in the dim, smoky light.

"Between the two of them we managed to come up with these sketches. They're close, though certainly not as good as photographs."

Lovelace looked up at his old friend. "They don't look like killers."

"Who does?" Gillingham commented, with a shrug. He took a drink of his beer. "So what happens next?"

"Can I have these?" Lovelace asked.

Gillingham nodded. "They're copies."

"Then send copies up to the D.C. police department, and let them help with the search."

Gillingham held his silence for a long time as he studied Lovelace staring at the sketches. "What's this all about, Michael?"

Lovelace looked up and smiled. "I can't tell you. All I can say is that it's damned important. Might be something you'll never know about—you'll just have to trust me."

"Sure," Gillingham said, and he went back to his beer.

From Boston, before he left on the train, he had called Willis at his apartment and set up a meeting for early in the morning. Willis had sounded strange on the phone, but had agreed to pick Lovelace up at Union Station when he arrived.

During the overnight train ride he had tried to sleep, but he had not been able to. He kept thinking about everything he had learned so far. It was a Russian operation of some kind. And the thought that Oppenheimer was at least suspected of having Communist leanings gave him little comfort.

But why go through such a terrible ruse to convince the Americans that a couple of Germans had landed? Why hadn't they just snuck their agents in, making sure no one would notice them?

The only conclusion Lovelace was able to come up with was that the man and woman were here to do something that was terribly dangerous, something that had a great chance of failing. If they were caught, they would be identified as Germans.

All that, of course, Lovelace had to admit, did not mean that they were here to sabotage the atomic bomb project. After all, maybe they were here to assassinate Roosevelt, as he had flippantly suggested to Kennedy.

Whatever their mission, however, he was going to find it out and stop it, but with the assumption that they were here to assassinate at least Groves.

Willis was waiting for him at Union Station on Massachusetts Avenue, but refused to say a word until they had gone outside and climbed into his battered Ford, and pulled away from the curb.

"I don't know what the hell you're working on, Michael, but whatever it is sure has got J. Edgar in a stew."

"What's he saying now?" Lovelace asked tiredly.

"Just two things," Willis said, glancing over at Lovelace. "Number one is that he's going to see you sent to jail if you don't stop interfering with Bureau business. And number two is that when he finds out who the sonofabitch is that's helping you, he's fired."

"I may be close," Lovelace said, "so I probably won't be needing your help much longer."

Willis started to protest, but Lovelace held him off, taking the police artist sketches out of his pocket and holding them up one at a time so that the FBI man could glance at them in the glare of a passing street light.

"These are the two who came off the sub, killed a man in Boston, and took a bus down here to Washington. Do their faces mean anything to you?"

Willis did a doubletake at the sketch of the girl, and he pulled over to the side of the road, flipped on the dome light, and stared at both drawings. When he looked up he was white-faced.

"What the hell are you involved with, Michael?" he asked softly.

Something clutched at Lovelace's gut. "What is it? You know these people?"

Willis studied the sketches a moment longer, and when he looked up there was a strange expression in his eyes. "This is it, Michael. After this tip I'm not doing a thing for you."

"What is it, for chrissake?" Lovelace asked, raising his voice.

"Last night. Dunbarton Oaks Hotel. Two military policemen followed a man they suspected of black market gasoline dealings to the hotel. Later in the night both MPs plus the hotel's night clerk were found shot to death in the stairwell. We were called in on it around midnight. I just left there."

Willis looked away from the sketches, out of the windshield, as a newspaper truck rumbled by.

"Go on," Lovelace prompted. "What do these two have to do with it?" The tight feeling in his stomach was almost unbearable now.

"Room 328. We found the man they had followed shot to death. Haven't seen the lab report yet, but it'd be my guess they were shot with the same kind of a weapon . . . probably a 9 millimeter."

"German Luger," Lovelace said softly.

Willis shrugged. "A page was torn out of the hotel registration book, but the house dick gave us a pretty fair description of the girl . . . she looks a lot like this one."

"And the man?" Lovelace asked, tapping the other sketch.

"Can't be sure. The house man said he didn't get a good look at him, but what he did see reminded him of a Prussian baron or something."

"Christ," Lovelace said, looking away. "Any clue as to where they went? What their names are?"

"None. But this is the kicker. The man was found dead in 328—the one the MPs trailed to the hotel—was the night garage man at the War Department."

It was as if a huge fist had slammed into Lovelace's gut, taking his breath away. After a moment, he asked, "No idea where they went?"

"None."

"That'll be two-fifty, bud," the cabby was saying.

Lovelace opened his eyes. They were at the airport already. "Sorry," he mumbled. "How much?"

"Two-fifty," the cabby repeated the figure, and Lovelace handed him three ones, told him to keep the change, and jumped out of the cab, hurrying across the walk and into the terminal.

He walked across the busy mezzanine to a row of telephone booths around the corner from the ticket counters and sat down, closing the door behind him.

This was a last-ditch gamble, but there would be no way for him to get normal air transportation out of

Washington and down to Santa Fe without a priority number . . . something Groves would have already put a stop to.

When he had the Washington operator he asked her to connect him with the local operator in the town of North Brookfield, Massachusetts, and as he waited for the connection to be made, he laid his head against the back of the booth and closed his eyes.

For more than twenty-four hours, ever since Willis had told him about the murders at the Dunbarton Oaks Hotel, he had pulled out all the stops, and the lack of rest was finally catching up with him.

He had talked to everyone he could at the hotel that morning, showing them the sketches Gillingham had given him. Besides the house detective, a maid and one of the other night clerks were certain that the man and woman were the ones from 328. But no one knew their names.

Then he had spent most of the afternoon talking with ticket clerks at the train and bus depots, as well as here at the airport, with no luck.

Gillingham had sent copies of the sketches to the D.C. police, who had started in on the search as well.

But as of this morning no one had seen either of them. They had been registered at the Dunbarton Oaks Hotel, but now they were gone.

"North Brookfield. Your number please," the operator was saying.

Lovelace sat forward. "I don't know the number, operator," he said. "But I'm trying to get in contact with a Hubert Briggs. He owns a farm in your area."

"Yes, sir, I am ringing that number. That will be three dollars and twenty-five cents for the first three minutes."

Lovelace frantically searched his pockets as he heard the telephone ringing at the other end, but all he came up with was about thirty-five cents in change.

The phone rang again, and a man's gruff voice answered. "Hello."

"One moment please, long distance calling," the operator said. "That will be three dollars and twenty-five cents for the first three minutes, sir."

"What's going on here?" Briggs shouted.

Lovelace took a deep breath. "Operator, ask the general if he will accept a collect call from Michael Lovelace."

"Yes, sir . . ." the operator started to say, but Briggs overrode her.

"Lovelace, you bastard, what the hell do you want?"

"General, this is an emergency, I must speak with you . . ."

"Sir, I will have to cut you off unless you deposit three dollars and twenty-five cents."

"Stuff it!" Briggs roared. "I'm accepting the call as collect!"

"Very well, sir, you may go ahead, long distance."

"You've got balls, Lovelace! Balls down to your knees! Now what the hell do you want?"

"General, I haven't got very much time, so I'm going to have to ask you to listen very closely to me. But I'll tell you right now that this is of extreme national importance."

"Go ahead," the general said tersely.

"Are you convinced in your mind, sir, that I am a man who tells the truth?"

"That's a hell of a question to ask of a man whose retirement you forced, goddammit, but yes, you are a truthful bastard."

"I need your help, general. Right now, this morning. Without it there is a very strong likelihood that General Groves will be assassinated this evening."

"Who the hell would want to put Leslie away, and why?" Briggs shouted. "What are you trying to pull, Lovelace?"

"General, I couldn't tell you all the details even if I had the time, but there are certain powerful people here in Washington, D.C., who will not allow me to leave town by any normal means. I must be in Santa Fe no later than seven o'clock this evening. Believe me, sir, this is a matter of life or death. I would not have called you if I had had any other choice. I think you know that."

There was a silence on the line for a long moment, and Lovelace was beginning to think that their connection had been broken, or that Briggs had hung up on him. But then the general was back, his voice low, guarded.

"Your word of honor that this is on the level?"

"Have you ever known me to be anything but, sir?" Lovelace replied. He had his fingers crossed, and he wanted a cigarette, but he was afraid to move, to make a sound.

"What do you want?"

Lovelace let out the deep breath he had been holding. "Have you got access to an airplane? Something that can pick me up here at Washington National, and get me down to Santa Fe by seven tonight?"

"I've got a DC-3 at my disposal. It's over at Bolling. I'll call ahead and tell them to expect you."

"No good, general. Bolling is out. Have your pilot fly over here and pick me up. But don't mention my name."

"This is on the level?" the general asked.

"I promise you, sir, this is not only on the level, it's of supreme national importance."

"Where will you be?" the general asked.

"At the terminal. Please hurry."

"What are you wearing?"

"Civilian clothes. Dark gray suit."

"Identify yourself as Michael Briggs. You're my son."

20

THE ATCHINSON TOPEKA & SANTA FE

Jada was in love. She found her knight in shining armor at long last, and his name was Aleksandr Petrovich Badim. With him she would spend the rest of her life, no matter what happened.

They walked along West De Vargas Street, the Santa Fe River to their right, the lovely smells of zinnias and squash blossoms rich in the early evening air, and she sighed contentedly, the day's memories flicking across her mind's eye like slides in a show.

From the moment she had decided to make love with him she had blocked out of her consciousness the murders of Harvey Dansig and their contact from the War Department.

It had not been difficult for her to do that. Not at all. For her entire life she had lived in a world of fantasy. Nothing was different now.

Besides, she told herself, hugging his arm a little tighter as they strolled through the lovely old Spanish town, he was tall, strong, and handsome, and yet there

was a gentleness about him . . . a consideration that
made her feel warm and protected deep inside. It was
much the same feeling she had had with her father, only
now there were sexual overtones. Overtones that created
an all-pervading glow in her spirit.

They had made love a second time on the train,
slower and more gently than the first, and then she had
fallen asleep in his arms.

He had awakened her a little past seven-thirty, and
she had gotten up and hurriedly dressed as they were
pulling into the station.

While she was checking their single suitcase in a
locker, Alek had gone outside to watch Groves, who
was picked up in front by an army noncom driving a
plain sedan.

And then they had had their day together, beginning
with a leisurely breakfast at a small café around the
corner from the depot.

They had turned the corner onto Sandoval Street, and
Badim had quickened their pace, but Jada hadn't really
noticed; she was still thinking about the lovely day they
had had.

After breakfast they had gone shopping together,
Alek purchasing three wide leather belts with heavy
buckles at three different stores, fifty feet of strong rope
at a saddle shop, and finally four iron rings, each about
five inches in diameter and a large, vicious-looking baling hook with a T-handle at a hardware store.

Before they went to lunch, they had returned to the
depot, where Alek had put the things he bought in their
suitcase.

When he had relocked the locker, he had turned to
her and said an astounding thing. "The rest of the day
is yours, Larissa. What would you like to do?"

For several long moments she had just looked at him,
her mouth hanging open, and then she had laughed with
joy and hugged him.

"First of all lunch, then an ice cream soda, and then a movie . . . maybe two of them."

Alek had laughed with her, and arm and arm they had left the depot and had done exactly that.

The movies had been wonderful adventures that even Alek had enjoyed, although he did not want to admit it. The first was a picture called *The Mark of Zorro* with Tyrone Power (who Jada thought was nowhere as good-looking as Alek), and the second, at a theater two blocks away from the first, was *Berlin Correspondent*, with Dana Andrews and Virginia Gilmore.

Andrews played an American newspaperman who helped a German professor escape from the Nazis. Although the picture was silly, she had felt almost a kinship with the actors on the screen, who were doing in make-believe what she and Alek were doing for real.

Afterward they had eaten a light supper downtown, and then had taken their stroll, Badim becoming more and more taciturn, and Jada delving into her memories in greater and greater detail.

They crossed the river and turned another corner and suddenly Jada was jerked back to reality, and she stopped short.

A half a block away was the Atchinson Topeka & Santa Fe Depot, and she shivered as she turned to look up into Alek's eyes. "Must we?" she asked foolishly.

He smiled. "We're almost there, Larissa," he said, that variation of her alias sounding soft and loving to her. "Don't freeze up on me now."

"What if Oppenheimer isn't with him?"

"Then we'll stay here and wait for Groves to show up again and I'll follow him to wherever Oppenheimer is," he said patiently. "We have been sent here to do a job. We will do it."

"Yes, Aleksandr," she said finally, her mind going numb. He was strong, he was handsome. She would trust him. Completely.

They turned, her arm still linked with his, and continued down the block to the depot, where he gave her the key to their locker and instructed her to retrieve their suitcase and wait with it for him on the platform.

It was just seven o'clock, and the overnight to Chicago was not due to leave for forty-five minutes. Groves and whoever he was taking back with him probably would not show up until later. From what they had been told about the man, he did everything in a rush, and although he was considered punctual, he was rarely early.

The station was teeming with people coming and going, and Jada had to jostle her way down the wide stairs to the lower level, where she took their now heavily laden suitcase out of the locker. Then she went outside to the platform, where the overnighter was waiting on the tracks.

She set the suitcase down next to an ornate iron railing and post holding up the wide roof directly across from their assigned car, and sighed deeply, trying to quell the butterflies in her stomach.

All through their training in Moscow, then on the submarine, and even back in Washington in their hotel room with a murder behind them, this assignment had not been real to her. It was nothing more than an exercise. Some kind of an elaborate game. But now that she was here, and they were very close, she was frightened.

Alek had gone over the details of what they were going to have to do this morning, and she understood everything. The risk would be minimal. And if everything went well, they would get off the train unnoticed in Kansas City. No one would stop them. No one would have any reason to stop them.

She shivered and stepped around the post so that she could get a look at the clock through the windows in the waiting room, when she collided with two men.

For a moment she lost her balance, until one of them,

a short, thin, effeminate-looking man, grabbed her arm and steadied her.

"Pardon me, miss," he said, his voice soft.

Jada looked up and very nearly fainted. The man who had helped her was Dr. Oppenheimer. The other man was General Groves.

"Are you all right?" the general asked, stepping forward.

"I . . ." Jada squeaked, and beyond Groves she could see Alek thirty feet away, staring at them. It gave her strength she didn't know she had, and she managed a smile. "Clumsy of me," she said. "I'm terribly sorry."

"You're sure you're all right?" Oppenheimer asked. He was still holding her arm.

"I'm fine," she said.

He returned her smile, touched the brim of his wide, floppy hat with two fingers, and he and General Groves hurried down the platform and boarded the train three cars away from theirs.

A moment later Alek passed her and, without stopping or even looking her way, said, "I'll meet you in our compartment," and he boarded the same car as Groves and Oppenheimer.

It was five minutes past seven when the DC-3 carrying Lovelace finally touched down at the air strip in Agua Fria, just southwest of Santa Fe. They had been delayed in Louisville with engine trouble, and again in Wichita when a squall line had rapidly moved through the area, causing them to duck down for shelter.

But there was still plenty of time if he could get some cooperation from the people here at the field. He would need a car.

The plane slowed at the end of the runway, turned, and taxied back to the terminal as Lovelace undid his seatbelt and went forward to the main door.

In Louisville he had remained aboard until the engine problem had been solved, but at Wichita he had gone into Base Ops and had called the depot here, where he had learned that the overnight to Chicago was scheduled to leave at 7:45 sharp. He had not been able to reach the Santa Fe police chief, and no one else at the police station knew what he was talking about . . . spies? assassins?

But he had made it on time. If he could get a car, he would be able to make the train.

The DC-3 finally pulled up, turned again, and then the engines clanked to a stop. Lovelace quickly undogged the hatch and shoved the door open as a ground crew was bringing up the boarding ladder. An open jeep carrying two military policemen came across the field at a high rate of speed, and as he stepped down the stairs and started across to the terminal, the jeep pulled up alongside him and screeched to a halt, both MPs jumping out.

"Captain Lovelace?" one of them called out.

Lovelace stopped and turned toward them. This was trouble. He could smell it. "I'm Michael Briggs," he said.

One of the MPs smiled. "Could we see some identification, sir?"

"What is it?" Lovelace said tiredly. He hadn't been able to get much sleep on the trip.

"You're under arrest, captain," the MP said apologetically.

"On whose orders, sergeant?" Lovelace snapped, and the MP stiffened.

"General Groves, sir. Said you were to be held here until we could contact a Colonel Lansdale, CIC."

"Well?"

"Sir?" the MP asked, confused.

"What did Lansdale say?" Lovelace roared.

"The colonel will be calling us soon, sir. He's in California."

"Bullshit," Lovelace swore. "I can't wait." He turned

on his heel and started toward the terminal when one of the MPs behind him shouted.

"Halt!"

Lovelace stopped and turned back in time to see both young men draw their .45 automatics and point them at him.

"You're going to have to come with us, sir," one of them said. "At least until we can get hold of Colonel Lansdale."

Badim lay on his back in the lower bunk and decided that they had a fifty-fifty chance of success, which was not particularly bad. He had accomplished other missions with much greater odds against him. Only this time he was worried, and he knew it was because of the girl.

After he had spotted the two army intelligence officers tailing Groves and Oppenheimer, and after he had nevertheless managed to get past them in time to see which compartment his targets had entered, he had come back to Jada, who was waiting in their compartment, white-faced.

Before he had said anything to her, however, he went to the window and carefully peered outside, watching until the two men who had followed Groves and Oppenheimer left the platform and went back into the depot, as he had expected they would. They had come along merely to make sure their charges got aboard safely. When that had happened, their jobs were done.

He had turned and gone to Jada finally, held her face in his hands, and kissed her. She'd jumped up from the bunk and clung tightly to him.

"Aleksandr . . . I was so frightened . . . I didn't know what to do . . . or what to say . . ." she had blubbered.

"It's all right, Larissa," he'd said soothingly. "It's fine, you did the correct thing."

They parted and she had looked into his eyes. "Are you sure?" she had asked fearfully.

"I am sure," he'd said. He stared into her lovely, large eyes for a long time, trying to read the emotions there. But then he sighed tiredly. "There will be much for us to do this evening, and I need my rest. I will sleep now, but you must be sure to awaken me when we come to Springer. That should be around ten o'clock. Maybe a little sooner."

Jada was nodding. "I understand," she said, and he could tell that she wanted to say more, but was holding back out of fear.

Again he kissed her, then lay down on his bunk to try to sleep. He kept thinking about her, though. About what would become of them after this night. If and when they got back to Moscow, he was certain Runkov would send him out on another assignment. And then another, and another, until either the war was ended or he was dead. Sleep eluded him.

Either way, he knew, it would probably be over between them. Over.

"Alek," Jada called softly to him. She was standing by the window, leaning her forehead against the glass.

"Yes?" he said, opening his eyes.

"We're approaching the little town ... Springer ... and it is nearly ten."

"Good," he said, half under his breath, and for just a moment he held tightly to his thoughts about Jada, but then he blocked all that out of his mind and got up.

She was watching him as he pulled the suitcase out and opened it on his bunk; he could feel her eyes on his back. He took out the things they had bought in Santa Fe and laid them aside, along with his silenced Luger and an extra magazine of ammunition. Then he closed the suitcase and pushed it aside.

"You know what you have to do?" he asked, as he worked.

"Yes," she said softly. "I will wait for ten minutes after you are on the roof, and then I will go down to their car and wait. When it happens I will be able to see if anyone has noticed and if an alarm is sounded. Afterward, I will come back here to wait for you."

"Very good."

Quickly now he checked to make sure his gun was loaded, a round in the chamber and the safety on, before he stuffed it in the holster strapped to his chest. He pulled on a lightweight dark jacket and zipped it up halfway.

Next he threaded two of the wide iron rings on one of the wide belts, and then loosely strapped the belt around his waist. Then he strapped the other two belts around his legs, first looping their ends through the belt around his waist, so that the three belts formed a crude mountain-climber's harness.

He cut a five-foot section of the rope off the coil and tied it firmly to the T-handle of the large baling hook, then tied the other two iron rings onto the rope.

Finally he threaded the main coil of rope through the iron rings attached to the baling hook, securing one end of the long coil to the rings on his belt, and leaving the other end free.

The spare magazine of ammunition went into a trouser pocket, and he was ready.

Lovelace had his gun, a car, and his freedom, but if he was wrong this time, there would be no second chances. This time Groves would make sure he never wore a badge again. Only Lovelace knew damned well, now, that he wasn't wrong.

He drove recklessly through the night east on U.S. 56 out of Springer. It was shortly after ten o'clock and he figured he could not be too far behind the train.

Lansdale had absolutely refused to order the train stopped, but had agreed at least to allow Lovelace his freedom if he promised to return immediately to Washington by the first available transportation.

"I'm going way out on the limb for you," Lansdale had said on the phone. "But I happen to think you're a damned good cop. This time, though, I have to agree with the general—I think you are chasing hobgoblins."

"But you're going to tell them to release me?" Lovelace asked.

"Yes."

"And return my gun?"

"Absolutely not . . ." Lansdale started to object, but Lovelace looked at his watch, which read nearly 8:00 P.M., and he cut him off.

"It's my personal property, colonel. Besides, I've given you my word. The only thing I'm going to do is borrow a car and go to the train depot in Santa Fe with a couple of police artist sketches. I just want to ask around if anyone saw these two."

"If you try to interfere with the movement of that train I'll join the growing line behind the general and Mr. Hoover to see you court-martialed and put in jail, captain. Do I make myself clear?"

"Yes, sir," Lovelace said, looking again at his watch. "I'll let you talk to the MPs now. And thanks, colonel."

One of the MPs had loaned Lovelace his personal car, a beat-up old Chrysler with a souped-up engine, and he had driven immediately to the train depot in Santa Fe, where within a few minutes he had found at least three people who were reasonably certain they had seen the couple at the station.

The ticket clerk said the woman was very pretty, and one of the others said the man had walked with a limp.

From there he had driven northeast out of Santa Fe through Las Vegas on U.S. 85, and then on to the town of Springer, where he had changed over to U.S. 56, most of the time pushing the old car to more than 65 miles per hour.

Although there was a clear sky and a bright moon, he was able to spot the lights of the train in the distance, and he jammed the accelerator pedal to the floor. If he could get to Clayton or one of the other towns down the line soon enough, he could signal for the train to stop.

It took Badim three tries, because of the wind from the motion of the train, to get the baling hook to catch on something above the roof. But then he had it.

"Ten minutes," he said to Jada, and then he swung out from the open window and started up the rope.

It was much harder to do than he had expected it would be, but his muscles were in perfect tone from his months of training, and despite the wind that tore at his body, and the heaving, lurching motion of the train over the uneven tracks, he made it to the roof, where he lay flat for a moment to catch his breath.

A few seconds later he pulled the rest of the rope from the open compartment window below, and freed the baling hook from where it had caught on an air-conditioner grille, and headed to the rear on his hands and knees.

He worked like a finely tuned, well-oiled machine now, all personal thoughts about Jada or about anything other than the job at hand erased from his mind.

At the junction between cars, the passageway below was covered by a flexible roof, which he gingerly stepped down on, nearly losing his balance and toppling over the edge. But in an instant he had scrambled up on the next car and noiselessly continued.

With any luck no one would be in the passageway when he fired except Jada, and no alarm would be sounded. The bodies would not be discovered until the train arrived in Chicago when Groves and Oppenheimer failed to get off. And even when they were discovered, it would be found that someone had apparently fired the shots at the passing train from outside. By the time anyone figured it out, if they ever did, he and Jada would be long gone. Mission accomplished.

He was more careful at the next junction between cars, and once he was safely over it, he stopped a moment to adjust the heavy coil of rope on his shoulder before he continued.

The countryside they were passing through now consisted mostly of barren rolling hills, mesas, and the mountains in the distance, brightly illuminated by the moonlit sky.

Eight minutes had elapsed when he finally made it to the roof of the car in which Groves and Oppenheimer were riding in the first compartment. Without hesitation he dangled the baling hook over the edge of the roof on the opposite side, catching it on the rain gutter.

Keeping tension on the rope so that the hook would not slip, he looped the free end around his buttocks from the right side, then up over his left shoulder, carefully stood up, and leaned back, his feet spread apart, his knees slightly bent.

He held the rope with his left hand, which he brought up so he could see his watch. Nine minutes. One to go and Jada would be heading toward this car. She would make it within two minutes.

For the moment he let the tension drain out of his body, riding easily with the uneven motion of the roof beneath his feet, almost like a water skier whose knees took up the shock of small waves.

At Kansas City they would rent a car, and from there drive to New York, where he would call their contact for transportation to Nova Scotia.

There would be a possibly pleasant sea voyage, depending upon the weather, and then they would be home.

He took a deep breath, letting it out slowly, looked at his watch again, which showed it was nearly time, and then began to slowly rappel down the slope of the roof and over the edge, just in back of the general's compartment window.

Here the motion of the train seemed more violent, and his rubber-soled shoes barely had any traction on the slick surface. Beneath him the ground was rushing by at a terrifying speed, but his eyes were only on the window. The curtain was pulled back and a light shone from inside.

In position, the toes of his shoes dug into a riveted seam, Badim withdrew his Luger with his right hand, flipping the safety off.

He tensed, ready to swing to the right so that he would have a clear shot through the window, when something snapped against the side of the car just above his left shoulder.

For a moment he was confused, not knowing what was happening, but then he looked up. There was a bullet hole in the car. Someone was shooting at him.

He twisted violently to the left, nearly losing his toe-hold, and looked over his shoulder in time to see the muzzle flash from the driver's window of a car less than 20 yards away on the highway. The shot was high again, to the right this time.

Badim fired four shots in quick succession at the car, which suddenly swerved to the left and braked hard, falling behind.

Stuffing his gun back in its holster, he quickly scrambled back to the roof, undid the belts holding him to the rope, and threw them aside, as the car again pulled up.

He yanked the Luger out and, taking careful aim, fired two more shots. At least one, he was certain, hit the driver, because the car swerved off the road and into the ditch.

Unmindful of the danger of a fall now, Badim raced forward, leaping over the connecting roofs between cars until he was directly above his own compartment.

He got down on his stomach and worked his way as close to the edge of the roof as he could get.

"Jada," he shouted over the noise of the wind and the clattering wheels against the tracks.

He looked back, but the car was no longer in sight.

Somehow they had been blown. But how? And by whom?

"Jada," he shouted again, this time louder.

"Alek?" her voice drifted up to him from the open window below. She sounded nearly hysterical.

"Find the emergency brake and pull it. We must get off."

"I can't," she shouted.

"You must! Listen to me, Jada, they know we are here. Hurry!"

There was no answer from below, and he was about to call her name again, when he realized that she was probably complying with his orders, and he scrambled up to the center of the roof as fast as he could go, and was about to reach for the air-conditioner vent, when the train lurched with unbelievable force, the wheels squealing on the tracks, and he was thrown violently forward and to the right.

At the last moment he reached out for a ventilating pipe of some sort, but he missed it, and went over the edge, headfirst.

21

NEW YORK CITY

Harry Gold, whose code name was Raymond, waited in front of St. Mark's on East Tenth Street in Manhattan for Klaus Fuchs to show up. The man had never been late before, but this evening he was already thirty minutes overdue.

Gold was a small man. Pint-sized, they called him. But his appetites were voracious. For freedom for the oppressed proletariat. For a workers' paradise in which big business and bigger government could no longer devour the output of honest men's toil. For those things, and others like them, Gold was a zealot.

He wore green gloves and carried a novel with a green binding, and as he paced fretfully up and down the block he scanned the passersby for Fuchs, who always carried a tennis ball. The accoutrements were their recognition signals that everything was all right for contact.

They had been meeting like this since March, rendezvousing sometimes in Central Park, sometimes on

Madison Avenue, or in Queens, and once in Brooklyn's Borough Hall. This evening it was to have been St. Mark's In The Bowery.

Fuchs had been transferred from the University of Birmingham in England to New York to work with the Kellex Corporation on the design of a uranium separation plant. And in five months he had passed on to Raymond everything he knew—which was considerable—about the American efforts to build the "gadget," as they were calling the bomb.

Dutifully, Gold had passed this information on to his contact, a man code-named John, who in turn had passed it down to the Soviet Embassy in Washington, where it went back to Moscow in the diplomatic bag every Friday.

But there would be nothing for the bag tomorrow unless Fuchs showed up. And that meant there would be no money for Gold. No money.

He checked his watch again, and for the tenth time tapped the crystal with a forefinger to make sure it was running. It was. Fuchs was late.

Gold knew about Fuchs' background. Knew about the man's early days in Germany, about his beating at the hands of Nazi ruffians, and then about his immigration to England.

But Gold also knew that the British, and therefore probably the Americans, were aware that Fuchs had Communist sympathies. Perhaps something had gone wrong. Perhaps he had been arrested and was now being interrogated. Perhaps he would break under pressure and lead them here, to his contact.

Gold forced a deep belch, trying to quell the rumbling in his stomach, and finally headed away from the church at a brisk pace. He could not wait here any longer. He was due soon across town to pass his information on.

As he walked he kept thinking about his contact; he simply could not go to the man empty-handed. But what to give him other than the information that Fuchs had not shown this evening?

He pondered that problem up Lexington Avenue until nearly East Thirty-fifth, when he finally came up with a possible solution, and a block later he came to a telephone booth.

Slipping inside, he dropped a nickel in the slot, dialed for the operator, and gave her a Cambridge, Massachusetts, telephone number from his little black book. It was the home phone of Mrs. Kristel Heinemann. Fuchs' sister.

He deposited the necessary coins for the long-distance call, and the phone was ringing.

His hand shook as he held the instrument to his ear. What he was doing was risky business. If Fuchs had been found out, the authorities would be watching his sister's house. Possibly even monitoring her phone.

On the fourth ring a woman answered. "Hello?"

"Mrs. Kristel Heinemann?" Gold asked.

"Yes, who is this calling?"

"I'm a friend of Klaus'. I'm wondering if he is there?"

"No, he is not. Is this his friend Raymond?"

Gold's heart nearly stopped, and for a moment he could not speak, his throat constricting.

"Klaus left a message for his friend. Is this Raymond?"

"Yes," Gold managed to squeak.

"Good," the woman said. "Well, Klaus went somewhere in the southwest. It's his work, you know. But he'll contact me when he's settled."

If this call was being monitored they were all dead. But what could he say to this foolish woman? What could he say?

"Have you a message for Klaus?"

"No . . . no," Gold said. "I will call later."

"Very good," the woman said cheerfully, and she

hung up, leaving Gold, a stupid expression on his face, staring at the phone.

MOSCOW

It had been well past one in the morning when Major Runkov finally left his office at Lubyanka and stumbled home to fall fully clothed into bed. The workload across his desk had been tremendous over the past week, and combined with the tension of not hearing a thing from Badim, had completely exhausted him.

Ever-faithful Sergeant Doronkin had practically forced him into leaving the office for at least a few hours' sleep at home. Only it was difficult with all the racket going on, and even asleep he could sense his anger steadily rising.

As he lumbered heavily out of his deep sleep he began to realize that the noise was someone pounding at his door, and for a confused moment he was certain it was the Nazis, who had finally taken over Moscow, and he reached for his gun, but it wasn't there.

He came fully awake, finally, and sat up in bed, the sweat pouring from him as the pounding on the door continued.

Swinging his legs over the edge, he got unsteadily to his feet and lurched out of the bedroom to the front door, which he yanked open, not bothering to slip the lock, the wood splintering and pulling away from the frame.

Two men in civilian clothes stood in the dark corridor, and Runkov reached out, grabbed the nearest one by his shirt front, and pulled him forward.

"What in fucking hell are you doing banging on my door at this hour . . . comrade?" he bellowed.

"Marshal Stalin wants to see you," the other man said, backing a few steps away. "Now, major."

Runkov turned his attention to the other man for a moment, then let go of the man he was holding. "Wait," he snapped, and he turned and went back into his apartment, where at the kitchen sink he splashed some water on his face, and brushed his hair back with his fingers.

In the dim light filtering in from outside, he could just make out the small clock on the wall above the gas ring. It was 4:30 A.M.

Without bothering to straighten his crumpled clothing, he went back to the front door, followed the two men downstairs, and climbed into the backseat of a dark green limousine. Within ten minutes he was inside the Kremlin and an aide was escorting him down a wide corridor, their heels clattering hollowly on the parquet floor.

Stalin was waiting for him in a small, plainly furnished office off one of the main conference rooms. His gray tunic was half-unbuttoned, his hair was mussed, and he was smoking a foul-smelling cigarette that was mostly cardboard filter.

His entire bearing and demeanor were the exact opposite of what they had been the last time Runkov had met with him. Then the supreme Soviet leader had seemed ebullient; now he seemed to be a dark, foreboding, malevolent force.

The aide quietly withdrew, closing the door softly behind him, and Runkov stood facing Stalin, who had been seated behind a desk, but now stood up, crushing the cigarette out in an ashtray.

"Valkyrie's mission is to be changed," Stalin said, his voice cracked and hoarse.

"Comrade?" Runkov said, but Stalin's face suddenly turned red and he slammed his fist on the desk top, making the ashtray jump.

"Do not argue with me, comrade major!" he screamed, spittle flying from his mouth. "Paris has fallen to the Americans and British, but all we have is Bucharest! We must have Berlin! We must have Hitler!"

For a moment Runkov was certain the man had lost his mind, or was having a seizure of some kind, and he just stared, unable to think of anything to say.

"Paris has fallen," Stalin said, regaining some of his composure, but evidently misinterpreting the expression on Runkov's face for complete understanding.

"Yes, comrade," Runkov said, hesitatingly.

"Yes, comrade!" Stalin exploded again. "Is that all you can say? Valkyrie must be diverted or everything will be lost!"

It was as if someone had slammed a fist into Runkov's gut. There had been trouble of some kind. But why hadn't he been told?

Stalin was shaking with rage, but with obviously great effort, he managed to control himself as he picked up an NKVD file folder from his desk and handed it across to Runkov.

"Valkyrie must be immediately called down from his assassination attempt on Groves and Oppenheimer," he said.

"Shall we bring him home, comrade marshal?" Runkov asked. He desperately wanted to look at the information contained in the file folder, but he didn't dare to move.

"No, you fool!" Stalin screamed. "He and the woman are to remain undercover in the United States. One of Beria's people in New York has learned that Fuchs has been sent to the southwestern part of the country, evidently to work on the bomb design itself. He'll send us all the information we need. I don't want the project interfered with!"

Now Runkov was totally confused. "Then why, comrade marshal, should we take the risk of keeping Valkyrie in place?"

Stalin's eyes opened wide in disbelief. "I want him to sabotage the test of the first bomb!" he shouted insanely.

OCTOBER 1980

OCTOBER 1995

22

ALBUQUERQUE, NEW MEXICO

It was late afternoon by the time Mahoney and Jada returned to the Holiday Inn just off Interstate 25 in Albuquerque. He had cleaned up first and went down to the bar, Jada promising to join him as soon as she had taken a bath.

They had registered as husband and wife in the name of Charles and Marion Anderson. McBundy had insisted on the precaution in case Washington KGB operations had somehow gotten a line on the woman. She was hot stuff, and would remain so until the dust had settled, which might not be for several months. Or as long as a year.

"It's not every day a KGB chief of station chooses to defect," McBundy had cautioned. "If you want to take her down to New Mexico, it's up to you. But you'll do it my way."

Mahoney had thought that the assumed identity bit was silly, but now that he had heard at least the first part of Jada's story, he wasn't so sure. Her assignment with Valkyrie was the sort of operation that could be politically embarrassing if it got out, even though it had happened more than thirty-five years ago.

He sat in a back booth in the cocktail lounge drinking a bourbon neat—no ice, no water—as he waited for Jada.

He spotted her as she hesitated at the doorway, obviously searching for him, but he did not immediately get up and beckon. Instead he watched her for several long moments.

She was wearing a fashionably cut, pale yellow jump suit with a scarf at her neck, courtesy of Sampson's wife, who had done the shopping for her with CIA slush funds. Her hair, which she had washed, was brushed to one side. She had put on a little makeup to give her face color, and from here she looked beautiful.

Combined with her clothes, her speech, which held little or no accent, marked her as western—definitely not Russian.

He waved. Jada spotted him immediately and came across the crowded room to him and sat down.

Close up he could see the lines of her age and of her sickness, and again he felt sorry for her. For just a fleeting moment he found himself wishing he had known her in the forties, but he instantly dismissed the thought.

"Would you care for a drink?" he asked.

She managed a slight smile, although it was clear she was still shaken and weary from telling her story out at the Trinity bomb-test site. "A cognac, plain, would be nice," she said softly.

Mahoney motioned for a waitress, and ordered them both a drink. When the young woman was gone, Jada leaned forward, placing her hands over Mahoney's.

"What I've told you so far, Mr. Mahoney, is the truth. You must believe me," she said earnestly.

"I do," he said. "But I'm puzzled by a number of things."

"For instance, where did I get all my information?" Mahoney nodded.

"You must understand that although I've given you the motions of our operation in strict chronological order, the details did not come to me until long afterward."

"You went digging," Mahoney said.

She nodded. "Yes, I went digging. After the war, I remained as a clerk in the NKVD, and then in 1953, when Comrade Beria was shot, there was the great reorganization of our intelligence *apparat*, culminating in the formation of the KGB in 1954. At that time I was promoted to the Cipher Division, and then later I was moved to the Second Chief Directorate."

A startled expression crossed Mahoney's features. "Did you know Yuri Zamyatin?"

"No," she said. "But I've heard of him. He took over Department One within the directorate after I left. Is he familiar to you?"

Mahoney had worked with Zamyatin on an Allied mission in Germany during the war, and later the man had been involved with the trouble Mahoney had had in Moscow. But his name now served to focus attention on the fact that, after all was said and done, Jada had been a high-ranking KGB officer. Defector or not, she was the enemy.

She noticed the sudden change in his expression, and she drew her hands back as the cocktail waitress came over with their drinks and Mahoney paid.

When they were again alone, she sipped at her drink and then held the balloon glass in both hands to warm the liquor. It seemed to Mahoney that she was stalling for time, trying to think of the right thing to say, and he held his silence. It was her story, but when it was finished, he would make sure he had all the facts.

"Everything I've told you, including Captain Lovelace's part in the business, is on file in our archives at Dzerzhinsky Square."

"Impossible . . ." Mahoney started to say, but then he closed his mouth. If what she was saying was true, it would indicate that nearly every level of government had leaked like a sieve in those days. Not a comforting thought, but not impossible, nevertheless.

"I've seen the files recently," she said, "including the reports I filed myself in the late summer and fall of '45."

Mahoney stared at her for a long time. She was indeed an extraordinary woman. But the story she was telling him was even more startling than she was.

She took another sip of her cognac, then set the glass down and took a deep breath, letting it out slowly. When she looked up, her face was composed.

"Lovelace knew we were there to assassinate Groves and Oppenheimer, and once he had them out of danger, he came looking for us."

"Lovelace hadn't been shot?" Mahoney asked.

"Yes, in the arm, but that didn't stop him. We very nearly didn't escape."

"How about Badim?"

She smiled wistfully. "Alek was a mass of scrapes, cuts, and bruises, but he hadn't broken anything and even managed to help me that night," she said. "We hiked back to Springer, stole a car from a ranch house, and drove to Oklahoma City. From there I rented a car and then we drove directly to New York."

"To your contact?"

"Yes," she said. "We were going to tell him that there had been a leak in our plans, but the man was frantic. Wouldn't listen to a word Alek said to him. Kept asking if Groves and Oppenheimer were still alive. Alek wanted to try again, but our contact said there had been a change in plans. We were to assume new identities and lay low."

"Because of the information Klaus Fuchs was supplying your government?"

Jada nodded. "That and the fact our scientists were having a tough time catching up with the bomb processes. More time was needed for us. Stalin wanted to let the bomb be developed, with Fuchs sending us back information. At the last minute we would be assigned to somehow sabotage the test."

"Would Badim have been able to kill Groves and Oppenheimer that night on the train had Lovelace not shown up?" Mahoney asked. "I mean, did you think it was possible?"

Jada nodded again. "Yes," she said. "It would have been easy. Alek was very good, you see."

"So what happened after you escaped and then contacted your man in New York?"

"That was the late summer of 1944. Our orders were to keep out of sight until the date of the first bomb test was set . . ."

In the comfortable and familiar surroundings of the Holiday Inn, Mahoney heard the rest of Jada's incredible story.

BOOK FOUR
JANUARY–JUNE 1945

23

CAMBRIDGE, MASSACHUSETTS

It was early evening and a cold wind blew plumes of snow up Western Avenue as Klaus Fuchs, driving a battered Buick sedan, pulled over to the curb just north of the Massachusetts Institute of Technology.

Despite the chill winter wind, Fuchs was sweating, a thin sheen of perspiration on his pale face, and his hand shook as he reached across the front seat to open the passenger door for his contact, Raymond.

Gold, bundled up in a heavy coat, wore his green gloves and in his left hand carried the novel with a green binding. When he got into the car and closed the door, Fuchs plucked a tennis ball from the pocket of his brown leather coat and held it up. Both men laughed nervously.

"I knew you would contact my sister," Fuchs said. His voice held a German accent. "That's why I left the message with her. There was no time to try to contact you. Besides, it would have been too dangerous . . . I think."

Gold patted the scientist on the arm. "You did the right thing, Klaus, believe me."

Fuchs shut off the car's headlights, but left the windshield wipers flapping, clearing the blowing snow from the glass as he stared down the nearly deserted avenue. "It's cold here. A lot colder than in Santa Fe."

"Is that where you've been keeping yourself these days, Klaus?" Gold asked, careful to keep the excitement out of his voice.

Fuchs turned back to him, his eyes behind his tortoiseshell glasses enlarged by the lenses. "The laboratory is northwest of Santa Fe at a place called Los Alamos. It's designated Site Y."

"And what is happening at this Site Y that has you so excited?" Gold asked. His voice was soothing.

"We're doing it, Raymond. We're actually doing it. We'll have the first gadget ready for testing sometime after March, but no later than July."

"Where is the test site—surely nowhere around Santa Fe?"

Fuchs shook his head. "No, of course not. It's somewhere to the south of us in the desert. I'm not sure yet of the exact location, but the place is being called Trinity."

A car passed them slowly and both men stiffened until it was out of sight, then Gold turned to the scientist, his heart racing. "Trinity?" he asked.

"Dr. Oppenheimer named it."

"You will be going back to the laboratory soon?"

"Yes. I've only got the rest of this week for my holiday, then I have to be back to work. But I get into Santa Fe and even Albuquerque from time to time."

"Fine," Gold said, thinking ahead. "Listen now. Before I get the details of your work I want to set up a meeting with you for sometime late in the spring, in Santa Fe. It's far enough away from Los Alamos and large enough so we won't create any suspicion. Is that all right?"

Fuchs nodded again. "Certainly," he said.

24

MOSCOW

The wind raged like a wounded beast through the city
of Moscow as Runkov drove across the Krimskiy
Bridge and passed through Gorky Park, turning right
finally onto Kaluzhskaya Street.

His mind spun with a thousand technical details,
many of which he could only guess the meaning of,
which had come in a few days ago from the United
States. Beria, as great a fool as he was, had put together
an effective organization there. An organization that
was getting results.

It was four in the afternoon, but already it was dark,
the lights shining from apartment windows and the occasional street lamp throwing its feeble illumination
only a few yards in the blowing snow.

To the west a whistle blew, and Runkov shuddered,
the action involuntary, with the mournful sound. It came
from one of the trains moving up the river on tracks
laid over the ice. At this moment it struck him as a
particularly lonely sound.

As he drove, taking care because of the ice and snow on the pavement, he thought about the past—about the friends he had never made, about his wife dead and gone now three years, and about his accomplishments.

At first he had been a dedicated man, fighting fiercely for the Party and the State. But lately over the past years, and especially over the past months, Runkov had begun to discover that he had a conscience. And it was a bothersome thing.

The war with Germany would be over soon, probably in the spring or early summer. So why were the Americans still going ahead with production of the atomic bomb? What reason was there for the fearful device, if not to stop the Nazis?

He smiled to himself as Gorky Park became Lenin Park out his right window. Besides having a conscience, he told himself, he was becoming maudlin in his old age.

Power. That was the name of the game. If the bomb was not to be used on Germany, perhaps it would be dropped on Japan. If not Japan, perhaps Moscow?

Kaluzhskaya Street curved to the right, turning into Vorobyevskoye Road, which followed the bend in the river. Three army trucks passed him in the opposite direction. A moment later he could just pick out the dim lights of Moscow State University in the distance.

For the past four months Runkov had worried about Stalin's orders that the test of the first atomic bomb be sabotaged. Although he had felt that such a task was impossible, he had not argued with the man. No one argued with Stalin and lived.

Instead he had gone back to his office, outlined the new problem to Sergeant Doronkin, and then had sent off a quick message to Badim: GO UNDERGROUND. AWAIT FURTHER INSTRUCTIONS.

Together, then, he and Doronkin began to break the impossible task into its much smaller and conceivably possible components.

First and foremost among them would be learning the exact time and date of the test, as well as its precise location and the layout of the test site.

That information was coming to them from the British scientist Klaus Fuchs through Harry Gold, who in turn passed the details on to NKVD agent Anatoli Yakovlev, who was working under the code name John.

The test site, called Trinity, had not yet been pinpointed beyond the generality that it was somewhere in the southern New Mexico desert. The exact information, however, was expected soon.

Second among the priorities was the exact method of sabotage. In this Badim and Jada would be severely handicapped.

No matter what happened or did not happen, they would have to maintain their secondary cover as Germans. But once the war with Germany was over, that cover would no longer be useful, which meant they would have to carry out the operation in total secrecy.

Still, those obstacles had not presented any absolute stumbling blocks. The operation would be difficult, but up to that point not impossible.

The problem did come, however, in the actual physical details of the sabotage itself. Undoubtedly the bomb, as well as its control mechanisms, would be highly complicated. Any little thing going wrong could possibly throw the test off. But what little thing? And would it be possible to sabotage the test in such a fashion that no one knew it had been sabotaged?

It was this last that most intrigued Runkov. Interested him to the point that he had forgotten all about his earlier dismal predictions for the outcome of the operation.

But until a couple of days ago when they had received the latest information from Fuchs, and then the technical report from Army Corporal David Greenglass, who worked in the machine shop at Los Alamos, Runkov had had no earthly idea how such a thing could be accomplished.

The reports had been passed on to the Special Physics Wing at Moscow State University, where much of the theoretical work on atomic bomb research was being done. Earlier this afternoon Runkov had made an appointment to speak with Dr. Leonid Yushenko, whose complicated position was one of liaison between the theoreticians, the industrial designers, and the military.

Yushenko had been somewhat cool on the phone, but had nevertheless agreed to the meeting in his office at 4:15 P.M.

The guards had been notified of his visit, and merely checked his GRU identification before waving him on. He drove through the gate and about a kilometer into the university grounds, then turned left to the physics building, parking his car around back.

One of the sentries just inside the door escorted him immediately down the busy corridor, knocked once at an office door, and then ushered him in. A tall, balding man with a pale white face and thick glasses was hunched over a drafting table. No one else was in the office.

"Dr. Yushenko," the guard said softly.

The scientist looked up, then came across the room, holding his hand out. "Major Runkov, is it?" he asked.

Runkov shook the man's hand. "Yes," he said. "It was good of you to see me on such short notice."

Yushenko's gaze flickered to the guard, who had remained by the open door, and the man flinched almost as if he had been struck, then quickly backed out into the corridor, quietly closing the door behind him.

"Now, what can I do for you this afternoon, major? You were not quite clear on the telephone as to the nature of your business with me."

"I need some information, comrade doctor."

A pinched smile briefly crossed the scientist's face. "You could have saved us both the trouble of your visit, major. Such requests must come through channels in writing for consideration. Then in a week or so, once the necessary clearances have been obtained, I'll see what I can do for you."

Runkov had anticipated just such a reaction, and he withdrew Stalin's letter from his breast pocket and handed it to the man. "If you'll just look at this."

Yushenko took the letter, scanned it quickly, then looked up at Runkov with new respect in his eyes. He read the letter again, this time more slowly, and finally handed it back.

"Quite an extraordinary document, major," he said softly. "In effect it makes you the second most important man in the Soviet Union."

"I'll need your complete cooperation," Runkov said.

"You have it, of course," the scientist replied.

"And whatever is discussed here this afternoon, between us, will not be mentioned to anyone, for any reason."

"You have my word on it," Yushenko said.

"Good," Runkov said ominously, "because your life will depend upon it."

Yushenko blanched, but said nothing.

"You have studied the latest information the NKVD has provided you about the explosive lens designs the Americans have come up with?"

"Yes, quite ingenious. I would have thought such a technical feat would be years in the future."

Runkov looked beyond the scientist toward the drafting table, then took the man by the arm and led him to it. He picked up a pencil and pinned a clean sheet of paper to the board.

"I want you to draw me a diagram," he said, handing the pencil to the scientist.

"Of what?"

"The American atomic bomb design. Exactly how it works . . . to the best of your knowledge . . . and how it could be sabotaged in such a fashion that no one would know."

25

NEWPORT NEWS, VIRGINIA

Alek Badim got to his car and was about to open the door when he spotted the crumpled cigarette pack on the front seat. For a moment he just stood there, oblivious to everything except his heart thumping against his ribs and the butterflies in his stomach.

It had finally come. After six months the message had finally come.

Around him hundreds of women, and a scattering of men, were streaming to their cars and to the bus stops outside the Newport News shipyards and dry docks. It was shortly past 11:30 P.M., and across the vast parking lot a few stragglers were still coming in for the greatly reduced graveyard shift.

Over the past months the workload had been severely cut back because of the way the war was going. In Europe, Soviet troops were within seventy or eighty kilometers of Berlin, while the Americans, British, and Free French were closing in on Cologne. When Berlin fell, which was expected sometime in late March or early April, it would be finished. In the South Pacific, the war with Japan was still at least a year away from completion, but no longer were as many ships coming into the Hampton Roads Harbor for repairs. And no longer were the Victory-class ships being built.

The war was finally winding down. Very soon now there would be peace. The mission would be scrubbed.

With a shaking hand Badim opened the door and slipped in behind the wheel. He dug his keys out and started the battered old Ford coupe, but before he switched on the headlights and pulled out of the parking lot, he reached over and picked up the crumpled pack of Chesterfields, and immediately felt something hard inside it.

He looked up to make sure no one was watching him, and then tore open the pack. Inside was a key with a large head. Holding it up to the parking lot lights, he was able to read the numbers 357 stamped in the metal beneath the words PORTSMOUTH R.R. STA.

Instructions for bringing them home? It had to be. Once the war with Germany was over with, his and Jada's secondary cover as German agents would be ruined. And in New Mexico they had nearly been caught. These would have to be their orders bringing them home. Anything else would be too risky.

He pocketed the key, switched on his headlights, and pulled away from his parking spot into the long line of cars heading out to Jefferson Avenue.

Jada would be happy. Over the past month or so she had become increasingly irascible, apparently anxious for something to happen one way or the other, although he had supposed all along that she had been happy playing house.

Until a few days ago, too, she had seemed to thrive on their new lifestyle. They had managed to rent a small house just north of Newport News in Grafton. They had the car, a large Stromberg Carlson upright to listen to the radio shows at night, and an electric fridge.

It had been quite a change for her from the old days in Brighton, and even more of a change from the austerity of Moscow, and at first she had been like a deprived child in a toy shop.

Hanging over them, however, during the past six months, was the knowledge that their life here was a temporary one; the new mission, whatever it would be, was waiting for them, and after that it would be back to Moscow.

Months ago he had come to realize that Jada did not want to go back, although he had said nothing to her, and in fact had played along with her little game of "Let's Pretend," just like on the Saturday morning radio show.

"Let's pretend," she would start the game, "that in July we'll go up to Long Island and spend a week. Or maybe take the train all the way down to Florida. Or maybe even down to Arizona. Neither of us has ever seen the Grand Canyon, you know."

"Long Island is for snobs. Florida is too hot in the summer. And who wants to look at a great hole in the ground, anyway," he would tease her.

"You're a big bore, Peter Bradley," she would say. She hardly ever used his real name anymore, not even when they made love. "I suppose you'll be suggesting we go to New York to see the big buildings, or maybe even to Louisville so you can lose our savings on the horse races."

A mock serious expression would cross his face then, and he would say something like, "If you're not careful, toots, I'll do just that, only I'll leave you home, and find some good-lookin' dish at the track."

She would smile, loving every moment of it. "Mr. Bradley, have I ever told you that I love you?"

"Nope," he would say.

He found himself smiling as someone behind him beeped a horn, and he looked up to see that the traffic had cleared in front of him, and he pulled out onto

Jefferson Avenue and headed toward the James River Bridge, which led across to Portsmouth.

Jada's feelings were perfectly obvious, or at least they had been until very recently. And more than once he had found it necessary to bring her harshly out of her little game when it threatened to become too serious.

She had invented parents for them in Chicago, and once she had even suggested they spend their summer vacation visiting them.

But even more dangerous than that gentle delusion was her longing to make friends. Someone to come over on Saturday nights for cards and a few beers. Maybe a girlfriend to go shopping with.

"Our cover wouldn't stand that close a scrutiny," he had said to her.

"Cover?" she had asked weakly.

"And what would those friends think when we were ordered to leave suddenly?"

"Leave?" she had asked.

He turned left on Mercury Boulevard, and headed across the bridge, sighing deeply as he drove. He was tired, but it was a good tired that made him want to do nothing more than go home, have something to eat, take a quick bath, and then go to bed.

Jada's feelings were obvious, but what about his? They were Soviet spies in an Allied country. They had been sent here to assassinate two men. That mission had very nearly ended in total disaster. It was only pure blind luck that they had managed to escape.

He shook his head in irritation. He was as guilty as Jada of playing "Let's Pretend."

Dammit, he too liked the feeling of belonging. He liked their little house, and the radio, and the fridge. He didn't particularly care for his job at the shipyards, but the war would soon be over, and he had even caught himself, from time to time, wondering about going back to school, maybe getting a degree in engineering.

It was another of the things he had never mentioned to Jada. It would have been like adding fuel to an already furiously burning fire.

Germany, Canaris, Oster, and the Abwehr seemed like a million miles and as many years ago to him. But curiously, Major Runkov, Moscow, and their GRU training seemed even more remote.

Across the bridge he continued along Highway 17, which led back into Portsmouth, and for just a moment as he sped through the night he toyed with the idea of ignoring the locker key, turning around, and going home. But his speed did not waver, nor did he.

The Portsmouth Depot, downtown, was nearly deserted at this time of night, and Badim had no trouble locating the correct locker. Inside he found a small, plain brown cardboard suitcase, secured with a cheap brass lock, and when he hefted it he was surprised at its weight. It was heavy, almost as if it was filled with rock or bricks.

Outside he carefully laid the case beside him on the front seat, and then headed for home, resisting the temptation to open it right then.

He knew that they were not being ordered home. Without looking at the contents of the suitcase, he knew their assignment had finally come through. But how Jada was going to take it was, at this moment, more worrisome to him than the actual job.

He crossed over the James River again, the shipyards directly across the harbor, and beyond them Forts Monroe and Wool, which guarded Hampton Roads, were brightly lit.

Work went on, he thought. The war went on. And so did their mission.

Jada would have to understand about their assignment. Understand that the past six months had not been a fairy tale, but had been nothing more than a carefully engineered cover for them. A waiting period until their real work began.

*   *   *

It was shortly after 1:00 A.M. when he finally pulled into the graveled driveway, killed the engine, and went up the walk to their small bungalow, the suitcase in his left hand.

He came up on the porch and the door opened. Jada stood there wearing a pale pink bathrobe and an intense expression on her face. "I was worried about you."

"Sorry," he said, brushing past her and coming into the tiny but comfortably furnished living room. The radio was on, playing soft music, and the tea things were on the small coffee table by the couch.

"Where've you been?"

"Portsmouth," he said over his shoulder. "Had to pick this up." He pushed the tea things aside, and laid the suitcase on the coffee table. "Close the door and lock it."

"What is it?"

He turned around to face her. She still stood by the open door, her face drawn, almost haggard-looking. At that moment he loved her more than he thought it was ever humanly possible to love another person. But there was the mission.

"Close the door, Larissa," he said gently, but the use of that name caused her to reel back, almost as if she had been hit.

Her eyes went from his, down to the suitcase lying on the coffee table, and then back to his again, as her right hand came up to her mouth.

"The door, Larissa," he said again, and after a long moment she complied, her motions mechanical.

When she turned back there was genuine fear in her eyes. "What is in the suitcase, Alek?" she asked, using his Russian name.

"I don't know. Our assignment, I suppose."

"I . . ." she started to say, but her eyes were suddenly filled with tears. "I knew it couldn't last," she said. "But the war is almost over, Alek. You said so yourself."

He resisted the almost overwhelming urge to go to her. She would have to be made to understand about the mission. Instead he dug a pocket knife out of his pocket, opened it to the largest blade, and then turned and knelt down on the floor in front of the coffee table, pulling the suitcase toward him.

He easily pried the cheap lock out of its frame, set the knife down, undid both latches, and opened the lid. The suitcase was filled with Bibles—twenty of them stacked neatly in two rows of five each, two deep. For a moment he just looked at them until he spotted the inspirational message attached to the inside of the lid. It was headed: THE SOUTHWESTERN AMERICAN BIBLE CO., DALLAS, TEXAS.

Beneath that was the inscription, "Remember sons and daughters of God, the words of our Lord, Psalm 94:1. 'Lord God, to whom vengeance belongs, let your glory shine out. Arise and judge the earth, sentence the proud to the penalties they deserve.' "

Badim smiled to himself, remembering the Bible lessons he and Jada had been given prior to this assignment. He had not questioned the extraordinary nature of study, assuming all along that it was for a purpose. Now he understood. They were going to become Bible salesmen. It was just one of many covers they had been given.

He picked the top left Bible out of the suitcase and quickly thumbed to the Ninety-fourth Psalm, the facing page of which was a picture, printed on very thick paper, of Jesus Christ looking down on a pastoral scene from a thundercloud. The page was loosely bound in the book, and came out easily. On the back was printed the psalm, and the message from the Bible company that this lovely rendering of our Lord was suitable for framing and its removal would in no way detract from the worth of the Good Book.

Jada had come up behind him and stood looking over his shoulder. "They're Bibles," she said.

"It's our orders," Badim corrected her, glancing up. "Get me a razor blade."

She was confused. "What?"

"A razor blade, Jada. And then make a pot of coffee."

She turned and went down the hall into the bathroom while Badim opened each of the twenty Bibles, working left to right through the rows, taking the suitable-for-framing Ninety-fourth Psalm picture out of each.

When he was finished Jada was back with the double-edged razor blade and she handed it to him. "Don't cut yourself," she said automatically.

He had set the suitcase aside, and stacked the twenty pictures in a neat pile. Taking the top one, he carefully slit the edge at the top right corner with the razor blade, and in a few seconds he had it apart. Written on the inside of the front half, in German, were their orders, with no signature other than the initials *S. R.*—Sergei Runkov.

Within ten minutes he had the other nineteen pictures slit apart and lying in order on the living room floor. Their orders covered three of the pages, while on many of the others were complicated diagrams, and on one, a map showing an area of New Mexico from Santa Fe down to the Mexican border.

Jada had made coffee, and she came back into the living room with a mug of it for him.

"Where are they sending us now?" she asked dully.

He took the cup from her, and looked up. "Albuquerque, New Mexico. Apparently to sabotage the atomic bomb test, although I'm not quite clear yet how he expects me to do it. But it's all here. Or at least most of it is. We'll get more information later."

"I don't know if I'm going to be much help," she said.

"Don't worry about it," he said absently, his mind on their orders. There had been a leak once before . . . it had probably come from their contact at the War Department garage. This time it was going to be different.

But something Jada had just said suddenly penetrated his understanding, and he looked up at her again. There was an odd expression in her eyes. "What did you say?"

She sighed deeply. "I'm not going to be much help to you, especially a few months from now. When is the test shot scheduled?"

"June, or possibly as late as July, according to these," Badim said. "What are you talking about?"

"I went to see a doctor last week," she said, almost timidly, and he jumped to his feet.

"What is it, Larissa? What's wrong? Are you sick?"

She shook her head. "No, Aleksandr, I'm not sick. I'm pregnant."

26

SANTA FE, NEW MEXICO

Michael Lovelace sat in the back of a plain brown grocery delivery van parked across Letrado Street from the small stucco bungalow, trying to convince himself that this time it was going to be different. But he was having a rough go of it.

He had not felt this out of touch, inept, or disillusioned about his work since he was a young man, learning for the first time that people were generally not interested in the truth, but only in power.

The adage "Keeping up with the Joneses" meant nothing more than keeping up with the next man's buying power.

Politics was power. The military was power. Knowledge was power only in that if you knew more than the next guy, you had the edge on him.

For eight months he had been sitting in restaurants, on tops of buildings, in railway depots, and outside factories waiting to catch a glimpse of the man he had seen on the roof of the train.

He was searching for the truth, but no one really cared, although he was being supported for his efforts. He was out of the way. And that's the way they wanted it.

For eight months he had been bitterly disappointed exactly seventeen times. And unless this lead panned out, it would make eighteen.

He had been given an almost absolute power to control and command as many Counter Intelligence Corpsmen as he needed . . . so long as he stayed out of everyone's way. And over the past few months he had done everything humanly possible to catch the man and woman, but with no results.

There had not even been so much as a hint of what had happened to them beyond New York City.

The police departments in every major U.S. city had copies of the sketches that Gillingham had come up with, along with a physical description of the man that had been gleaned from the coroner's report in Boston, as well as the details he himself had added.

He had seen the man hanging onto the side of the train outside Springer. He had seen him in the bright moonlight. Had even managed to fire two shots, high and to the left because he had not wanted to risk hitting anyone inside the train.

And then when the assassin had crawled back up on the roof of the train, Lovelace had been certain he had won.

He could see the man now. He could see the muzzle flash. Could feel the hot, sharp, numbing pain in his arm. Could see his car skidding to the right, into the ditch, up on the other side and then over.

The next day they had learned that a car had been stolen from a farmhouse near Springer. One week later the car was found in Oklahoma City. Two days after that they had determined that a woman matching the girl in the sketch had rented a car. And ten days later the rental car had been found abandoned in New York City.

After that, nothing.

Lovelace sat back from the peephole in the rear door of the van and lit a cigarette, inhaling deeply.

Groves had been apologetic . . . hell, even solicitous . . . after the incident on the train. Hoover's complaints against him had suddenly stopped, but so had any further information from Willis. And President Roosevelt himself had called Lovelace to the Oval Office to offer congratulations on stopping the assassination attempt.

He looked toward the front of the van, where the CIC driver, his head back against the door frame, was sound asleep, and he had to smile.

One hundred creeps with one hundred copies of the sketches, all working from Los Alamos in ever-widening circles, in search of . . . who, or what? Assassins or saboteurs or will-o'-the-wisps?

"They won't give up, Mr. President," he had said, and Roosevelt, who had looked definitely ill, had taken off his glasses and wiped the lenses with his handkerchief.

When he had them back on his nose, he had peered over the huge desk at Lovelace. "You do not believe they have left the country then, captain?"

"No, sir," Lovelace had said.

"Extraordinary," the President had replied softly. He had taken a cigarette out of a plain silver case and fixed it in an ornately carved bone holder, but before he lit it he gazed thoughtfully at Lovelace. "Nor do you believe the man and woman are Nazis."

"No, sir, I do not."

"I take it you believe them to be Soviet citizens—am I correct in that as well? Something to do with a Russian-made fuse on that submarine?"

"Yes, Mr. President," Lovelace had said, sitting forward, but Roosevelt had waved him back.

"Undoubtedly then you have no plans to give up your search once we've finished in Europe."

"No, sir."

"Nor, I take it, will you give up until they are caught."

"Then, sir, or when the bomb is successfully tested."

"Admirable, captain, simply admirable. I wish I had more men like you around me."

Roosevelt had had a charisma that was impossible to deny. The man was the President of the United States. Yet Lovelace had found himself leaving the Oval Office that day a deeply confused and disturbed man. On the one hand he had felt almost like a high school football player charged up for the Saturday afternoon game after a pep rally. While at the same time he had the gut feeling that some vital piece of information was being held from him. Something that would change everything. Something that would have a profound effect on his work.

The pep rally enthusiasm, however, had been ground away by the events—or lack of them—over the past months. His confidence had begun to erode so that he was finding it difficult to believe any longer that given enough time and manpower and persistence and luck, the man and woman would be found.

They had scoured New York. They had turned Washington, D.C., and then Boston and Cape Cod upside down through the fall and into the winter, with no luck. Finally, two months ago in mid-February, Lovelace had finally moved his operation down to Los Alamos.

The bomb was rapidly nearing completion, and the test shot was expected sometime in the summer. July Fourth was a date he had heard mentioned more than once.

The test site had been selected from a half-dozen that ranged from desert areas in California to sandbars off the coast of Texas and the San Luis Valley region near the Great Sand Dunes National Monument in Colorado.

Oppenheimer and some of the others on the project had finally settled on the northern portion of the Alamogordo Bombing Range near the town of Socorro, New Mexico, 140 miles south of the laboratory at Los Alamos.

That remote section had a number of advantages, among them the fact that it was already owned by the government, its relative proximity to the lab, and finally its isolation.

The engineering problems of constructing the pumps and barriers for the separation of the uranium isotope had been solved, and bomb material was beginning to come from the plant at Oak Ridge.

The reactors and plutonium separation facilities at Hanford, Washington, were operational now, and bomb material was beginning to come from that plant as well.

At Los Alamos, the thousands of technical problems were being solved for the test shot, among them bomb casings and recovery vessels, blast monitoring devices, detonator timers, and a unique design for TNT charges shaped like lenses that would implode in such a fashion that the nuclear material would be compressed into a critical mass within a millionth of a second, which it was hoped would create a chain reaction and blast.

The stage was set. The players were all assembling on the desert. And yet Lovelace was frightened. Worried not only about the man and woman who had disappeared from New York without a trace after nearly succeeding in killing Groves and Oppenheimer, but deeply worried about the fact that this was probably a Russian operation and that no one seemed to care, or want to know.

He stubbed his cigarette out on the floor and as he leaned forward to peer out of the peephole at the house across the street, he told himself for the thousandth time that he was doing everything that could be done. In three months, no matter what else happened, his job would be finished.

An old pickup truck was just pulling into the drive-way across the street, and Lovelace's stomach tightened into a knot. A man was driving. A woman was in the passenger seat. Her hair was long and light brown.

"Wake up, you stupid bastard," Lovelace said over his shoulder, and the driver grunted.

The man was getting out of the pickup truck, his back to Lovelace. He wore a brown jacket and his hair was dark.

Lovelace's heart was accelerating as he pulled his .38 out of his belt. It was him! Goddammit, he was sure of it!

"Let's go," he said to the driver, and he flipped the handle down, shoved the door open, and jumped out on the street just as the man was going around the front of the truck.

"Hold it!" Lovelace shouted, as he raced across the street.

For a moment he could not see the man on the far side of the truck, and his hands were sweating as he raced to the right, running in a crouch.

Bells started ringing from somewhere downtown, but it did not register on him, as the woman opened her door and stepped out onto the driveway. She was hold-ing something in her right hand.

"Drop it!" Lovelace screamed, as he leaped over the curb and started to raise his pistol with both hands.

The woman, startled, dropped her small purse at the same moment the man came around the front of the truck, and for a long moment Lovelace stood rooted to his spot, his pistol wavering at a spot halfway between the couple. And then he could feel the bile rising up in his throat, and his hand shook as he lowered his gun.

"Jesus Christ . . ." the CIC driver shouted from the van.

Lovelace half turned and shouted over his shoulder. "Easy, it's not them."

"Lovelace, for chrissake, shut up and listen," the

driver was shouting, an hysterical edge to his voice.

The man and the woman by the pickup truck were staring across the lawn at Lovelace, who shrugged tiredly at them, but then he could hear the radio in the van blaring, and the bells ringing in town, and he turned around.

The driver was standing by the open door of the van, looking across the street at Lovelace, tears streaming from his eyes.

"What the hell . . ." Lovelace started to say, but the CIC officer waved him off.

"He's dead . . . Christ, he's dead . . ."

And then Lovelace began to hear what the radio announcer was saying, and his knees began to go weak.

". . . had gone to his retreat at Warm Springs, Georgia, only thirteen days ago to recuperate from his recent conference at Yalta.

"Franklin Delano Roosevelt, the thirty-second President of the United States, dead at sixty-three, on this Thursday, April the twelfth, 1945."

27

ALBUQUERQUE, NEW MEXICO

Badim felt like a cornered animal, and for the first time in his life he was seriously contemplating not obeying a direct order.

His regular Tuesday night telephone contact, a man somewhere here in Albuquerque, had wanted his address. Christ, he had wanted to meet Badim face to face, and had damned near mentioned Runkov by name for his authority.

Badim had agreed to think about it, and call the man back at two the next afternoon.

It was nearly that time now, and as he limped along West Copper Avenue downtown, he was seriously considering not making the phone call after all.

Soviet troops had completely encircled Berlin, according to the newspapers, and the war with Germany was virtually ended. It would only be a matter of days, or a couple of weeks at the most, before a peace treaty would be signed, and the Third Reich would no longer exist. Nor would his and Jada's cover.

He stopped in front of a shop window and stared at his reflection in the glass for a moment. His hair, streaked with gray, was long, almost completely covering his ears, and his thick, luxurious beard made him look the part he had been playing now for the past six weeks . . . that of a religious fanatic who sold Bibles.

But such a disguise was only superficial at best. And if he actually made contact with his man today, and later the man was caught, he could give the authorities a fairly accurate description. A description that would lead them back to him and to Jada and to the child she was carrying.

He looked at his watch, which showed it was a couple of minutes before two, and then glanced up, spotting a telephone booth across the street on the corner, but he did not immediately move away from the window.

The reflection in the glass was that of an old man. And at this moment he felt, in many ways, old and used up. Confused. He did have a choice. He could turn away, return home to Jada, and they could completely forget about the assignment. When the war was finished he could go to engineering school, get his degree, and open a small firm of some kind. They had been supplied with plenty of American funds.

Jada could have the baby, and their lives could continue normally. They would have more children. Eventually grandchildren. And in forty or fifty years, they would be dead and nothing would matter anyway.

Just thinking along those lines, however, made Badim's gut tighten. All his years in Germany would have been in vain. His work for the State, and the State's protection of him, would be lost.

He shook his head in irritation. Christ. It was all so senseless now. So damned useless.

But *did* he have a choice? He looked up again at the telephone booth. He had known something like this was bound to happen. The information that had been passed on to them at Portsmouth in the Bibles had been sketchy at best. In order for him to carry out the assignment he would have to have a lot more information. He supposed now that that was what the contact had for him.

But in the months they had been here in the States he had never been ordered into a face-to-face confrontation with someone from home. Nor, during his entire nine years in Germany, had he ever actually met one of his contacts. Information was passed back and forth through dead-letter drops, or by shortwave, or in some cases by telephone or the mails. Never face to face. It was simply too dangerous.

But Runkov had apparently ordered this, which meant it had to be very important.

He moved away from the shop window finally, and at the corner waited for a break in traffic before he crossed the street to the phone booth.

Inside, he closed the door, dropped a nickel in the slot, and dialed the number he had been given in his general instructions with the Bibles. It was answered on the first ring.

"It's a nice day and it's your nickel," a man's voice came over the line.

"Uncle Wilbur?"

"He's not here. Thank God you called, Bradley. Why wouldn't you talk to me last night?"

"Is there trouble?" Badim asked, ignoring the man's question.

"No, but I have a package for you. It's come from New York from a mutual friend who lives a long ways off."

The man was a messenger boy, nothing more. But worse than that, he was an amateur. "I'll give you instructions where to leave it."

"No," the man said, his voice rising in excitement. "I have to see you. We must talk."

"Impossible."

"This comes from S. R."

The man was even more dangerous than an amateur. He was a complete fool. Badim's mind raced to a dozen different methods and solutions, finally coming up with one that would work. "Do you live alone?" he asked.

"Yes," the man said hesitantly.

"Then listen to me," Badim said. "Do you know where the National Trust and Savings Bank is located?"

"On Central Avenue, I think."

"Central and Second Street. How soon can you get there?"

"Five minutes," the man said, after a brief hesitation.

"All right," Badim said. "I want you to go there right now. In your right hand you will carry two books, and in your left, a newspaper."

"Two books right, newspaper left."

"Right. Just walk past the bank, and if it's safe for me to contact you, I will. Otherwise I want you to go directly home, and we'll try again tomorrow at 2 P.M. Is that clear?"

"I'll be there in five minutes . . ." the man said, and Badim hung up, left the phone booth, and quickly headed for the bank, which was one block away.

Badim got to Central and Second with one minute to spare, and he started down the avenue away from the bank at a leisurely pace, as if he was having difficulty walking because of his limp.

He spotted his contact halfway down the block, head bent down, the books in his right hand and a rolled-up newspaper in his left. The man was short, somewhat on the thin side, and from across the street he looked to Badim to be no more than twenty-four or twenty-five. He wore a brightly checked sport coat.

At the corner, Badim crossed the street and headed back toward the bank, which was a one-and-a-half-story brownstone building with tall arched windows and a large clock at the corner.

The man in the bright coat hesitated several moments at the corner, setting his watch from the overhead clock, then looked around before he finally crossed the street, and headed slowly back the way he had come.

Before he had reached the corner at First Street, by the railroad tracks, he had looked back toward the bank three times, making it perfectly obvious that he suspected he was being followed.

Badim was across the street and slightly ahead of the man, and as he walked he scanned the passersby for any sign of a tail, but so far as he could tell his contact was clean. It was a wonder, though, Badim thought. The man's actions, and his dress, made him stick out like a sore thumb.

The man turned north on First Street, walked three blocks up to Grand, and then turned into a nondescript hotel. Badim had to run to catch up with him, and entered the hotel just as the elevator doors were closing, giving him a brief glimpse of the bright sport coat.

Two old men sat in a broken-down couch in one corner of the small lobby, talking and smoking, and the clerk had his back to Badim, who ducked around the corner, found the stairwell, and raced up to the second floor.

In the corridor he watched the elevator indicator stop at the third floor, then went back into the stairwell and raced up to the next floor, just as the man with the sport coat was entering a room halfway down the corridor.

The hotel smelled of age and dirt, but Badim was aware of none of that now, intent on his immediate task. He pushed open the stairwell door, limped past the elevator to the door his contact had entered, and knocked.

He could hear someone moving around inside, and then the man was at the door.

"Who is it?"

"Bradley," Badim said softly, looking both ways down the corridor. No one had seen him so far.

The door opened, and Badim pushed his way past the

man into the room, shoving the door closed.

"What the hell?" the man was saying, as Badim turned around to face him.

"It's a nice day and it's your nickel. Uncle Wilbur? He's not here," Badim said.

For a moment the man just stood there, his mouth hanging open, but then relief spread across his face. "Christ, you gave me a scare," he said.

"Who'd you expect, the FBI?"

"Don't even joke about it," the man said. He turned and put the chain lock on the door; then crossed the room to a small radio set atop a bureau and turned it on, fiddling with the dial until he got a station that was playing music.

Badim watched all this with amusement. His first assessment of the man had been correct. He was indeed a rank amateur, which made him very dangerous.

"I didn't know what to expect," the man said, kneeling down beside the bed, and pulling a thick manila envelope out from between the mattress and the springs. He got to his feet and turned to stare at Badim, a smile on his lips. "But I can tell you that I sure as hell didn't expect anyone like you, in a getup like that. What the hell are you supposed to be, anyway . . . a holy roller?"

The term was unfamiliar to Badim, but he suspected it held some sort of religious connotation, and he nodded. "Something like that."

"Is it real?"

Badim's eyes narrowed.

"The beard, I mean."

"Yes. Is that for me?" Badim asked softly, indicating the envelope in the man's hands.

"Down to business right away, huh? I like that. Real professional. John told me you'd be that way."

"John?"

The man nodded effusively. "Right. He's your contact up in New York. Real name is . . ."

Badim held up his hand, and the man fell silent, for a moment.

"Sorry," he said finally. "I guess I shouldn't go spouting off like that. It's just that you Reds have got a good thing going for you and I think you've been screwed over. I aim to help change it."

This was all wrong. Badim could feel it in his gut. "Were you ordered to come here and see me personally?"

The man nodded. "Yes, sir. John gave me this package, and told me to make sure I put it into your hands. It's very important, I gather." He stepped forward and held out the envelope. Badim took it.

"Anything else?"

"I'm to stay in case you need any help."

"What about my regular Tuesday night contact here in Albuquerque?"

"He's been sent away."

"There is no one here now who knows of my existence?"

The man shook his head. "Nope. Just me."

Badim thought a moment. "And if I don't require your services, what are you supposed to do?"

An odd expression crossed the man's face. "Why . . . I don't know. John didn't tell me."

Badim stuffed the envelope into his jacket pocket, finally understanding what was happening here, and what was required of him. The mission was apparently even more important, more critical now than it had been before. "Tell me something, how did you come to know John's real name?"

"It's me and my snoopy nose," the man said sheepishly. "I saw it on some papers in his apartment."

Badim looked around the small room, understanding exactly what John had done to this man, and now, why. He nodded toward a narrow door. "What's in there?" he asked.

The man glanced that way. "The bathroom."

"Has it got a tub?"

"Yes," the man said hesitantly.

Slowly, Badim told himself. "Good. I want you to start filling it with water."

"I don't understand."

Badim forced a smile. "I have something very important to tell you. It is a message you must bring back to John."

The man nodded.

"Your radio here playing while we talk is all right—I'm happy you thought about it. But it's not perfect. Running water in a tub, combined with a radio playing, makes it totally impossible for us to be heard."

Understanding and pleasure crossed the man's features. "I see. Of course," he said. "I'll get it ready."

While the man was running the water in the tiny bathroom Badim went to the bureau, unplugged the radio, and brought it over. "Is there someplace in here to plug it in?" he asked in the doorway.

The man was bent over the tub and he looked over his shoulder. "Sure, by the sink," he said.

Badim found the wall socket, plugged the radio in, and set it on the edge of the sink over the tub.

"How long have you worked for us?" he asked conversationally. The man straightened up and turned around.

"Just a short time," he said.

Badim nodded toward the edge of the tub. "Have a seat," he said, and he leaned back against the sink.

The man perched on the edge of the rapidly filling tub, crossed his arms over his chest, and looked expectantly at Badim. "I've got a pretty good memory," he said. "So don't worry if it's a long message. I can handle it."

For a moment Badim wondered at what his life had become, and what it could have been had he and Jada been born here in America, gotten married, and had a family. But at the thought of her, and the child she was carrying, he realized just how vulnerable this fool had made them.

He made as if to shift his weight against the sink, but instead shoved the unsuspecting man backward into the tub, and in the next instant tipped the radio off the sink into the water, then stepped back.

Sparks flew for just a second, the man shrieked and then his body convulsed as the electric charge coursing through him caused his muscles to contract his knees and elbows banging against the side of the tub.

Badim went out of the bathroom, and at the corridor door listened a moment before he eased it open. The dingy hallway was still deserted, and within two minutes he had made his way down to the ground floor, and had let himself out the back way.

28

TRINITY

"I think you've lost touch with reality, Michael," General Groves was saying.

Lovelace, sitting in the passenger seat of the general's car, looked over at him more surprised by the use of his first name than the content of Groves' statement.

"I didn't know you cared," he said.

Groves glanced at him, a scowl on his heavy features. "Don't be flippant with me, captain," he snapped. "I'm trying to save your ass so you can retire with an honorable discharge."

Lovelace started to smile, but then thought better of it, and shrugged tiredly. He took a deep drag on his cigarette and tossed the butt out the window.

It was a pleasant early spring afternoon, and the drive down from Los Alamos had been at least relaxing, if not enjoyable. Lovelace found himself glad now that the general had ordered him to come along. Los Alamos had been getting on his nerves.

"Can you tell me one thing?" Groves asked, the anger

that had suddenly come to his voice gone again.

"You're the boss."

"What have you accomplished since the Springer incident?"

How like an officer's mentality, Lovelace thought. The Springer incident. He closed his eyes and once again he could see the man hanging onto the side of the train. Christ, if he hadn't frozen up, he could have had him. Yet he had blown it.

"Besides pissing off the Santa Fe and Albuquerque police departments, and half the people at the site, you mean?" he asked.

"I think you've got the drift of what I'm asking."

Lovelace just looked at the general. "Is everything so clear to you, general?" he said, and Groves glanced sharply at him, the scowl back on his features. "No, I didn't mean that as a smart-ass comment. Honestly. I meant it exactly as it sounded. *Is* everything so clear to you that you never find yourself worried about what the next step is going to be?"

The general seemed to consider his question for a moment. They had passed through Albuquerque a couple of hours ago, and from time to time they caught glimpses of the Rio Grande out the left side of the car as nothing more than a wide band of green in the valley against the pale, yellow-brown of the desert, the blue mountains surrounding them in the hazy distance. The country here, except for a couple hundred yards on either side of the river, was barren, bleak, and forbidding.

"To tell the truth, Lovelace, I'm worried all the time. Have been ever since the President gave me this assignment."

"Do you ever discuss those feelings with your wife?"

Groves smiled. "No," he said. "I'm a man who leads two lives. One is with my family, and another very separate life is my work. I never mix the two."

Lovelace envied the general for his other life. He had never been married. Hell, no woman would ever have put up with his monkey business. And yet he had often found himself pining for a sympathetic ear. If he were in Groves' shoes, he would definitely share his work with his wife.

"What about me, general? Are you worried about me?"

Groves again glanced at Lovelace. "I was worried about you even before the Springer . . ."

"Don't," Lovelace said sharply, and the general let out his breath. "Don't say it. I was merely doing my job, and I blew it. I should have had him."

"And now he's gone."

"Bullshit," Lovelace snapped, but the instant he said it he had to wonder if Groves and Hoover and Lansdale and even FDR himself had not all been right.

He tried to put himself in the man's shoes. He had been given an assignment: Kill Groves and Oppenheimer. The assignment had failed. Now it was time to bail out. To haul ass for home.

He could not buy it, though. Dammit, he just could not buy it. Yet everything had been calm in the past months. In a few more months the test shot would have come and gone, and the assignment would have been completed. What the hell *was* he worried about?

They passed through the town of Socorro and a few miles south turned left on Highway 380 passing through San Antonio and then crossing the Rio Grande. Once they were across the river, Groves sped up along the narrow road that wound its way through the wildest, most forbidding countryside Lovelace had ever seen.

"How far away are we now?" he asked.

"Not far. We're at the northern edge of the bombing range right here. We'll be going into the site at a place called Stallion Range Gate."

"Why are you bringing me down here today?"

"I thought you'd better see it," Groves said, a little too quickly.

"Why?"

Groves hesitated a moment. "You don't miss a trick, do you?"

"Are you going to strand me here on the desert, keep me out of everyone's hair? Is that it, general? Is that how you're going to save my ass so I can retire with an honorable discharge?"

"Don't be more impossible than you normally are, Lovelace. I'm bringing you down here because I'm worried you just might be right."

"Good god, an admission. The first I've heard to date."

"You really don't give a damn, do you?"

"About what, general?" Lovelace said bitterly. "About my honorable discharge? Hell, no. About the bomb? Hell, yes. It has me scared silly. About him . . . whoever the hell he is, Russian or Nazi . . . hell, yes. About . . ." But he had run out of steam.

"I want you to remain frightened, captain. I want you to remain scared silly, because I think you're the only one around here who understands what could happen if something went wrong with the test. We're counting pretty heavily on it."

"The Germans surrendered two days ago."

"The Japs. If we have to invade the mainland, it'd mean a million or more casualties. Maybe another entire year of bloody fighting. We've had enough."

"The bomb is going to end it?"

"Truman thinks so."

"And you?"

"I'm an officer, not a politician. I told you that before," Groves said. Once again he glanced over at Lovelace. "Don't give up on me now."

Lovelace had to smile at that. "A few minutes ago you told me I had lost touch with reality. Which is it to be, general? Do you want a crazy man working for you?"

Up ahead of them, a couple of miles, parked on either

side of the road, were a number of army trucks and cars, and a canvas lean-to shelter.

Groves slowed down. "I don't know whether the attempt on mine and Oppie's lives was a Nazi or a Russian operation. I guess I don't want to know," he said. He was staring straight ahead. "When I said you were losing touch with reality, I meant political reality."

Lovelace started to object, but Groves cut him off.

"I know what you were going to say, and I don't blame you. I've been spouting off about being a military man, and not a politician. But I'm also not blind. Something may be going on, Lovelace, and dammit, I do mean *may*, and I think the signals have been coming back pretty strong and clear that you're to keep your mouth shut about our allies."

"Find the spy, but don't name him."

Groves glanced over. "I don't know if you're serious now or not. But I am. And so is everyone else, as far as I can judge."

They had come to the vehicles at the sides of the road, and Groves stopped the car as a pair of military policemen approached. They saluted.

"I'm taking responsibility for this man," Groves said. "He'll be issued a badge at base camp."

"Yes, sir," the MP said, and he waved them on.

Groves put the car in gear and, a few hundred yards farther down the road, turned to the right down a wide dirt road that threaded its way through a series of hills and mesas, a long, low wall of mountains clearly visible far to the east across the desert.

After they had driven a few miles in silence, Lovelace lit another cigarette, inhaled, and then picked a bit of tobacco off his lower lip. "If there is a spy, I'm to find him but not name him. Once I find him I'm to kill him."

Groves turned white. "I never said that, captain."

"No," Lovelace said. "You never said that."

In the distance Lovelace could see swirls of dust marking a great deal of activity over a huge area, but since they were heading that way he did not ask about it.

"What I'm saying," Groves continued, "is that I don't want this test interfered with."

"Surely the site is being guarded?"

"Of course," Groves said. "By men on foot, by men in jeeps, on horseback, in airplanes. We're guarding the place."

Another thought struck Lovelace. "How do you suppose he knows so much about us? After all, he did trace you down to Santa Fe, and evidently boarded the train the same time as you and Oppenheimer."

"I'd just as soon not think about it."

"How the hell am I supposed to catch him if someone doesn't start thinking about it?"

"Possible traitors you're looking for? Someone feeding out the information?" Groves snapped bitterly. "Shall I start with suspicions about Oppenheimer himself and work down, or should I start with some of the lesser technicians who come from foreign countries and work my way up?"

Lovelace said nothing.

"Keep doing what you're doing. If he's here you'll find him. You did it once before."

"Then I should be back in Santa Fe and Albuquerque. If he's around, he'll be hiding there someplace until the day before the test."

"Agreed," Groves said, "but first I wanted you to see this."

The farther into the desert they went, the flatter the land became. Far to the south were several mountain peaks, and way off to the west, nearly lost in the distance, was another line of mountains. But to the east, what looked like ten or twelve miles away, was a solid wall of low mountains that seemed like one large cliff rising straight off the desert floor.

"The San Andres and Sierra Oscura mountains," Groves said. "They should block off much of the blast effect from the town of Bingham on the other side."

They turned left on an intersecting road, this one blacktopped recently, and once again Groves sped up. Now Lovelace could see dozens of trucks hauling supplies from the railhead twenty-five miles to the west, dozens of earth movers scraping new roads, jeeps bouncing across the desert in every direction, all at breakneck speed, men stringing wires on low poles as if their lives depended upon them completing their task within the next ten minutes, and then just off the road a huge concrete and earthenworks bunker was nearing completion, at least fifty men working on it.

"The west ten thousand," Groves said, as they slowly passed it. Several men looked up from their work and waved, but Groves kept his eyes on the road, his knuckles turning white from gripping the steering wheel.

They were driving due east now, directly toward the wall of mountains, and Lovelace could feel his gut tightening.

"That bunker we just passed," he said. "It'll be used for test instruments?"

Groves did not take his eyes off the road. "Mostly cameras and searchlights, plus personnel. The north ten thousand bunker will be used for shock-recording instruments and searchlights, and the south ten thousand for the main controls. There are five other bunkers, unmanned, closer in, just for equipment."

Lovelace turned in his seat and looked back toward the massive bunker they had passed. "Ten thousand yards from ground zero?" he asked softly.

"Yes," Groves said.

Lovelace turned back. "In God's name, how big is this thing going to be? Ten thousand yards from ground zero and you're building a bunker strong enough to withstand a direct hit by a blockbuster. What are you people building?"

Still Groves did not turn his gaze from the road. "We

have no idea how big it will be. Or even if it will explode."

"How far is base camp from ground zero, then . . ." Lovelace started to ask, but the words died on his lips as he caught sight of a huge steel tower rising up from the desert directly ahead of them.

As they got closer, he could see dozens of workmen setting girders in place, installing guy wires, and running control cables to the tower base.

Groves licked his lips. "Can you feel it?" he asked.

"Ground zero?" Lovelace asked without turning, like Groves unable to tear his eyes away from the rising tower.

"The bomb will be hoisted to the top of the tower. It'll be a hundred feet up."

"And the nearest people will be ten thousand yards away?"

Groves nodded, as they pulled up near the tower and he shut off the car. For a long time they both stared at the work in progress, until two men broke away from the others, and came toward them.

"I've watched this entire thing develop, Lovelace, from the moment it was just a theory in a few scientists' minds, until this."

But Lovelace wasn't listening to the general. Instead he was staring across at the mountains. Groves had told him the bomb would be fired at night so that the light and heat it produced would be easier to accurately measure. He was also thinking about the fact that no one would be within ten thousand yards of the bomb just before it was triggered. That was five and a half miles.

But who would have the guts to come down from the mountains, cross the desert, and climb a hundred-foot tower? Either a fool or a very dedicated man.

Lovelace had the strangest feeling at that moment that the man he had seen clinging to the side of the train outside Springer was just such a person.

29

ALBUQUERQUE, NEW MEXICO

It was a much-shaken Lovelace who pulled up and parked in front of the seedy little hotel on First Street by the railroad tracks and hurried inside.

He had borrowed a car and left Trinity at 7:30 P.M., making the long drive in record time. It was just 10:00 P.M. now, and Bobby Cripps, one of the CIC creeps assigned to his team, was waiting for him. He looked relieved when he saw Lovelace.

"Am I ever glad to see you, captain," he said, coming across from the desk. "All hell has broken loose down here."

No one else was in the lobby except for a bedraggled old man behind the counter, who was looking at them with sad eyes. "How about him?" Lovelace asked, keeping his voice low.

"Sergio Valdez. The hotel desk clerk. He's the one who discovered the body and called the police."

"Anyone else in on this?"

"A whole truckload, I'm afraid," Cripps said. "They

sent out a couple of uniformed cops, who took one look, realized it was murder, and called in the detectives. When they got here they called the coroner, the police lab people, and the photographer. The newspaper picked it up and sent a man . . ."

Lovelace interrupted. "Where the hell are all these people now, Bobby?"

"We've got them upstairs," Cripps said. "Stewart is with them."

"With the body?" Lovelace asked incredulously.

Cripps shook his head. "No, sir, in a room across the hall. The detectives began searching the place before everyone started showing up and found the notes mentioning Los Alamos. They called us right away and sealed off the room."

"Thank god for small favors." Again he looked over at the desk clerk. "How much does he know?"

"Not a thing, except he's got a body in one of his rooms that a lot of people are interested in."

"Where is it?"

"Third floor."

"All right, let's go up and take a look before we see the others."

Cripps led the way to the elevator, and they rode up to the third floor. A uniformed policeman greeted them when the elevator doors opened, and beyond him Lovelace could see another cop standing guard in front of a room door.

"Captain Lovelace," Cripps said to the cop, who stood aside.

"Has the hotel been searched?" Lovelace asked.

"Room by room," Cripps said, as they went down the hall. The cop by the door stood aside as they approached. He looked bored.

"Anyone been in this room since it was sealed off?" Lovelace asked.

"No, sir."

"Keep it that way."

Cripps opened the door and the stench hit them immediately. They went inside, Lovelace first, Cripps closing the door behind them. The room was small and was furnished only with a narrow bed, a dresser, a small table, and a rickety wooden chair. The place had obviously been searched. Thoroughly.

"How long has he been dead?" Lovelace asked.

"Twenty-four hours, no more," Cripps said. He indicated the bathroom. "He's in there. His bowels loosened up when he died. That's what you're smelling."

Lovelace nodded, went across the room and looked in at the body contorted in the tub. The man's eyes were open, and blood was crusted around his mouth where he had bitten through his tongue. A radio, still plugged into the wall by the sink, was lying in the water. The stench in the bathroom was overpowering. Lovelace backed out into the room and closed the door.

"Have we got an ID on him yet?"

"Lawrence Tragger. Conscientious objector, laborer. Boston. The FBI dug the file out on him pretty fast."

Lovelace looked sharply at the man. "The FBI is in on this as well?"

"They haven't been told a thing. The request came from the Albuquerque police. They got the name off the man's driver's license."

"I thought they didn't touch anything."

"They didn't once they found the notes taped to the dresser drawer bottom."

Lovelace looked over at the bureau from which three of the four drawers had been pulled out and stacked upside-down on the floor. "All right, let's see it."

Cripps went over to the bed and pulled aside the covers. Laid out in neat rows were at least twenty sheets of white, unlined paper filled with what appeared to be hastily scribbled notes, diagrams, and several maps.

Lovelace stood next to Cripps looking down at the notes, and he was about to tell the CIC man to bundle them up when one of the sheets caught his eye. He reached down and picked it up, sweat suddenly popping out on his forehead.

It was a map, with the city of Albuquerque clearly marked at the top center. The Trinity test site was shaded in crosshatch marks, and the exact location of the bomb tower was pinpointed by a small dot. A route was penciled in from the railroad siding to the west of the tower, across the desert, around the west ten thousand bunker, and to the tower itself.

Lovelace stared at the roughly drawn map for a long time, conscious of nothing other than the sight of the tower in his mind's eye, and of the mountains to the east, and the fact that the nearest manned bunker was ten thousand yards out.

He finally looked at Cripps. "These look like copies," he said softly.

"That's what I figured."

"I mean copies of the originals he probably already delivered."

Cripps was nodding. "He may have been planning on playing both ends against the middle."

"But he delivered the originals already. Our man has got the originals."

"More than likely."

Lovelace's breath was coming shallowly now. All these months the man and the woman had been laying low. Hiding. Waiting until just this moment. There was no doubt in his mind now that a sabotage attempt was going to be made. It was one thing to gather information on the bomb and send it back to the Germans or to the Soviet Union, but that would not have included the location of the tower. There would have been no need for that information unless they wanted to sabotage the test.

"He's here," Lovelace said very softly. "Christ, he's here in Albuquerque."

"We've got better than two months to find him," Cripps said.

"We won't, you know," Lovelace said. "Not unless he makes a mistake."

"He's made two already. The first on the train, and now this one."

Lovelace had turned around and was staring at the bureau. "The notes were taped to the underside of one of the drawers?" he asked.

"That's what the detectives told us."

"Then he hasn't made a mistake, at least not one that he knows of. As a matter of fact, he's covered his trail rather nicely."

"I don't follow you," Cripps said.

Lovelace looked at him. "Why did he kill his contact in there?"

"Because the man was playing both ends against the middle . . ." Cripps started to say, but then stopped in mid-sentence. "No, that's not right. If Tragger had said anything, made any indication that there was another set of notes for sale, our man would have found them."

"Right," Lovelace said. "So why kill this contact?"

"I don't know," Cripps said, confused. "It doesn't make any sense."

"Oh, yes, it does," Lovelace said. "Because Tragger was the only one in Albuquerque who knew of our man's existence. There will be no one here now to make a mistake. He and the woman are on their own."

"But he still doesn't know the date of the test."

Lovelace looked down at the notes. "If he's learned this much, he'll have a way of finding out that last bit of information. You can count on it."

"He'd never get in."

Lovelace smiled. "Yes, he will. He'll find a way unless we stop him first."

30

ALAMOGORDO BOMBING RANGE

Badim had gone exploring for the gold of San Vittorio Mountain.

The horse shivered beneath his legs and he reached down and gently patted the animal on the side of its powerful neck as he gauged the distance and height of the barbed wire fence the rancher had just jumped with his horse.

"Señor, come," the man called softly. He was drunk and his words were slurred.

It was after one in the morning. They had been out here for more than two hours and had covered, twelve miles or more from Oscuro.

Somewhere to the northwest, at least another eighteen miles over the Oscura Mountains, which they were approaching from the east, was Trinity. Straight ahead was a place the rancher had called Mockingbird Gap, which was a low cut through the mountains, and somewhere to the south was San Vittorio and a billion dollars in gold bullion.

Jada had come up with the idea two days after he had gotten the envelope from his contact in Albuquerque, but at first he had ignored her suggestion.

For a couple of days she had sulked around their apartment, her mood volatile partly because of the advanced stage of her pregnancy, and partly because of her intense desire, all of a sudden, to help him finish this job.

Finally, if for no other reason than to keep the peace with her, he had agreed to listen, and what she had laid out for him was nothing less than amazing.

Out of self-defense against boredom during the long days while Badim was away selling Bibles to the ranchers south of town, Jada had spent some time at the public library and at the State Historical Society.

Albuquerque and the area had intrigued her, and she had wanted to learn more about its history. It was during one of these forays that she had discovered the story of the gold of San Vittorio. When Badim had shown her the map pinpointing the Trinity site, she had seen exactly how he would be able to get to the tower, with a fail-safe if he was discovered.

In the sixteenth century, when the Spaniards had had missions in Mexico, a group of monks discovered a rich vein of gold, which they mined, reducing the ore to ingots.

The Spanish government got wind of the monks' cache of gold and sent troops to fetch it for the king and queen. The monks, however, had no intention of giving up their wealth. Instead they loaded the gold bullion on the backs of donkeys and headed north, up the desert, and into the San Andres and Oscura Mountains, through an area called Journada del Muerto . . . Journey of Death.

The monks, so the legend went, hid the gold in a cave in or near San Vittorio Mountain, and then perished in the desert trying to return to their monastery in Mexico.

For nearly four centuries the gold had remained hidden, although many expeditions were sent to search for it.

In the 1920s, a local rancher was said to have found the cache of gold, and had brought one ingot out of the mountains to prove it. But he was killed in a barroom brawl before he could tell anyone the exact location.

San Vittorio, Jada excitedly pointed out, was less than twenty-five miles south of the Trinity site.

It had taken Badim nearly a week to find the right man: a rancher who knew the area well, who was not afraid of the government, which had cordoned off the entire Journada del Muerto, and who had enough greed to keep his mouth shut.

He jammed the heels of his boots into the horse's flanks, and the animal shot forward, easily clearing the fence, and a moment later he and the rancher, Victor Gonzales Reyes, continued through the rugged desert, skirting the southern edge of the Oscuro peaks, and entering the eastern flank of Mockingbird Gap.

They had gone another six miles in silence, only the horses' hooves thudding softly against the desert hardpan, when Badim noticed a flash of light off to the north, and then a second and a third wavering flash. It looked to him like the headlights of a moving vehicle, but a long way off.

He pulled up even with Reyes, and pointed toward the lights. "What's down there?"

"Jesus motherfucking Christ, shut your mouth," Reyes ordered, pulling his horse up.

The rancher was looking down through the gap toward the desert. "Just a minute now and I'll show you, Bible man," he slurred, "but for the love of Mother Mary, keep quiet."

Badim followed the man farther down into the gap, until they came around the southern edge of the Oscura Range, the ground here hard and littered with huge stretches of lava flow.

Then he could see it. A long way off, down on the floor of the desert. A large group of lights to the south, which would be the base camp, and three, no four, other sets of lights, which from their position Badim guessed would be the north, south, and west bunkers, as well as the tower itself.

He could feel his heart accelerating. His mouth was dry. He took the canteen hanging from his saddle horn, unscrewed the cap, and drank deeply as he kept his eyes on the sight far below.

The bomb was relatively simple, according to the notes he had gotten from his contact. Two hemispheres of pure plutonium, which were coming down from the separation plant at Hanford, Washington, would be set in close proximity to each other, at the center of which would be a device called the initiator.

Surrounding the plutonium spheres was a spherical array of ordinary TNT charges that were shaped in the form of magnifying lenses.

Each of the charges was connected with a timer-detonator, and the entire assembly was encased in a steel jacket.

When the TNT charges were set off, in a very precise order, the blast would force the plutonium spheres together into a critical mass within a millionth of a second, crushing the initiator, which would then release a stream of neutrons—nuclear bullets, the scientists were calling them. This would create a sudden, runaway chain reaction that in turn would, it was hoped, create an explosion of up to twenty thousand tons of TNT.

If the timing of the lens-shaped TNT charges was off, by even the slightest fraction of a second, the bomb would melt . . . not explode.

On the surface, the plan Runkov had worked out for Badim was simple.

The bomb was to be placed on a steel tower one hundred feet off the desert floor, with the nearest manned bunker a little less than six miles away. At least one hour before the blast, the tower area would be cleared, and it would be during this time that Badim would sneak under cover of darkness to the tower, climb to the top, and simply switch a few of the detonator wires that were attached to the TNT lenses.

He would then climb back down the tower and get away.

The bomb would not explode, so there would be no real danger to Badim even if he was only a few hundred yards away when the switch was thrown. But the bomb would melt, completely destroying all evidence of his sabotage. The scientists would be led to believe that the bomb design had failed, and a new design and test would not be ready in time to circumvent the invasion of the Japanese mainland. It would also give the Soviets more time to finish their own bomb.

"That's the fucking government down there," Reyes said softly, and Badim looked at him.

"What are they doing?" he asked. Reyes was a man who had no regard for his own government, and Badim found it distasteful being with him.

Reyes looked at him and smiled. "Heh," he said. "They're building submarines. Go like the devil wind. They're using the power of the atom."

Badim was startled, and it evidently showed on his face because Reyes pointed a finger at him.

"Reyes doesn't always tell the truth you know, gringo. You have to keep on your toes. Nobody gets up earlier than Reyes. Don't forget it when we find the gold." He reined his horse around savagely, cutting the animal's mouth with the bit. "Come on, motherfucker, we're going to find us some gold."

31

ALBUQUERQUE, NEW MEXICO

The nurse helped Jada down from the examining table when the doctor was gone, then busied herself tidying up the room, putting away instruments and changing the paper sheet over the leather cover as Jada went behind the screen to dress.

"When you're finished, dear, doctor would like to see you in his office," the nurse called to her. "It's just across the hall."

Jada peeked around the screen. "Is there something the matter?" she asked, suddenly worried.

"Heavens, no," the nurse said, looking up from her work. She was a large-boned woman with a pleasant face and red hands. "He just wants to talk with you, is all. Probably will write you a prescription of some sort."

"I see," Jada said uncertainly, and she stepped into her underpants, then pulled on the half slip, and then the maternity skirt, tieing it in the front in a bow.

As she buttoned up the loose smock, and stepped into her flats, she began to imagine all sorts of things wrong with her baby. And for just a moment she had a powerful dread of crossing the hallway and entering the doctor's office.

She had heard some of the other women out in the waiting room talking about sisters or cousins or friends who had had troubles with their babies—stillbirths, deformities, blindness, retardation, and some things even worse.

She had tried to block out those conversations from her mind, but each time she came here, it seemed like the same women were sitting in the same chairs and couches, saying the same kinds of things. And now she was beginning to wonder if she wasn't carrying some kind of monster.

Her back ached, her belly seemed to be stretched so tightly that it would split at any moment, her breasts were heavy and tender, and now she was sore where the doctor had examined her.

Tears began slipping down her cheeks and suddenly the nurse had come around the corner, clucking solicitously.

"There, there," the woman crooned, holding Jada for a moment. "We're ugly and fat, and we don't feel good, we ache all over, and no one loves us . . . that's it, isn't it?"

Jada looked up at her, and had to smile, but the tears continued nevertheless.

The nurse led her around the screen and at the door she pulled a handkerchief from her pocket and dried Jada's tears. "Your first one, isn't it?"

Jada nodded. "Yes," she said softly. "But what if something is wrong with my baby? What if it's . . ."

The nurse looked at her sharply. "The doctor will probably be giving you iron tablets to build up your blood, but I have my own prescription for you." She leaned a little closer. "Don't listen to those old hags out in the waiting room. The only thing they manage to do well is gossip."

Jada had to laugh, suddenly understanding just how silly she had been. "Thank you," she said.

"Chin up," the nurse said, and she opened the door for Jada. "Right across the hall. Doctor is waiting for you."

"Thank you," Jada said again, and she went across the hall, knocked once at the doctor's door, and opened it.

The doctor was seated behind his desk, staring at what looked like a photograph, as a tall man stood watching him. They both looked up when she came in.

"Excuse me," she said, and started to back out of the office, but the doctor had gotten to his feet.

"No, that's all right, Mrs. Bradley, come in. This gentleman was just leaving."

The man nodded politely as Jada came all the way in, crossed the room, and sat down in a chair that he held for her.

"I'm afraid I can't be much help to you," the doctor was saying. He looked at the photograph one last time, then handed it over to the man, giving Jada a brief glimpse of it, and her heart seemed to leap up into her throat.

It was a photograph of two sketches, sketches of her and Alek. They knew! Somehow they knew, and they were here in Albuquerque looking for them.

"Well, thanks anyway, doc, sorry to have bothered you," the man said, and he turned to Jada and nodded. "Ma'am," then he was gone, and the doctor was sitting down, pulling Jada's file to him and opening it.

Her heart was beating rapidly, her breath was shallow and her hands were cold and sweaty. They knew!

The doctor looked up, sudden concern in his eyes. "Are you feeling all right, Mrs. Bradley?" he asked.

She nodded, barely trusting herself to speak. "I'm fine," she mumbled. "Just a little nauseous."

"Would you like to lie down for a moment?"

She shook her head. "No . . . I'll be fine."

The doctor smiled. "If it's any consolation, it happens to a lot of women." He looked again at her chart. "I'd say you have about thirty-five days yet." He counted from a desk calendar. "July nineteenth, perhaps the twentieth."

They knew their faces. It was all she could think about as the doctor prescribed several medications he wanted her to take to build up what he was terming a slight anemia.

"Nothing out of the ordinary," he was saying finally, and then they were standing, and he had come around his desk to show her to the door.

She had to think. She had to use her head, and not fall apart. Alek's life depended upon it. "I hope I wasn't interrupting anything," she said, trying to keep her voice nonchalant.

For a moment the doctor apparently did not know what she was talking about, but then understanding dawned on his face. "The soldier," he said.

"Soldier?"

He nodded. "Looking for a couple of murderers, or spies, or something. Wondered if I had seen either of them."

"I see," Jada said, her knees weak.

"Take care of yourself now," the doctor said. "Plenty of rest, plenty of liquids, and stick with your diet. I'll want to see you back here next Friday."

Her doctor's appointment had been for 9:00 A.M., and it was just noon when she got off the bus and walked the last two blocks to their apartment. She let herself in and locked the door behind her.

Alek would be gone for the entire weekend. Before he had left yesterday evening, he had told her that he and Reyes would be spending the entire weekend in the mountains, and would not be coming out until late Sunday night or sometime Monday morning before dawn.

He had been excited, showing her on a map how he

had planned to get within a couple of miles east of the tower and hide until everyone cleared out and went back to the protection of the bunkers.

Meanwhile, he said, he would have to keep Reyes convinced that they were actually looking for the gold.

"But after this weekend, Larissa, when we find nothing, I'm going to tell Reyes that I'm giving it up. That my nerves can't take all that prowling around on government land."

"Then what?" she had asked him. They were lying together in the big bed.

He was on his back, smoking a cigarette, staring up at the ceiling. "I won't need him any longer. As soon as Yakovlev comes up with the exact time and date for the test, I'll rent a horse . . . I've already seen to it. You'll drop me off at Oscuro, I'll get to the tower and switch the wires and return to Oscuro, where you'll be waiting to pick me up. Shouldn't take more than twelve hours at the outside."

"Then back to Moscow," Jada had said, watching the smoke curl up from his cigarette.

He rolled over so that he was propped up on one elbow facing her, and he looked deeply into her eyes. "Alek and Larissa and baby makes three. Back to Moscow."

She had fallen asleep soon after that, and when she awoke a couple of hours later he was gone.

And now, what were they going to do? They had figured the baby would be born sometime around the middle of August, giving them plenty of time to get out of the States beforehand. But now, if the doctor was correct and her baby was due much sooner, that would be impossible.

On top of all that, the army knew their faces, and knew, or at least suspected, that they were here in Albuquerque.

She turned on the radio, found a station playing music that wasn't Mexican, and then went into the kitchen to make a cup of tea as she tried to think this thing out.

The mission would have to be scrubbed after all. There was no help for it. The army knew they were here, and probably knew why they were here. The man in the car who had fired at Alek on the train was probably behind it. Alek had suspected the man had seen his face.

She closed her eyes tightly as she felt the baby moving, a foot or a fist jamming into her ribs.

Alek was relatively safe for the moment, out of Albuquerque. But once he got back on Sunday night or early Monday morning he would be in danger again.

She laid her right hand on her stomach, and could feel the new life stirring within her. It was pleasurable, more deeply pleasurable and satisfying than anything she could imagine.

When Alek returned they would have to leave. Call their contact in New York to arrange for transportation out of the country, and then get out quickly.

Yet she could not travel like this. Especially not with the possibility that they could run into some trouble.

Dear god, she thought, as a very dark, foreboding image swam into her mind.

She turned off the burner under the pot, the thought of tea suddenly not very appealing, and went back into their tiny living room, where she stood looking toward the front door.

"Alek," she said, half to herself. "Aleksandr." How she loved him. How she loved the baby in her womb. How she had loved their life in Newport News.

For a few wild seconds she thought she had a solution to their problem. The Soviet Union and the United States were still allies, so what she and Alek had been doing here really wasn't spying. They could turn themselves in and trade amnesty for everything they knew about the NKVD and Runkov's GRU operations.

But then she remembered poor Harvey Dansig. And she remembered their War Department contact, and the hotel clerk, and the two MPs. Alek had told her about them. He was a murderer.

She stared hard at the front door, willing Alek to come home, to open the door and take her into his arms this instant. But nothing happened. The door remained closed.

With her right hand on her distended belly, she turned finally and went into the bedroom, her movements rigid, mechanical. From the closet shelf she pulled out a small suitcase, and laid it open on the bed. Then she went to the bureau and took out her nightgown and some clean underwear, which she packed in the suitcase. From the closet she took down a pair of lightweight slacks and a blouse that she had worn before she was pregnant, and packed them as well.

When she had the suitcase closed, she picked it up, grabbed her purse from the coffee table in the living room, and opened the front door.

The radio was still playing, but she ignored it as she debated for a moment whether to leave Alek a note. She was sure she would be back before he returned, so she went out, carefully locked the door behind her, and then trudged slowly the two blocks to the bus stop.

The day was bright and warm, but to her it seemed dark and cold, and somehow hopeless.

The city bus came a few minutes later, and she climbed up, paid her fare, and sat in one of the back seats for the ride downtown.

For a while, as she watched the houses out the window, she thought about Brighton, and the beach, and for that time she felt calm, and unafraid. If her father were alive now, he would know what to do. She could call him and he would tell her what was necessary.

She could almost hear him now, his voice clearly recognizable, but she couldn't quite make out the words he was saying. She strained to listen, but it was no use, and gradually the image faded.

Alek loved this baby as much as she did. In some

respects, even more. But she would have to make him understand that as much as she loved their baby, she loved Alek even more.

She got off the bus at Second and Silver across from the Trailways Bus Depot, crossed the street, and went inside to one of the ticket counters.

An old man, thin, with a bald head and thick glasses, looked up. "Yes, ma'am," he said.

"I'd like a ticket to Juárez," Jada said softly. Her knees felt like rubber.

The clerk took a blank ticket from a slot, and began writing on it. "Round trip?"

"Yes."

"When will you be returning?"

"Sunday," she said. "Sunday afternoon."

BOOK FIVE

JULY 12–16, 1945

32

MOSCOW

Sergei Dmitrevich Runkov stood by the barred window in a small room on the second floor of the Lubyanka Compound looking across the cobblestoned courtyard. From where he stood he could just make out the edge of the black statue of Felix Dzerzhinsky, the founder of the State Secret Police, and over the wall the Polytechnic Museum a few blocks away.

He was confused in some ways. He had served his country well during and since the Revolution, and was willing to continue serving his country in any capacity.

But there was something else happening, something much larger than him and the project, and as frightening as the prospect seemed, perhaps even larger and more powerful than Stalin himself.

The gates opened below in the courtyard, and a canvas-topped lend-lease truck pulled through the opening. It swung around and stopped so that its tailgate was facing the outer wall about fifteen meters away.

The Berias and Merkulovs of the world were the true

survivors, he thought, as he watched two soldiers jump down from the cab of the truck. He was merely a fighter.

He had only two real regrets at the moment—for Sergeant Doronkin, who had chosen to be loyal to the wrong master, and for the fact that he would never know the real reason they were being executed.

The project, which was nearing its final hours, was only a small part of some other much larger scheme . . . he was almost certain of that now. But what was confusing was the apparent fact that Stalin was only a pawn. The supreme Soviet leader himself did not have all the answers.

Who did, then? And what was the larger scheme?

He focused again on the truck. The stage was set, he thought grimly, as he turned away from the window. The tray of food they had brought him an hour ago sat untouched on the low stool next to his cot. He had not been hungry, even though his stomach had rumbled all morning.

He crossed the small room to the tray, opened the bottle of vodka, and half-filled the metal cup with it.

There were no sheets or blankets on the bed. They had taken his belt and tie. The overhead lightbulb was encased in a sturdy wire mesh. They had given him no utensils with which to eat his food, and had given him a metal cup out of which to drink his liquor.

He smiled. Yet they had forgotten the glass bottle of vodka, although how anyone could break the bottle and then cut his own throat or wrist was beyond him. It was a distinct possibility, however, which despite their supposed meticulous attention to detail had completely escaped them.

He turned, drink in hand, to stare at his reflection in the polished metal mirror on the wall across the room.

His shirt collar was open, exposing a large, angry red welt on the side of his neck where the soldier had hit him with the butt of his rifle.

He toasted his reflection, drinking deeply, the vodka smelling and tasting faintly metallic from the cup.

Six days ago it had begun, he thought now, trying to make some sense of what had happened.

Doronkin had come into his office flustered. A series of files on the project were missing.

Runkov had immediately alerted Center Security, but no search had been ordered.

Next he had tried to get an audience with Stalin, but he was denied the request. Nor would Beria or Merkulov speak with him.

That night General Yenikeev was found dead, an apparent suicide, in his apartment on Kutuzovsky Prospekt.

And at that point Runkov began to become seriously concerned about his own safety. It seemed as if someone was closing all the doors on him, and he wanted to know why.

Two days ago he had gone into NKVD archives on a routine file search, but instead had begun looking through cross-references to the Trinity project. One name popped up from time to time in the supporting documents that made absolutely no sense to him.

In the signature block for the orders transferring the captured German submarine they had used on the project to the GRU was the name Leonid Ilyich Brezhnev, who was the chief of political administration for the Eighteenth Army.

Why was an army party hack involved with a highly sensitive secret service operation?

Later that day he had made some quiet inquiries about the man, but just yesterday an NKVD captain with four enlisted men, all of them armed, had come to Runkov's office and arrested him and Doronkin. The signature on the arresting orders had been Brezhnev's.

Footsteps sounded in the corridor, and he looked toward the heavy metal door. A moment later a key grated in the lock and the door swung open, two soldiers entering the room, while four others remained out in the hall, rifles at the ready.

"Dyee tyeh!" one of the men snapped nervously.

Runkov managed a slight smile. "It is time, comrade?" he asked in a clear voice.

A lieutenant also standing in the corridor poked his head through the doorway. "We wish no trouble, Major Runkov."

"It is you offering me the trouble, lieutenant," Runkov said, but he immediately tired of the little game. "If you are to shoot me, I'd rather it be with my sergeant out in the courtyard than in here. I'll come peacefully."

The soldiers were obviously relieved. Now, Runkov thought for just an instant, while their nerves were settling. But he just sighed, set his cup down on the stool, and stepped out into the corridor, three guards ahead of him, the three other with the lieutenant falling in behind.

As they walked down the long corridor, past the rows of cell doors, he thought about all that had happened since he had recalled Badim from Germany.

Most of all, at this moment, he thought about the men aboard the submarine, now lying dead at the bottom of the Atlantic somewhere off the coast of the United States.

Officially his and Doronkin's deaths had been ordered for the conspiracy to murder seventeen of their fellow officers and men aboard the sub. A measure that had caused Runkov great pain, but one that had nevertheless been authorized by Stalin himself as a necessity of war.

It had worked beautifully. Everything had worked except for the business with Groves' and Oppenheimer's assassination in New Mexico. That had been the only blot on the entire mission, and yet it had been a stroke of fortuitous luck.

Sabotage, not assassination, Stalin had ordered, and he and Doronkin had complied. Even now it was too late to recall Badim. Two weeks ago they had received the final word from Yakovlev in New York: the test shot was set for sometime in the early morning hours of Monday, July sixteenth.

One week ago Runkov had sent a terse message to Yakovlev that Badim was to be informed of the date and time, and then all further contact was to be eliminated until Badim and Jada requested a way home.

They came to the end of the corridor, turned left, and went down the stairs that led to the courtyard.

Everything was set. Badim could not fail.

At this moment the new American President, Harry Truman, was aboard the *Augusta* steaming across the Atlantic for Antwerp, where he would continue on to Potsdam to meet with Churchill and Marshal Stalin.

At Tinian, a tiny speck of coral in the Pacific, the men and aircraft of the 509th Composite Group were waiting for the arrival of the first atomic bombs, which they would drop on Japan.

From the latest intelligence reports Runkov had seen, four Japanese cities had been selected as possible targets—Hiroshima, Kokura, Niigata, and Nagasaki—two of which would be bombed.

Plans for the invasion of the Japanese mainland, code-named Downfall, had been drawn up by the American military establishment, which was still almost completely unaware of what was happening in the New Mexican desert.

If Badim was successful, and the test shot was a failure, then Downfall would be carried out with the Soviet Union waiting in the wings to grab off her share of the Japanese empire, as they were doing in Europe.

All was going well. Very well. And yet . . .

They had come to the ground floor, where the guards opened a door and stepped outside, Runkov following.

Sergeant Doronkin had already been escorted out into the courtyard, and he stood near the wall, facing the truck's tailgate, smoking a cigarette. When he saw Runkov he threw the cigarette aside and stiffened to attention.

The day was bright, a warm breeze smelling of the river pleasant against Runkov's face. He hesitated a moment just outside the door and turned to the lieutenant.

"What time is it?"

The lieutenant, a young man with pockmarks on his face, looked sharply at Runkov for a moment, and then, evidently deciding it was not some kind of a trick, looked at his watch. "Two minutes before noon, comrade major."

Runkov breathed deeply of the fresh air, and then he and his guards continued across the courtyard to where Doronkin stood, his back barely a half-meter from the already bullet-scarred wall.

"Good morning, Vladimir Nikhailovich," Runkov said, as if this was nothing more than a chance meeting of an old friend.

Doronkin nodded, but did not speak, his Adam's apple bobbing up and down. Runkov moved closer to him, then reached out and hugged him, and then kissed him on the lips.

When they parted there were tears in Doronkin's eyes. "I am sorry, major . . ."

"Not to be sorry, Vladimir. We have done our job well. The mission will come out. And maybe after all is said and done, we will end up knowing more than the rest of them put together."

"Do you wish a cigarette, comrade major?" the lieutenant asked, his voice shaking.

Runkov turned calmly to the man. "No, you little faggot, I do not wish a cigarette."

"Bind them," the lieutenant snapped, red-faced.

Two guards came forward and quickly tied Runkov's and Doronkin's hands behind their backs.

"Do either of you wish blindfolds?"

Runkov shook his head, and a moment later so did Doronkin.

"You know, Vladimir," Runkov began conversationally, "I have been doing some thinking, now that the war is nearly over, that a vacation on the Caspian would be pleasant."

The tailgate on the truck clanged open and Doronkin flinched, but his eyes never left Runkov's. "Why are they really executing us?" he asked.

"It is simple," Runkov said, as he heard the slide snap back on the machine gun mounted in the rear of the truck. "But it is something I only recently figured out . . ."

The .50-caliber bullets tore into Doronkin, killing him instantly, and a fraction of a second later Runkov felt the wind being knocked out of him as something hard and very hot slammed into his stomach, his chest, and then his neck, and his last conscious thought was about the soldier whose nose he had broken when the man had tried to arrest him yesterday. . . .

33

Now that they were so close to going home, Jada had
lost all of her fear. An icy calmness had descended over
her, settling her nerves, making her less jumpy and taking away some of the sorrow for the thing she had done
in Juárez five weeks ago.

She was in the kitchen making up a large packet of
sandwiches, but she stopped a moment and looked out
the window at the neighborhood children playing base-
ball in the sandlot next door.

Most of the pain from the induced labor had stopped
by the first week, and the soreness had gradually faded
as well over the following days. Yet she and Alek had
not made love since then.

It had been a stunning blow to him, and at this moment she could still see the expression on his face and
hear his first words when she had returned to their apartment that Sunday evening.

He had been waiting for her in the dark, and she had

not seen him until she had closed and locked the door behind her and turned on the light.

The color had instantly drained from his face, and he had stood up. "My god," he said, "you've killed our baby."

"Alek," she said, taking a step closer. "I had to," she cried. "They have our pictures. They know we're here. I had to do it. It was for you."

Badim looked at her for a long moment, every muscle in his body tense, but he made no move to come to her, nor did he say anything. Instead he turned away, went into the kitchen, and poured himself a half-tumbler of brandy, which he drank in one swallow.

She came to the kitchen door, her insides on fire, her head buzzing, and her knees weak. "I love you," she said.

He turned to her. "Why, Larissa? Why did you do such a thing?"

"There was a man at the doctor's office with sketches of our faces. He was from the army. They know we're here in Albuquerque."

Badim seemed to think for a moment. "How did you see the sketches?"

"The man was in the doctor's office when I came in. I saw the sketches there."

"Did the man see you?" Badim asked, absolutely no inflection in his voice. "I mean, did he get a clear look at your face?"

She nodded weakly, but suddenly understanding flashed into her mind like a bright explosion. The man had seen her face and yet he had not recognized her. And looking at Alek, she could see that his beard and long gray hair made him nearly unrecognizable.

It had been for nothing. She had killed their baby for nothing. "No," she had cried weakly, and she'd fallen to the floor in a faint.

Today was the fifteenth of July, and in five days, she thought with sadness, she would have had their baby.

"How's it coming in there?" Badim called from the bedrôom, and she looked up.

"Just about finished," she said loudly enough for him to hear. "What time do we have to leave?" She looked over at the kitchen clock on top of the icebox. It was 3:00 P.M.

"Not for another two hours," Badim said. He had come to the doorway from the living room, and she snapped around with a start.

"I . . . I'm just about done with your lunch," she said.

His eyes flickered to the counter, where the four meat and cheese sandwiches she had made were wrapped in waxed paper. "Wait," he said, and he turned and left the kitchen.

A moment later she could hear cloth tearing, and then he was back with a large, ragged piece from one of their bed sheets. He handed it to her.

"Wrap the sandwiches in this. Waxed paper makes too much noise."

She managed a slight smile. "They'll dry out," she said.

"I want to live long enough to eat them. No waxed paper."

"Yes, Alek," she said, averting her eyes.

He sighed deeply. "When you're finished in here, Larissa, come into the other room. There's something I have to say to you."

It was the first time he had used that name in five weeks, and she looked up, but he had already turned and was going into the other room.

"Alek . . ." she said.

"Finish what you were doing first," he said without looking back, and then he was around the corner.

She stared at the doorway for a moment, and through it into the living room. The radio was turned to a news broadcast, and she heard the words Potsdam, and the names Truman, Churchill, and Stalin, but she paid no attention to it as she turned back to the counter, unwrapped the sandwiches from the waxed paper, and bundled them up as best she could in the cloth.

When she was finished, she took a deep breath, let it out slowly, and then turned and marched resolutely out of the kitchen, around the corner, and into their bedroom, where Alek was just reassembling his Luger.

He looked up when she came in, set the gun down, and took the sandwiches from her, stuffing them carelessly into a small, dark-brown canvas pack.

"Do you want a cup of tea or something?" Jada asked as she watched him.

"Nothing," he said, without turning around. He picked up his Luger again and screwed the silencer on its barrel, then snapped a magazine of cartridges in the handle, and put the gun in the pack, folding the flap over the top. Then he set the pack on the floor at the foot of the bed.

He looked around the room critically, as if he was searching for something, then turned and brushed past Jada, going into the living room, which he also inspected. He did the same in the kitchen, and when he returned to the bedroom he seemed satisfied.

"When we leave here this evening, we're not coming back," he said by way of explanation. "I don't want anything left behind that would give us away. We'll need at least a week to get up to New York and then out of the country."

For a moment she didn't know him. He had the same expression in his eyes that he had had when Harvey Dansig died, and when he had killed their Washington contact, and again just before he climbed up on the roof of the train.

He was a professional. A trained saboteur. A trained spy. A murderer.

She half turned away, but Badim came across the room, took her by the hand, and led her to the bed, where he made her sit down.

He squatted down in front of her on his haunches so

that her face was a little bit higher than his, and looked up into her eyes, his hands resting lightly on her knees.

"I have a lot to say to you, my little Larissa, and there isn't much time," he began.

"Alek, I . . ."

"No, Larissa, I want you to listen to me very carefully, because our lives may depend upon at least part of what I am going to tell you."

She blinked, but said nothing. She loved him so desperately; if only he would forgive her, everything would be all right. There would be nothing they couldn't do together.

"Are you listening to me?"

She nodded. "Yes."

"All right, then. We're going to leave here at five o'clock, and drive immediately down to Oscuro. We should get there by ten or ten-thirty. But there will probably be roadblocks between here and there, with many military men. They'll be excited about the upcoming test and it'll be dark, so they will not recognize us."

Jada could feel her stomach beginning to churn, and Alek tightened his grip on her knees.

"You're going to have to keep yourself together. We're a couple on vacation. We're going down to El Paso. We have hotel reservations there."

"Yes," she said weakly. He had taken a bath earlier, and he smelled fresh and clean now. She wanted to reach out and touch his cheek with her fingertips, but she didn't dare.

"I'm going to get out of the car near Oscuro, and you're going to continue down to El Paso alone, where you will check into the hotel. If the night clerk asks any questions about why your husband isn't with you, tell him that I was delayed and will arrive in a day or two."

She nodded again. Pregnant, and so close to delivery, she could not have driven the car tonight. And yet they had wanted a boy who would have grown up strong and tall like his father.

"In the morning you will drive back up to Oscuro, where I will be waiting at the coffee shop on the main street. Be there by ten o'clock."

She had been looking at his hair, wishing that it was its natural color, and the length he normally wore it, when the things he was telling her penetrated. "What if something goes wrong?" she asked, suddenly frightened for him. "What if you're not there?"

He smiled, but the expression was not a happy one. "The hotel room I reserved for us faces north. I want you to be up from three in the morning until dawn. If the bomb goes off, you'll see the flash. I'm sure of it."

"If it goes off . . ." Jada said, half rising from the bed, but Badim pushed her back down.

"If the bomb goes off, Larissa, it will mean I was not successful. In that event, you are to drive immediately to New York, make contact, and return home."

She was shaking her head. "No, Alek, I will not leave without you."

"Yes," he snapped, his voice like a pistol shot. "You will do exactly as you are told for once."

The rebuke stung.

"If the bomb does not go off, I will be at the coffee shop by ten. If I am not there, you will wait one half-hour, no more, and then you will continue on to New York alone. Is that clear?"

"Yes," she said dully. She felt light-headed, and distant. It seemed as if Alek's face was at the end of a very long tunnel. His mouth was opening and closing, and she strained to hear what he was saying.

". . . one last thing I have to tell you, Larissa," he was saying. "I love you."

For a moment she wasn't certain that she had heard him correctly, and she held her breath.

"I love you more than I could ever properly express," he continued, the expression on his face much softer now, much less the professional. "And I loved our baby that you were carrying, but I understand why you did what you did. It was necessary. But if there was anything within my power that I could do to change it, to take away the hurt you must have felt, must still be feeling, I would."

Jada was crying, she could feel the tears slipping down her cheeks. "I love you, Aleksandr," she cried. "God, how I love you."

And then he had gotten to his feet and they were in each other's arms, kissing deeply, holding onto each other, and he was lifting her up and laying her on the bed, pulling her blouse over her head, undoing her bra, and kissing her breasts, her nipples, and then her belly.

And she forgot then about the danger, about the roadblocks, about the atomic bomb on the desert, and even about the baby, because Aleksandr loved her.

Lovelace had done everything humanly possible to find the man and woman, and make it impossible for them to interfere with the test. And yet he knew that he had not done nearly enough.

Every cop in Albuquerque had been supplied with a photograph of the sketches of the two, who were being identified as murderers, and for the past seven weeks they had kept a constant watch on the railway and bus depots, on the airport, on the car rental and sales lots, on the hotels and boardinghouses, on restaurants and coffee shops, on doctors' offices and hospitals (in case either of them got hurt), and had even searched abandoned buildings and ranches within a twelve-mile radius of the city.

Earlier this afternoon, CIC Captain Rhodes, whom everyone called Dusty, had left Los Alamos with a contingent of twenty-five creeps, supposedly to monitor fallout in the area when the bomb went off, and to help evacuate civilians if necessary. Their real mission was to find the man and woman before the rest.

Here in Albuquerque, up in Santa Fe, and in each of the small towns ringing Trinity—Socorro, San Antonio,

Bingham, Carrizozo, Oscuro, Three Rivers, Tularosa, Truth or Consequences, and a dozen others—two or more creeps were stationed with fallout monitoring equipment. They also had been supplied with the photograph and the instructions, "Shoot first, ask questions later."

Closer to Trinity itself, on the bombing range, roadblocks had been set up every six miles or so, stopping all traffic. The MPs had the photograph. In addition, checkpoints had been set up on the surrounding highways.

At Trinity, there were more than three dozen MPs constantly searching the desert—some driving jeeps on which spotlights had been mounted, and others on horseback. They did not need the photograph, and their instructions were much simpler: "If it moves, shoot it."

Groves had flown in from Riverside, California, around noon, along with a number of scientists and other VIPs who had been in on the planning stages of the bomb from the beginning; most of the other project scientists and technicians had already been bused down from Los Alamos.

Everything was ready. But Lovelace had the strong feeling that he had forgotten something, that he had overlooked some crucial detail, leaving a hole a hundred yards wide for his man to slip through.

Yet he could not seem to make his mind focus on that one thing. For some reason he was drawing a blank.

The elevator doors slid open on the Hilton Hotel's lobby, and he stepped out, stopping around the corner to light a cigarette as he inspected his image in one of the tall mirrors.

He was dressed in civvies. They were a mess; his suitcoat rumpled, his shirt wrinkled and stained with food and cigarette burns, and his tie loose. His hair was tousled, and his eyes were red-rimmed and bloodshot.

"Not really that bad," he told himself, "for a scared-shitless man who hasn't had a decent night's sleep in a year, and no sleep in the last forty-eight hours."

He inhaled deeply, the smoke burning deep into his lungs, and he coughed. On top of everything else he had been smoking too much, at least four packs of Luckies a day, so that now even his cigarettes tasted like hell.

He shrugged, turned away from the mirror, and started across the lobby toward the front doors. Upstairs in 518, Bobby Cripps was filling in the details for a half dozen other creeps who would act as roving monitors along Highways 85, 380, 54, and 70, which surrounded Trinity.

Two of them would remain in the room, which had been set up as the Albuquerque command center for the search.

Everything that could be done was being done. And yet . . .

Lovelace was halfway across the lobby when Cripps and one of the other CIC men burst out of the stairwell door and came across to him in a dead run.

"We've got them this time," Cripps said, out of breath.

"What have you got, Bobby?" Lovelace asked, forcing himself not to get excited. He had been on these wild goose chases before.

"We'll explain on the way," Cripps said in a rush. "Is your car out front?"

"Right," Lovelace said, and without another word the three of them hurried to the main street doors, went outside and piled into the front seat of Lovelace's government-issue four-door Dodge sedan.

"Where are we going?" Lovelace asked, as he started the car. The sky had clouded up and toward the south they could see occasional flashes of lightning. Just for a moment he wondered about the bomb, which had been hoisted to the top of the tower yesterday; it was equipped with an electrical detonator, was sitting atop a steel tower, and now there was lightning. The scientists, he suspected, were beginning to sweat.

"Four-oh-seven Dartmouth Avenue. It's on the east end, just off Garfield."

Lovelace pulled away from the curb and headed around the corner. "What's there?"

"An apartment," Cripps said.

"I'm sorry, captain," the other man said. "I should have been thinking, but she was pregnant and it just didn't dawn on me until just a few minutes ago when the doctor called."

Lovelace glanced over at the man. "Who the hell are you?"

"Sorry, sir," the man said. "I'm Tech Sergeant David Bates, assigned to . . ."

"Never mind the bullshit, Bates. I'm Lovelace, now what have you got? Tell me everything, but slowly and in some kind of chronological order."

"About five or six weeks ago I was given the photograph and assigned to check the local medical facilities. It was at Dr. Collin Smith's office that I saw her."

"You saw her?" Lovelace snapped. "The woman?"

"I think so," Bates said. "Or at least I'm fairly certain now."

"Go on," Lovelace said, pressing harder on the gas pedal.

"I was showing the photograph to the doctor, when this woman came in. She was pregnant. Her name was Bradley. I just didn't connect her with the photo. But I remember that she got a look at it, and she seemed like she was about ready to faint or something."

"Then what happened?" Lovelace asked. They had come to Garfield, and he turned east.

"I didn't think anything more about it until the doctor called this evening. He told me the Bradley woman had not shown up for her appointments since that day, which got him to thinking, and he remembered the photograph. He was almost certain it was the same woman."

"And you got the address from him?"

"Yes, sir."

They came to Dartmouth Avenue about the same time it started to drizzle, and Lovelace turned onto the street as he flipped on his windshield wipers. He doused the headlights in the three-hundred block.

"Four-oh-seven?" he asked.

"Yes, sir," Bates said, and Lovelace turned at the corner, parking a quarter of a block up the street.

"Has either of you got a gun?"

"I do," Cripps said, but Bates shook his head.

"All right, Bobby, you take the back entrance, if there is one. Just stay out of sight. If anyone comes your way, shoot. We'll shout, uh, Mickey Mouse, if we're heading your way. Bates can come with me."

Lovelace looked at his watch. It was just a couple of minutes past five.

"All right, let's go," he said, and the three of them got out of the car. Cripps disappeared into the shadows behind the line of two-story Spanish-style, stucco apartment houses, as Lovelace and Bates hurried back up to Dartmouth and then ran down the street, finding 407 three houses down.

They went up the sidewalk, which was heavily in the shadows of several thick trees, and stepped softly up onto the porch. There were no lights shining from any of the windows.

Two mailboxes were labeled, one with the name Ramierez for the ground floor 13 and the other with Bradley for upstairs.

The front door was unlocked, and Lovelace carefully opened it, stepping into the darkness of a hallway. A flight of stairs with a wrought-iron railing led up to an ornately carved wooden door.

Bates closed the front door softly behind him and Lovelace took out his .38, cocked the hammer, and started up, his heart pounding. They were too late, he could feel it. The man and woman were already on their way to Trinity.

At the head of the stairs, Lovelace motioned for Bates to stand to one side of the door, and when he was in place Lovelace stepped back and then rammed the door with his shoulder, once, twice, and on the third time the lock burst and he was inside, leaping to the left and then rolling to the right.

The apartment was dark, and, lying near the end of the couch, he pointed his pistol at a spot between the open kitchen door and another that appeared to lead into a bedroom. And then he knew for certain they were too late, and he got slowly to his feet.

"They're gone," he said. "Call Bobby."

Bates came cautiously into the room.

"Come on, move your ass," Lovelace snapped, releasing the hammer on his gun and stuffing it back in his shoulder holster. "They're on their way to Trinity right now. If we're going to have any chance whatsoever of stopping them we're going to have to find out what they look like, what they're driving, and if she's still pregnant."

34

ALBUQUERQUE, NEW MEXICO

Badim got out of the car, walked across the street, went up the walk, and mounted the steps to the front door of their apartment building, an odd feeling up in his gut.

They had gotten less than six blocks when Jada had remembered the bus ticket stubs for Juárez in the top drawer of the bureau beneath her maternity clothes. It wasn't much of a clue, but it could lead someone to the conclusion that Jada was no longer pregnant.

This time Badim wanted to make perfectly certain that there could be no slipups—that he would be able to do the job and that they would be able to get away cleanly.

Out of years of habit, he opened the front door very softly, and went up the stairs to their apartment door, moving on the balls of his feet.

He had his key out and was about to insert it when he suddenly noticed that the lock had been broken. The entire door frame was broken, and then he heard a noise from within. He froze.

Voices. Definitely voices. Two of them. He was sure of it. But how?

He turned on his heel and silently raced downstairs to the front door, and carefully let himself out, then ran across the street to their car.

"What's the matter, Alek?" Jada asked, alarmed by his sudden return, but for the moment he said nothing as he started the car and headed down the street as slowly as he could go so as to make the least amount of noise possible.

At the corner he spotted an army-issue Dodge sedan parked partway up the block, and he flipped on his headlights and accelerated normally down the street.

"What is it?" Jada demanded.

"There were two men in our apartment," Badim said, trying to think out their next moves. It had begun to rain, and to the south he could see an occasional flicker of lightning, the thunder taking a long time to faintly reach them. There was the distinct possibility, if the rain kept up, that the test would be postponed. Only now they were running out of time.

"My god," Jada said softly. "Let's get out of here now, Alek. Let's drive to New York and get out of the country."

Badim shook his head. It wouldn't take long for the army men to reach their landlord, and from him to get an accurate description of a pregnant Jada and a long-haired Bible salesman by the name of Bradley.

Ramierez, their neighbor downstairs, would be home around midnight, and from him they would also get a description of them, as well as this car. They would have it even sooner if they traced him at work.

The ticket stubs might take a little longer to figure out unless they were really sharp, and noticed that there were too many maternity outfits in the closet and bureau, and not enough normal clothing.

But how, he kept asking himself. How in hell had they come so close so fast?

"Alek, this is insane," Jada said, raising her voice. "We can't go through with it. I won't let you."

"We must," Badim snapped. Renting a horse here in Albuquerque was out. If by some chance they found that out, it would tell them his method of penetration, and they would find him.

"They've come this close. They know what we look like. They'll be waiting for us. You'll never make it."

Badim turned on Garfield and headed west across town toward Five Points, where they would pick up U.S. 85 south.

"Alek," Jada shouted. "Listen to me!"

"I listened to you, Larissa, now you listen to me," he said, glancing at her. "It's after five, and the bomb is scheduled to go off at four tomorrow morning. That gives us less than eleven hours. They may be close, but they don't know how close they are—they don't know yet what we look like now, and they have no idea how I intend getting to the tower."

"That doesn't matter," she said, an hysterical edge to her voice. "They'll get our descriptions from Ramierez or our landlord sooner or later, so even if you do succeed in stopping the bomb test, we'd never make it to New York."

"Shut up, Jada," Badim snapped, trying to think it out. "We're here to do a job, and we're going to do it!"

"The war is nearly over," she said. "Leave it alone!"

And then he had it. He did not need to rent a horse here in Albuquerque as he had first planned. He could go back into the desert one last time with Reyes. The rancher would do it. And if he refused it wouldn't matter anyway. The man had no wife or children, and he lived alone just outside of Oscuro. He had a pickup truck as well; Badim remembered seeing it near the ranch house.

He glanced again at Jada, who had a wild expression in her eyes; she seemed like a cornered animal. The army would be looking for a couple. A man and a woman.

"Listen to me now, Larissa," he said gently, but she flinched at the sound of his voice.

"One last time, Alek, please don't do this. Please."

"I must, but you're right, we might not be able to get out together after the test."

"Together?" she cried. "What are you saying now?"

"You're going to drop me off outside Oscuro just as I planned, and from there you're going to continue on down to El Paso. Only you're not going to stop at the hotel. You're going to drive through Texas, all the way up to Dallas, where you can take a train to New York. You can make contact and get to Nova Scotia. I'll meet you there as soon as I can."

"No," she said flatly.

"Yes, goddammit," Badim exploded. "You *will* do as you're ordered."

"And if I don't?" she said defiantly. "What then, Aleksandr, will you shoot me?"

"If need be," Badim roared.

Jada turned away and stared out her window, her hands clasped tightly in her lap.

"I didn't mean that, my darling," Badim said, but she did not respond. "Please, you must believe me. I don't know why I said it."

She turned finally to look at him. "Do you mean to go through with this?"

He nodded.

"Then I will help you as far as Oscuro, as you have asked. I will drive to Dallas, and from there take a train to New York, also as you asked. But I will not wait for you there or in Nova Scotia or in Moscow. When I leave you in Oscuro you'll never see me again."

Badim wanted to stop the car, take her in his arms, and tell her how much he loved her. He wanted to turn around and head north for anywhere. California.

Oregon. Canada. Anyplace they could have a life together.

But he could not. It was as simple as that. He had
been assigned a job. He was going to do it. Jada leaving
immediately for New York was the best solution of all.
And if she meant what she had just said, if she really
intended never to see him again, it would be for the
best. She was too fine a woman to be involved in the
life that he led. She would be unhappy for a time, but
she would forget. And later, she would be thankful that
it had ended when it had.

They made it to Isleta Road, which was U.S. 85, ten
minutes later, and headed south at exactly the legal
speed limit, toward Trinity.

"I want you to round up as many men as you can get
your hands on and send them over here immediately,"
Lovelace said into the telephone.

"Did Bobby's lead pan out after all?" the man at the
Hilton Hotel CIC command center asked.

"If it hadn't I wouldn't be calling for backup, you
idiot!" Lovelace roared. Out of the corner of his eye he
saw Bates starting to turn on one of the table lamps.
"Don't touch that, Bates," he snapped, and the man
looked up, surprised.

Lovelace turned back to the phone. "We're at 407
Dartmouth Avenue. It's on the east side of town. Now
hurry."

"Yes, sir," the man said, and he hung up.

Lovelace slammed the phone down, and went across
the dark living room to the table lamp that Bates had
been about to turn on. He reached under the lampshade
and touched the lightbulb, pulling his fingers back immediately. It was hot.

"Jesus Christ," he said. "They just left. Minutes ago!"

Cripps was standing by the kitchen door. He was a
good man, Lovelace thought, but Bates wasn't too
sharp. If they worked fast they might have a chance,

just a chance, of stopping the man and woman.

"Bobby, I want you to get on the phone and find out who owns this building, or who the rental agent is. Get in contact with them as fast as you can and ask for a recent description of Mr. and Mrs. Bradley."

"Yes, sir," Cripps snapped, and he came across the room and picked up the phone as Lovelace turned to Bates, who stiffened to attention.

"Bates, I've got a big job for you. A slightly illegal job."

"Yes, sir!"

"Go downstairs and break into Ramierez's apartment. Find out if he's in there sleeping, or if he's not at home find out where he is, and get in touch with him."

"Yes, sir," Bates snapped, and he headed for the door, but stopped before he reached it. "What do you want me to ask him?"

"A description of the Bradleys, how long they lived here, where they might be now, what kind of car they drive. Anything."

"Yes, sir," Bates said, and he hurried out the door and rushed down the stairs.

Lovelace turned and went into the bedroom just as a loud crash came from downstairs, and he had to smile despite himself. He had told Bates to break into Ramierez's apartment and that was exactly what the man had done.

For a long moment he stood in the bedroom looking at the bed, the closet door, and the bureau. The room was neat, almost too neat, except for the bed, which was rumpled where someone had evidently thrown the covers over it, and then lain down.

From the living room he could hear Cripps talking on the phone as he crossed to the bureau and began opening drawers, starting at the bottom, dumping the contents of each drawer out on the floor and sorting through them.

In the bottom two drawers were some men's under-

wear and socks, as well as one shirt. In the top two
drawers were women's clothes. But all maternity
clothes, as well as a bus ticket stub for Ciudad Juárez,
Mexico.

Juárez, he thought. Why Juárez?

In the closet he found only one pair of men's trousers,
but several maternity dresses, blouses and skirts.

Maternity clothes again.

Juárez.

He stepped to the bedroom door and called to Cripps,
who looked up and said "Excuse me a moment," to
whoever he was talking to.

"Why would a man go to Juárez?" Lovelace asked.

Cripps shrugged. "To get a piece of ass at one of the
whorehouses."

"How about a pregnant woman?"

Cripps chuckled. "Only one thing," he said.

"Which is?"

"To get an abortion."

Lovelace turned back to the bedroom. The woman
was no longer pregnant, which explained why she had
not returned for her doctor's appointments, and which
explained why she had left her maternity clothes.

He went to the bed and flipped back the covers. A
section of the bed sheet had been torn out, and Lovelace
stared at it for a long moment. They needed a piece of
cloth for something. For what?

The answers were here. He was sure of it. He could
feel it.

He looked at his watch, which showed it was just 5:30
P.M. The bomb was scheduled for four in the morning,
which gave them ten and a half hours.

He wanted to leave immediately to jump in his car
and head to Trinity. The couple had left this apartment
only minutes ago, and Lovelace was certain he could
catch up with them. But would he recognize the man
again? Or would he miss him?

Ten and a half hours, he told himself. First an up-to-date description, and then if possible the make and color of their car.

Also there was the significance of the piece of cloth torn from the bed sheet. Somehow Lovelace felt that the missing bit of cloth was an important clue.

35

OSCURO, NEW MEXICO

It was well after 9:30 P.M. by the time Badim turned off the main highway from Albuquerque and onto U.S. 380, passing through the tiny junction town of San Antonio. A few cars and a couple of dirt-streaked pickup trucks were parked outside Jose Miera's bar and gas station as he drove by, and then they were back in the dark, forbidding countryside, the drizzle coming down harder.

Jada had not spoken a word since they had left Albuquerque, nor did she say anything now, as Badim sped through the night. It was nearly eighty miles from San Antonio to Reyes' ranch outside Oscuro, and the way it looked at this point, Badim figured they would not make it until after eleven o'clock.

From the ranch, over a narrow lava flow, it was almost twenty-two miles to the eastern edge of Mockingbird Gap, and from there still another twelve miles or so along the western face of the mountains and then across the desert to the tower.

Time was running out, and Badim began to seriously wonder if he was going to make it before the bomb was set off.

If they were held up for any length of time by road-blocks along the way, if Reyes was gone with the horses, if he encountered any trouble out on the desert, he would never make it by four in the morning.

Originally he had planned on going out into the desert twenty-four hours before the test, and hiding during the day. But he had decided against it at the last minute, not wanting to leave Jada alone that long in El Paso. If there were military intelligence officers in the area, and he suspected there were, they might pick her up.

As he drove he also thought about Oppenheimer and Groves, glad in a way that he had been stopped outside Springer, and that later Yakovlev in New York had called them off, although he wondered why Runkov had changed his plans in midstream.

Back in Washington, what seemed like a thousand years ago, he had told Jada the truth when he spoke to her of his feelings about killing. There were times at night when he would awaken in a cold sweat, remembering every single person he had ever killed. Remembering in vivid detail not only the circumstances of each kill, but the expression on each victim's face when they knew they were about to die.

His hands tightened on the steering wheel, his knuckles turning white, and he pressed a little harder on the accelerator pedal, the car surging ahead into the night, as he wondered what he had actually contributed to his country.

Little or nothing of actual value, he supposed now. All of it had been so senseless.

He glanced over at Jada, who had laid her head against the window, and seemed to be sleeping. When this assignment was over, he was not going to let her go. He was going to get out of the GRU, tell Runkov he was quitting, and once his life was straight he was going to find her.

The killing, and the spying, and the sabotage had been senseless. A life with Jada was the only reality he ever wanted to face after tonight.

They had gone a little more than nine miles from San Antonio when Badim spotted a military jeep, its top up, and an olive-drab van parked on the right side of the road ahead, their lights out.

He slowed down as he approached, and for a moment he thought about waking Jada, but decided against it.

His canvas pack was lying on the seat between them, and with his right hand he reached over and undid the flap, withdrawing the Luger from within, and laying it beside his right leg on the seat.

As he drew closer he could see two military policemen, their raincoats glistening in the rain, standing beside the jeep, but they just waved him on, and a few seconds later he was past, accelerating again, his heart hammering.

Security was loose, at least out here on the highway, and for that he was thankful. It would mean that they would not be delayed in getting down to Oscuro.

Jada awoke with a jerk. She pushed her hair back from her face with both hands and looked sleepily over at Badim. "Where are we?" she asked thickly.

"Between San Antonio and Bingham," he said, glancing at her. "It'll be a couple hours yet before we reach Oscuro, so you can get some more sleep. It'll be a long night."

She stared at him for a long moment, then looked out the windshield, the wipers flapping back and forth, clearing a streaky swath across the glass.

"It's raining," she said. "Won't they call the test off?"

Badim shrugged. "They might, if the rain continues."

"What will you do then, Alek?" she asked.

Again Badim shrugged. "Remain on the desert until the way to the tower is clear for me."

"Insanity," she said, but there was no emphasis in her voice.

"I love you, Larissa," Badim said, but she glared at him.

"Don't say that, Aleksandr," she snapped, on the verge of tears. "Don't ever say that. You do not have the right."

"Then I'll just think it, my little Larissa, but it is true, nevertheless."

She glared at him for a while longer, but then turned away, laying her forehead against the window, and Badim concentrated on his driving.

The drizzle had turned to rain by the time they passed through Bingham, which was almost directly north of Trinity, and sixteen miles outside Carrizozo they passed another military checkpoint, but this time no one even bothered to wave them on, and Badim barely slowed down.

The highway ran southeast then to Carrizozo itself, where Badim turned to the southwest on U.S. 54, which followed the South Pacific Railroad line down to Alamogordo and eventually to El Paso.

They were south and east of Trinity now, the Oscura mountains between them and the tower, affording a certain amount of protection from the bomb blast, the scientists hoped.

With luck, Badim thought, there would be no need for the protection of the mountains tomorrow morning, because the bomb would not explode.

He watched the car's odometer, and fifteen miles out of Carrizozo he slowed down, watching for the dirt road that led west to Reyes' ranch.

It was quarter to eleven. A little more than five hours before the bomb was scheduled to go off.

"Are we there?" Jada asked in a small voice, at the same moment Badim spotted the road ahead.

"Yes," he said. There was no other traffic on the highway, and in the heavy rain he could not even see the lights of Oscuro, which was a little more than one mile away.

He doused the headlights, and a hundred yards later slowed down to a bare crawl, turning into Reyes' dirt driveway.

"What is this place?" Jada asked, peering out the windshield, trying to penetrate the almost absolute darkness.

"This road leads to Reyes' ranch. It's about four kilometers from the highway," Badim said, and around a gentle curve he stopped the car, put it in neutral, set the parking brake, and turned to her. "Now listen to me, Larissa, and listen carefully."

"You can't go through with this, Alek," she said, obviously starting to panic.

He reached out and took her hands in his. Her palms were ice cold and sweaty. "I'm getting out here. You are going to turn around, go back to the highway, and continue south. El Paso is about two hundred kilometers away."

"No," she said weakly.

"Yes," Badim said firmly. "Drive as far away as you can this night. I will meet you either in Nova Scotia or in Moscow. I'm telling Runkov that I'm quitting. I'm getting out of the GRU. I will go back to school and become an engineer. I will find you, Larissa, and I will love you."

"Alek . . . oh god, my Alek," she cried, and she threw herself, sobbing, into his arms.

For a long time he held her, conscious of nothing other than her hair soft against his cheek, and his heart, which was pounding nearly out of his chest.

When they parted finally she had stopped crying.

"Do as I say and everything will be all right," he said.

"How will you get out?"

"Reyes has a pickup truck. I will steal it when I am finished with the bomb. I'll be in New York less than twenty-four hours behind you."

"I'll wait there for you."

"No," Badim said. "Make contact with Yakovlev and get out of the country. Immediately. If you must wait for me anywhere, make it aboard one of our ships in Nova Scotia. Promise me that."

"I'll get out of the country as soon as I can," she said.

Badim stared into her eyes for long time, kissed her deeply, then stuffed his Luger back in the pack, zipped up his jacket closer around his neck, pulled his hat low over his eyes, and opened the car door.

"Do as I say, Larissa," he said, and she nodded.

"I love you, Aleksandr," she said softly.

"And I love you," he said, and he got out of the car and headed away.

A few steps down the road and Badim had completely disappeared into the downpour, but Jada knew that he would be standing out there a few yards away waiting for her to turn the car around and drive back to the highway.

That much, she thought resolutely, she would do. She released the parking brake, put the car in gear, and jockeyed it around in the narrow driveway, careful not to let the wheels go off the road into the ditch.

When she had it around, she drove slowly back to the still deserted highway, flipped on the headlights, and turned right, heading toward Oscuro.

Sound would not carry very far in this rain, she figured, so she drove less than a half-mile before she slowed down, made a U-turn on the highway, and headed back toward the road to Reyes' ranch.

They were in this together. They *both* had been given the assignment. And they loved each other.

There was no way, she thought, that she was going to leave him here as he wanted her to. No way in hell.

36

TRINITY

Lovelace was operating on borrowed energy, and he knew that when the crash came it would be bad, knocking him out for at least a couple of days, if not longer. He had not smoked a cigarette in more than an hour because of a raw throat and a heavy feeling in his chest. And that, plus his fatigue, plus the weather, plus the sheer insanity of what was happening here in the desert, had combined to drive him into a deep funk.

He sat behind the wheel of a canvas-topped jeep, the side curtains buttoned up against the cold and the rain, the engine ticking over, and the headlights shining on the tower one hundred yards away.

It was just midnight. A few minutes earlier one of the scientists—Wilson, he thought it was—had started up the tower with a last-minute piece of test equipment, which would be placed in position above the bomb.

The man had seemed frightened to death, but not of the bomb. He was frightened of the climb up the hundred-foot tower.

Lovelace could see him now, about halfway up to the corrugated iron shed in which the bomb was resting in its cradle. One of the other scientists, Donald Hornig, had climbed up earlier to babysit the bomb, making sure none of its delicate firing circuits shorted out in the rain.

He was still there.

Out on Route 380 to the north, 54 to the east, and 85 to the west, were a hundred or more soldiers with orders to begin the evacuation of all civilians from the area if something went wrong this morning.

Back at base camp, ten miles from the tower, General Groves, along with Oppenheimer and dozens of other scientific and military brass, were watching the weather and getting ready to man the bunkers, or head over to the observation area at Compania Hill, which was twenty-five miles away from the tower.

In the west and north ten-thousand-yard bunkers, the camera crews were feverishly making last-minute adjustments to their equipment.

And in the south ten thousand, where the firing circuits were located, other scientists were gathering.

Meanwhile, crisscrossing the desert by jeep, by horse, and on foot, were several dozen jittery MPs, all searching for Bradley, or whoever he really was.

Everything that could be done had been done, thought Lovelace. Or had it?

Despite their best efforts, the man had somehow managed to slip through the net. Literally hundreds of law enforcement officers, civilian and military, had the sketches.

Earlier this evening Cripps had come up with a new description of Bradley, the long-haired, bearded Bible salesman, and Ramierez, from where he worked as a janitor at Kirkland Field, had confirmed it.

Yet Bradley and his wife, whose up-to-date description matched the sketch of her they had, had disappeared.

There were three ways of getting into Trinity and

reaching the tower, each of them seemingly impossible.

One was from the west, along the railroad tracks and then across a wide, forbidding lava flow. That route had been marked out on the map they had found in the hotel room in Albuquerque seven weeks ago.

Another way in was across the Oscura Mountains, through Mockingbird Gap, and then down into the desert. At Lovelace's insistence, Groves had ordered a contingent of troops up into Mockingbird Gap, where the men had cut slit trenches and were waiting and watching. Yet this weather could conceal an entire army of spies from detection by his men.

The only other way in was with false papers, a haircut, a shave, and a uniform or clothing a scientist might wear. But that method seemed impossible as well. Every single person who was allowed anywhere near this place had his or her photograph and name on file right here. In addition, the roads leading to the various bunkers, Compania Hill, base camp, and the tower itself, were on a restricted, need-to-be-there, basis. Certain badges were good only for certain areas. Only a handful of scientists and military personnel were actually allowed near the tower.

And then there was the piece of cloth torn from the bed sheet. It meant something. It had to.

But goddammit, Lovelace could *feel* the man's presence as a palpable thing—as real, as intense, and as malevolent as the bomb itself.

Someone tapped on the canvas top, and Lovelace nearly jumped out of his skin, immediately reaching for his .38. But the jeep door was opened to reveal an army noncom, an MP band around his thoroughly soaked jacket sleeve.

"Captain Lovelace?" the man asked hesitantly.

Lovelace looked up into his eyes. "What the hell do you want, Sergeant?"

"Lieutenant Bush is on his way out with a few of the scientists at General Groves' orders, sir. They want to make some last-minute checks for saboteurs," the man said. "And begging the captain's pardon, sir, but you look like hell sitting here."

Lovelace had to laugh. Too little too late. "You don't look so hot yourself," he heard himself saying.

"To tell the truth, captain, I'm mightily scared." He spoke slowly, in a Southern drawl. "Would you like a beer before the brass gets out here?"

Lovelace laughed again. "Hop aboard, sergeant. A beer would taste great about now," he said, and as the man came around to the other side of the jeep, Lovelace pulled out a cigarette, lit it, and inhaled deeply, the smoke searing his throat and lungs. "What the hell," he said.

37

MOCKINGBIRD GAP

Badim had come at least twelve miles from Reyes' ranch, riding hard through the rain, jumping over the seven barbed-wire fences that stood between there and the eastern approach to Mockingbird Gap, when he realized that he was being followed.

At first he was convinced that the sounds from behind him were a trick of his overworked imagination, of his concern for Jada's safety, and of his nerves, which were at the raw edge. But the farther he went, the harder he listened, finally knowing that the sounds were those made by horses' hooves.

Reyes.

Badim tried to think it out. The man's pickup truck, keys dangling from the ignition, the engine still warm, had been parked in front of the ranch house when he had come up the road.

There had been no lights on in the house, and Badim had figured that the rancher was asleep in the back bedroom.

He had silently opened the front door, crept across the living room, gun in hand, and had looked in at the bed. But it had been empty. A quick search, then, came up with nothing. Reyes had been nowhere in the house, nowhere in the barn, and nowhere in any of the outbuildings.

The man's three horses were in their stalls in the barn, and within a few minutes Badim had managed to saddle one of them and take off into the darkness.

Only Reyes had either been there hiding, or had come home just in time to see someone making off with one of his horses.

At least he didn't have to worry about Jada, he told himself as he slowed his horse down and pulled the silenced Luger from his pack. He had clearly heard her turn the car around on the gravel road and drive back up to the highway. She was long gone by now. Well on her way to El Paso.

He turned in his saddle and looked back the way he had come, following the depressions in the wet sand his horse's hooves had made. They were rapidly filling with water from the downpour that gave no hint of letting up.

He reined in and the animal beneath him stopped, shivering in the chill night air. Now he could hear the sounds quite plainly, but a moment later they stopped.

Badim shifted his weight to his left foot, swung his right leg over the horse's rump, and stepped softly down, holding the reins lightly in his left hand, as he brought the Luger up.

"Reyes," he called softly into the night.

There was a sound of leather creaking, and then a horse coughed. It was close. Probably no more than a few yards.

Badim ducked under his animal's neck so that his horse was between him and Reyes. "Reyes," he called softly. "It's me . . . Bradley."

Grasping the reins between the fingers of his left

hand, he clicked the Luger's safety off, and holding the weapon in both hands, his finger on the trigger, he rested his arms on the saddle.

A sound, like a rock falling, came from the left, and his horse jerked as a dark figure loomed out of the night, rushing directly toward him.

Badim fired twice, the Luger making only a soft spitting sound, barely audible over the rainfall, and a horse stumbled and fell to its knees barely a yard away from his own horse.

An instant later Reyes was on top of him from the right, swinging a rifle like a club.

Badim released the reins from his horse and fell backward, the rifle stock barely missing his head, and then Reyes kicked out, his sharp-toed boot catching Badim squarely in the ribs, causing the air to rush out of him in one breath.

No noise, his brain screamed over the pain in his side. There could be no noise!

He rolled with the blow, tangled for just a moment with his horse's hooves, and then he sprang to his feet, as the heavier man swiveled on his heel, bringing his rifle into firing position.

Badim was around his horse in a moment, shifting his Luger to his left hand. As Reyes started to swing his rifle around, Badim brought his right hand back, tightly curling his fingertips so they just touched the upper edge of his palm, and drove his fist forward, careful to keep his thumb tucked in, as he cried, "Hai!" sharply, but very softly.

His fist, driven with every ounce of his strength, penetrated Reyes' soaking wet jacket, shirt, and undershirt, just grazed the lower left edge of the sternum, and in an eruption of blood, he had his fingers curled around the man's beating heart.

A split second later he yanked back with all of his strength, as Reyes emitted a sickening grunt, and the man fell to the ground, his heart hanging by several major arteries out of the devastated remains of his chest.

38

MOCKINGBIRD GAP

Corporal Alfred Grankowski climbed up out of the slit trench in which he and the other three MPs had been getting soaked to the skin since before midnight, and then stepped a half-dozen paces into the nearly impenetrable darkness.

The bomb had been scheduled to go off at 4:00 A.M. sharp, but just a few minutes ago someone from base camp had called on the field phone to inform them that the test would be delayed at least until 5:00.

Roger was the only one of the four of them up here who wasn't afraid of what might happen when the longhairs threw the switch.

Hell, Roger's only complaint was that this trick made the 210th consecutive night of guard duty they had pulled as a team.

Grankowski slung his rifle over his shoulder by the strap, then unbuttoned the fly on his trousers and pulled his penis out, holding it lightly between his forefingers and thumbs.

Below, to the northwest, he could just vaguely make out the reflection of a dim light through the rain, and figured that it must be the tower.

On top of the tower was the bomb. The bomb was connected with wires all the way to the south ten thousand bunker. In the bunker was the switch. And at the switch was one of the longhairs, ready to . . .

Grankowski's legs felt like rubber, and although he had to piss like a racehorse, nothing would come.

And then he heard it.

Something to the left, from the mountains, farther up the gap.

Without bothering to button up his fly, he pulled his rifle off his shoulder as another noise came faintly to his ears over the patter of the rain, this time straight ahead.

His heart was hammering, but he suddenly realized that he was still exposed, and he fumbled with his fly.

"Grankowski," someone called softly, and he raised his rifle, sure at any moment he would shit in his trousers.

"Grankowski," the voice called. "This is the ghost of the mountains."

And suddenly relief flooded over him, making his whole body shake.

The right side of Badim's body was on fire, each shallow breath he took causing him pain.

He sat stock-still in the saddle, listening again for the voices ahead of him in the darkness. Someone had called a name. And then had repeated it moments ago.

"All right, you cocksucker, get out here where I can see you," another man shouted, this time only a few yards directly ahead.

Badim reached into his pack and withdrew his Luger, softly releasing the safety catch, barely daring to breathe. Could they see him?

"Roger, you son of a bitch, get your miserable ass out here now," the voice shouted angrily.

Badim carefully eased his right leg over his horse's rump, and got down out of the saddle, the pain so excruciating that he had to bite his lip, drawing blood, to keep from crying out.

He let the reins loose, got painfully to his hands and knees, and began crawling through the mud and water toward the voices.

About five yards from his horse, he heard someone walking to the right, ahead of him, and then someone laughed, and he could suddenly see the glowing tip of a cigarette. He flattened his body into the mud.

"I damned near shot you, you stupid bastard," the one man said. He had to be no more than two yards away.

"What the hell are you doing out here, playing with yourself?"

"I had to take a piss."

"That's why your donger is hanging out?" the second man said, and he laughed.

"Let's go back to the trench."

"It's only 2:30. They're delaying the test shot at least an hour, which gives us two and a half easy. Relax."

A few moments later one of them said something, but their voices were receding and Badim didn't quite catch it. Then the desert was silent, save for the falling rain and the wind.

There was a trench somewhere ahead with at least two and probably more soldiers. But what were they doing up here, unless they suspected that this would be a logical route to the tower.

Badim crawled backward, carefully, every movement sending sharp pains coursing through his side, until he could hear his horse behind him, and then he stood up and went back to it.

The luminous dials on his watch showed it was exactly 2:37 A.M. which, if the soldiers had been correct, gave him an extra hour to get around the trench and down to the vicinity of the tower.

He patted his horse on the side of its neck. The trip would have to be on foot from here, though. He would never make it around the guards with the horse.

He quickly pulled his pack down from where it was tied to the saddle, withdrew his spare pair of trousers from the pack, folding them into a thick pad, and then took off his belt.

Next he unzipped his jacket and pulled it and his shirt off, the rain cold on his bare back. Within a couple of minutes he had tightly strapped the pad around his side with the belt, and had put his soaked shirt and jacket back on.

Finally he unsaddled his horse, took its reins off, and hit the animal sharply on its rump. The horse jumped and then headed off into the night.

It would find its way back to its stall in the barn sooner or later, but without the horse Badim knew he would have to spend all day tomorrow hiding somewhere in the mountains, and then tomorrow after dark he would have to make his way back to the bodies of Reyes and his horse, and bury them before he could go back to the ranch.

Even at that, he might not make it the next night. It might take two.

He got down on his hands and knees and scooped as deep a hole in the wet sand and mud as he could, then buried the saddle, blanket, and reins. On the way back out he would check to make sure they were still buried, but for now this would have to do.

Finally he got painfully to his feet, shouldered his pack, and with his Luger in hand, headed back toward the northwest. His thoughts about Jada, and the life they would have together when this was all over, rode with him like a warm blanket.

39

TRINITY

Lieutenant Howard Bush put the field telephone down in its cradle and looked at the several men gathered around the jeeps and one sedan at the tower.

It had stopped raining nearly an hour ago, and the wind too had died down, although the sky was still heavily overcast.

His voice cracking with utter fatigue and emotion, he said, "It's a definite go for 5:30."

Lovelace, who had been leaning against the hood of his own jeep, brought his wrist up and looked at his watch. It read 4:45 A.M. Just forty-five more minutes and his job would cease to exist.

"We've got fifteen minutes to get out of here," Bush, who was the Trinity camp commander, said, and he turned back to the field telephone and cranked the handle.

Three of the scientists who had been waiting for the order headed away from the tower in their jeep to a small pit dug into the sand nine hundred yards out, where they would close all the switches arming the firing mechanisms.

Lieutenant Bush was saying something on the field phone, and when he hung up, he began directing his people to pack up everything they didn't want destroyed by the blast and load it aboard one of the jeeps.

Lovelace pulled out a cigarette, lit it, and inhaled, the smoke burning all the way down. But he didn't give a damn any longer. In fact, he told himself, his raw throat was the only thing keeping him awake.

The three scientists, Bainbridge, McKibben, and Kistiakowsky, were back from the arming pit in ten minutes, and Dorothy McKibben jumped out of the jeep, raced to one of the tower legs, and flipped a battery of switches, which turned on the bright aiming lights to help guide the B-29 that would make a flyover with test instruments.

"Are we about ready?" Bush called over to the trio.

"Just a minute, Howard," one of them said, his voice tense.

The three of them moved to the base of the tower, where Bainbridge unlocked a heavy wooden box, which looked very much like a coffin, and threw a series of switches. When he had the cover closed and relocked, he looked up.

"The bomb is armed at this end," he said, and he and the two other scientists moved back to their jeep.

Lieutenant Bush got back on the field phone. "West ten thousand?" he said. "Bush at the tower. Give me a searchlight on the shack. We're getting out of here now."

He hung up and looked around, finally spotting Lovelace, who was the only other one not in a vehicle. "Let's go, captain," he shouted across.

A powerful searchlight stabbed through the darkness, then moved to the right, finally centering on the tower about twenty yards up.

Lovelace watched as the light climbed farther up the

tower, finally coming to rest on the corrugated iron shed in which the bomb was waiting.

"Let's go, captain," Bush shouted again, and Lovelace looked his way.

"Go ahead, Bush. I'll be right with you."

"If your jeep breaks down you're on your own. We're not coming back."

"Get out of here," Lovelace snapped. "And that's an order, lieutenant!"

The scientists watched the exchange with curiosity, but no one said anything, and one by one the jeeps and the sedan left the tower.

Lovelace watched as their taillights receded into the distance toward the bright spotlights that marked the south ten thousand bunker. Behind him, lights marked the west ten thousand, and to the left a third set of lights marked the north ten thousand.

But straight ahead, past the tower, was darkness. The Oscura Mountains. Mockingbird Gap.

Lovelace pushed away from his jeep, its headlights still on, its motor still running, and walked slowly around the tower, then twenty yards out into the desert.

"You're out there, you bastard," he said, half to himself. "I know it. I can feel it."

Slowly, conscious of every muscle in his body, conscious of the tower rising up behind him, the spotlights shining on it, the red aircraft aiming lights up top, and conscious of the massive wall of mountains to the east, Lovelace withdrew a cigarette from a half-crumpled pack and lit it.

For just a fleeting moment he thought about a girl he had once dated in San Antonio, Texas. He could clearly remember her face, and the way she had felt in bed, but for the life of him, he could not think of her name.

He wondered, though, if she was still in San Antonio, and if she had gotten married and had the large family she so desperately wanted.

Whatever. He hoped she had found happiness.

He also thought about Major Faircloth and Colonel Woodsworthe back in London, and Willis in Washington, and Gillingham in Boston, and Gannt, the strange Navy officer in Portsmouth.

He thought about all those people whose paths he had crossed on this project, and he wondered how their lives would be changed after the bomb exploded.

Groves would probably retire. He had gotten his second star, he had accomplished a seemingly impossible task, and after the test his work would be completed.

Oppenheimer would return to his post at the University of California, and the other scientists would scatter as well.

But most of all Lovelace wondered about the man he was certain was out there in the darkness.

A German, or a Russian? Or didn't make any difference?

There was a burst of static from the loudspeaker on the tower, and as Lovelace turned around, the national anthem blared forth for just a few bars, over which came the voice of one of the scientists, echoing and reechoing across the desert.

"It is now zero minus twenty minutes."

Lovelace glanced one last time out toward the mountains, then flipped his cigarette away, the glowing ash making an arc in the night. And suddenly he was frightened, deeply frightened of the monstrous thing in the corrugated shed a hundred feet above his head.

He hurried back to his jeep, climbed in between the wheel, put it in gear, and headed as fast as he could drive to the south ten thousand bunker.

"God help him," he said to himself. "God help him."

Badim lay in a small depression barely a hundred yards from the tower. He had been there for nearly forty-five minutes, waiting for the remainder of the people to leave the area.

Only now, as he watched the taillights of the jeep

heading south, he knew there would not be enough time for him to escape.

The voice from the loudspeaker still echoed in his ears. Twenty minutes. Not enough time to make it to the tower, climb the one hundred feet, switch the wires, make it back down the tower, and away the required thousand yards.

No time.

Did they know? Could they possibly know that he was out here? Had they gotten to Jada? Was she now a captive?

He would never see her again. No matter what happened here this morning on the desert, he would never see her. He would never lie with her in bed. There would be no vacations at the seashore, something she had spoken about often. There would be no dinners at fancy restaurants. There would be no apartment in Moscow. No children.

But he had a job to do. Runkov had given him this assignment with Marshal Stalin's approval. The State had entrusted this mission to him. He could not let them down. Not even now.

He had lain absolutely still for the last three quarters of an hour, but now he moved his right hand, ready to push himself up, when he felt something long and cold lying next to his side. An instant later it moved, he heard a brief rattle, and then something very sharp pierced his wrist.

He flung his right hand out and rolled away from the rattlesnake that had evidently slithered next to his body for warmth against the cold night air, as it lethargically moved away from him.

He had been bitten. God, he had been bitten!

He held his wrist out to the dim light spilling from the tower area, and he could clearly see two small red spots on his arm just above his wrist, with a tiny amount of blood oozing from them, and his heart began to hammer.

It would not take long for the snake's venom to incapacitate him. But how long? Less than twenty minutes?

He pulled his pack around, opened it, and with shaking hands pulled out his knife, extending the smallest blade. Without hesitation he cut deep crosses over each of the puncture wounds, the tip of the blade grating against the bone.

The jeep was finally out of sight, and as he crawled across the desert toward the base of the tower, he sucked at the deep wounds, the venom bitter with the blood.

He would have to stay calm, he remembered from one of his briefings. Stay calm. The faster his heart beat, the faster the deadly poison would circulate through his system.

"Jada," he called, half to himself.

His wrist was on fire, and his elbow felt like someone had hit it with a hammer by the time he made it to the tower and stood up, his body fairly well-hidden behind one of the legs.

There were spotlights aimed at the corrugated iron shed on top, something he had not been warned about.

But a minute or two before the blast, all observers would be turned away to protect their eyes. It would be during that time that he would be able to get inside. It would only take a couple of seconds to switch the wires.

Pushing his pack around so that it was out of his way, he ducked down and raced to the opposite side of the tower, then shinnied up one of the legs to the lowest rungs of the access ladder that was three or four yards off the ground.

Painfully he pulled himself up and, flattening himself against the wide tower leg, started up toward the metal shack that was bathed in lights.

The pain from the snakebite had traveled up to his shoulder by now, and he was starting to get cramps, and a deep chill that made it almost impossible to think, let alone continue to climb the tower.

His concentration was reduced to the pain in his arm and side, and the metal rungs of the ladder he was climbing. Rung after run, the pain deepening, the cramps coming at him in waves.

A siren sounded in the distance to the south, breaking him out of his near-delirium, and he looked that way as a green rocket arched into the sky.

With great care he hooked his right arm around the ladder rung directly in front of his face, and brought his left arm around so that he could see his watch. It was 5:25. Five minutes!

The corrugated iron shed seemed to be a hundred yards above him as he looked up and tried to focus his bleary eyes.

Five minutes, his brain screamed, and he grasped the next rung, and continued up. Five minutes, he told himself over and over. Five minutes.

The public address speaker far below him, near the base of the tower, hissed with static as Badim's head came even with the platform on which the shack was resting.

"Zero minus sixty seconds and counting," a voice rolled across the desert.

Badim could barely see now, even in the bright light from the spotlight shining from the west ten thousand bunker.

He heaved himself over the edge, and on hands and knees crawled to the doorway.

"Zero minus forty seconds," the speaker far below blared.

Just inside the shack Badim collapsed, panting, every breath causing deep pains across his chest.

He was here to do something. He knew it. But he could not quite remember what it was for just a moment.

A gong sounded from somewhere in the distance, as he somehow managed to push himself up again to his hands and knees and crawl forward. And then he saw it.

The bomb, encased in a huge black steel ball, a maze of wires surrounding it like a spider web, was just below him through a hole in the floor.

He fell forward on his chest, and reached out with his left hand, his fingers barely four inches from the nearest bundle of cables.

"Five . . ." the loudspeaker intoned.

"Five what?" Badim asked himself. It was important.

"Four . . . three . . ."

There was something he had to remember, he told himself as he wiggled forward, his fingertips just brushing the nearest cable.

"Two . . ."

And then he had it. Jada. That's what he had to remember. He wanted to tell her just one more time that he loved her.

"One . . ."

Her face came clearly into his mind's eye, as his fingers curled around the cable and he tried to make his arm pull up.

Someone screamed *"zero,"* from far below him, and Badim started to roll over to see who was speaking. . . .

OCTOBER 1980

40

"The night was like day for just an instant, and then a few moments later the terrible thunder came," Jada said. Her voice was far away, and held a dreamy quality.

Mahoney stood, drink in hand, at the window of their second-floor hotel room, looking down at the swimming pool. A few late-night revelers were playing in the water, and their shouts and giggles could be heard even over the sound of the air-conditioner.

Most of what Jada had told him could be checked, and he damned well was going to do it, because she had hinted too strongly that there may have been collusion between the Soviet and American governments at the highest levels.

Between Stalin and Roosevelt, he mused? He doubted it, but there could have been cooperation between other men at high levels. Like Brezhnev.

If that were the case, then it would explain a great many anomalies from that time. For instance: Why hadn't the extensive network of Soviet spies been discovered until *after* the bomb had been tested? Or, why hadn't Oppenheimer, with strongly suspected Communist leanings, been kicked off the project at the beginning? Or why, he thought—and this was the most curious fact of all—had the Russians developed their own atomic bomb sooner than the British, who shared openly in our research? The Russians had certainly received a great deal of technical information from spies; but enough so that they could successfully build the bomb before the British?

He turned away from the window. Jada was propped up on the bed, her glass of white wine that Mahoney had ordered from room service untouched on the night table. Her eyes were moist.

"There are a lot of holes in your story, Jada," he said softly.

She smiled tiredly. "Some of it I've made up. Some of it is fantasy," she said. Her voice was hoarse from talking the entire day.

"The last part of your story," Mahoney said. "There is no way you could have known that Alek was bitten by a rattlesnake, or that he actually made it to the top of the tower."

"No," she admitted, but a look of defiance flashed in her eyes. "He made it to the tower, though. I'm certain of that. And he would have been successful except that something slowed him down. A rattlesnake?"

"How about the rancher . . . Reyes? How did you know about him? Or about the MPs in the trench up on Mockingbird Gap?"

"General Groves, before he died, told many of the details about the project in his book, *Day of Trinity*, including the four MPs up in the Gap."

"But nothing about Lovelace or about you and Alek, or about Reyes?"

"No," she said. "Nothing has ever been publicly written about that aspect of the project."

"Did Lovelace know about Reyes?" Mahoney asked.

Jada shook her head. "As far as I know he was not aware of Reyes, although he strongly suspected that Alek would penetrate the site through Mockingbird Gap."

"Then how did you know?" Mahoney asked, greatly curious.

"I was there," she said. "I saw it."

"Good god," Mahoney said softly, and then her illness was suddenly made clear. "You were on the desert. You got caught in the fallout."

She was nodding again. "As a result, I have leukemia. It took a while to develop, but it is a result of my exposure."

"How close were you when the bomb went off?"

Jada closed her eyes, and for a long moment she did not speak. Mahoney supposed she was back in the desert, that early morning in 1945.

"Reyes had been in the outhouse, the one building Alek hadn't checked. I watched him come out, button up his trousers, saddle a horse, and then ride off into the desert. I knew I would have to get out there and somehow warn Alek, but I knew very little about horses. I did manage to get the reins on the last horse, and I rode it bareback." She opened her eyes and looked across the room at Mahoney, who had not moved a muscle. "I fell off the horse seven times," she continued. "Each time it jumped a fence, I fell." She smiled. "I fell seven times coming back that morning, too."

"But you didn't get to warn Alek in time."

"No," she said. "By the time I caught up with Reyes, he and his horse were both dead. I buried them."

"Then what?" Mahoney asked, after a long silence.

"I was just about finished when the bomb went off, and I knew Alek would not be coming back."

And that was the story, except for the most monumentally important detail of all: Did the American government under Roosevelt and then under Truman cooperate with the Russians?

She had been watching the play of emotions across his face. "You are bothered, Wallace," she said softly.

He nodded, but said nothing. It was her story. It was her defection, and he wanted to hear it from her lips.

"You are bothered by the Russian fuse aboard the submarine?"

"No," he said. "I'm bothered by my government's lack of reaction to it."

"And you think that I'm going to tell you about some deep dark plot between my government and yours during the war?"

Mahoney said nothing.

She smiled sadly and shook her head, then reached over for her wine and took a delicate sip.

"I suspected there was contact between our governments at the highest levels. But we're going to have to talk with Lovelace about it. I suspect he is the only man who will be willing to talk."

Mahoney was startled. "Lovelace is still alive?"

"Very much so," Jada said. "He is an active seventy-three-year-old man. He married his girl back in San Antonio, Texas. He lives there now at 703 Craig Avenue, although I think his wife is dead."

Suddenly it was as if a veil had been lifted from in front of Mahoney's eyes. "That's why you defected."

She nodded.

"You wanted to confront Lovelace. But surely not for revenge."

"No, not for revenge. We were all soldiers doing our jobs, him included. I just want to hear from him that he knew for certain Alek was coming across the desert."

"And Brezhnev?" Mahoney asked, after a moment.

Jada smiled. "I found out about him when I made my inquiries into Runkov's death. By then, of course, he was quite powerful in my government, so I backed off. My inquiries were never traced back to me."

"Otherwise you would have been assassinated."

She nodded. "But there are others," she said. "I'm sure of it."

41

SAN ANTONIO, TEXAS

"You're damned right I knew he was out there," Lovelace croaked. He was a little old man, his sparse hair completely white, and the skin on his face and neck slack. But his eyes were alive as he stared at Jada.

"Why didn't you call off the test?" she asked, her voice very controlled.

She and Mahoney had flown to San Antonio this afternoon, and had called Lovelace on the telephone. He had instantly agreed to see her, and in fact had sounded most anxious for the meeting. They sat now in lawn chairs behind his one-story bungalow, the evening warm and very pleasant.

"No need to call off the test, comrade," Lovelace said. "I stuck around the tower after Bush and the others left, until the twenty-minute warning was sounded. Then I got the hell out of there. I knew there'd be no way he'd get up the tower and fiddle with the bomb. Leastways, not in time."

Jada just stared at him.

"It was the same fellow on top of the train outside Springer, New Mexico, the year before, wasn't it?"

Jada nodded.

"You called yourselves the Bradleys?"

Again she nodded.

Lovelace leaned forward. "Just one question for you, young lady," he said, his voice eager. "Why in Christ's name did you tear a piece out of the bed sheet back in Albuquerque?"

Jada tried to think. Bed sheet? And then she remembered, and she had to smile despite herself. "I made a lunch for Alek . . . some sandwiches. I had them wrapped in waxed paper, but he wanted them wrapped in cloth."

Lovelace slapped his right hand against his leg, and laughed long and hard. "Goddamn, you don't know how that has bothered me. Never could figure it out." He shook his head. "Goddamn. It makes sense."

"But you knew he was coming through Mockingbird Gap?" Mahoney asked.

Lovelace looked sharply at him. "That's not why you came here, Mahoney. Let's cut the bullshit. You want to ask me about the Russian fuse aboard that Nazi sub. You want to know why Hoover had a bug up his ass and wouldn't cooperate."

Mahoney nodded. He liked Lovelace, and wished he had known him during the war.

Lovelace took a deep breath, letting it out slowly, then reached in the side pocket of his sweater and took out a rumpled pack of Lucky Strikes. He looked over his shoulder toward the house before he lit one. "When my wife was alive she wouldn't let me smoke. But since she died I've taken up the habit again. The nurse doesn't know her ass from a hole in the ground, and if I'm careful I can usually sneak a half dozen smokes a day."

When he had his cigarette lit, he inhaled deeply, a pleasured look on his face.

"I've been waiting for someone to show up," Lovelace said. "I knew someone would come knocking at my door sooner or later."

Jada was sitting on the edge of her chair, her eyes bright.

"Your little operation was nothing more than a double cross . . ." Lovelace started to say, when a bright red hole appeared in his forehead, and he was flung backward off his lawn chair.

Before Mahoney could react, Jada jerked forward, doubling over, the back of her head erupting in a mass of blood and bone.

"No," he shouted, rolling left off his chair as he pulled his .38 out of its shoulder holster. In the next instant something incredibly strong slammed into his side, literally lifting him off the patio blocks, and his vision began to blur.

He was dimly aware of a woman screaming, and he managed to turn his head enough to see Lovelace's nurse, a buxom woman, jerk backward off her feet, and fall through a patio window, two large red stains on the front of her white uniform.

For a few moments he was able to focus on the nurse's feet and legs, but then his consciousness was reduced to nothing more than the feel of the rough stone against his cheek. He was drifting for a time . . . his mind a hodgepodge of Jada and Lovelace, of Brezhnev and FDR smoking a cigarette in a holder, and of a mushroom cloud rising over a city.

The Soviet operation against the atomic bomb project had been only one factor in a much larger operation. The Trinity factor. But who was running the operation? And why? What were they trying to accomplish?

He was vaguely aware of a car engine revving up and then tires squealing on pavement, and then he could feel his heart beating against his chest and he began to understand that if he lay here he would bleed to death.

Somehow he managed to turn his head, and he could see Jada's lifeless body curled up in a fetal position.

Across from her Lovelace's body lay spread-eagled on the lawn.

They were all dead. They had been murdered. But why, Mahoney silently screamed as he tried without success to sit up. By whom?

And then his mind locked on to the obvious. Whatever had happened thirty-five years ago was still going on. Whatever collusion there had been between the American and Soviet governments in 1945 was still intact today.

Was still intact. It was monstrous.

He pulled his right leg up and then pushed out, forcing his body a few inches forward.

A telephone. He would have to contact the Company. Tell them what he had learned. What he suspected.

His side was on fire, and a deep ache spread throughout his body as he continued to push himself toward the house while holding his arm against the wound.

If such an operation were still going on, however, who could he trust? Surely the CIA was involved. It had to be. And who else? The government? Business?

It took him nearly ten minutes to reach the nurse's body, and another ten to get past it into the house, where he spotted the telephone sitting on a low coffee table.

The living room seemed dark, and yet he could see that a table lamp was lit in the corner, and he began to get frightened that he would not make it.

He wanted nothing more now than to get home and talk with his wife Marge. He had a lot to tell her, including the fact that for a time he had found himself falling in love with Jada, who had been an extraordinary woman. A very extraordinary woman, indeed.

"Operator," a voice was saying to him, and he knew that he had the phone to his ear.

"Operator," the woman's voice repeated.

"Operator?" Mahoney mumbled.

"May I have your call, please?" the woman said.

"My call," Mahoney stumbled over the words, but

then it was clear to him what he had to do, and he managed to give the woman the duty officer's number at Langley, and a few seconds later it was ringing.

The Trinity factor. That had been in 1945. What else was there? What was happening right now?

"Night desk," a man's voice was saying.

Mahoney knew the words to say, but he was having difficulty in speaking. Christ.

"Night desk," the man's voice came sharper.

"This . . . is . . . a triple six," Mahoney said.

"Who the hell is this?" the man snapped. It was a familiar voice.

"Mahoney . . ."

"Wallace?" the man said. "Where are you? What's the matter?"

Then he had it. "Switt?"

"This is Switt. Are you in trouble, Wallace?"

He had worked with Switt in Moscow what seemed like a century ago. He was a man to be trusted. "Listen, Darrel," Mahoney forced himself to speak clearly. "I'm wounded. San Antonio, Texas. Seven-oh-three Craig Avenue."

"I'll get someone to you . . ." Switt started to say, but Mahoney cut him off.

"Listen, Darrel . . . listen. Erase the tape. Don't tell anyone from the Company. No one. This is important. Get me help, and then get down here yourself. This is important."

Mahoney could feel himself slipping away again, and he tried to concentrate on what Switt was saying to him, but he could not. He wanted Marge, and he wanted Switt to be here. He had so much to tell them both. So much, but he did not know if there was enough time. He worried that they were already too late. Thirty-five years too late.